THOSE IN PERIL

THOSE IN PERIL

Fay Sampson

This first world edition published 2010
in Great Britain and in the USA by
SEVERN HOUSE PUBLISHERS LTD of
9–15 High Street, Sutton, Surrey, England, SM1 1DF.
Trade paperback edition first published
in Great Britain and the USA 2010 by
SEVERN HOUSE PUBLISHERS LTD

British Library Cataloguing in Publication Data

Sampson, Fay.
    Those in peril.
    1. Fewings, Suzie (Fictitious character)–Fiction.
    2. Women genealogists–England–Fiction. 3. Missing
    persons–Investigation–Fiction. 4. Detective and mystery
    stories.
    I. Title
    823.9'14-dc22

ISBN-13: 978-0-7278-6915-9   (cased)
ISBN-13: 978-1-84751-255-0   (trade paper)

All Severn House titles are printed on acid-free paper.

Severn House Publishers support The Forest Stewardship Council [FSC],
the leading international forest certification organisation. All our titles that
are printed on Greenpeace-approved FSC-certified paper carry the FSC logo.

Mixed Sources
Product group from well-managed
forests and other controlled sources
www.fsc.org Cert no. SA-COC-1565
© 1996 Forest Stewardship Council
FSC

3 1813 00432 0551

Typeset by Palimpsest Book Production Ltd.,
Falkirk, Stirlingshire, Scotland.
Printed and bound in Great Britain by
MPG Books Ltd., Bodmin, Cornwall.

To Alan

ONE

'**N**ice funeral.'

Nick Fewings threw an affectionate smile at his older brother as they walked to the crematorium car park. On either side of them, the green lawns were vivid with crocuses in gold, white and purple.

'Thanks,' said Leon. 'I had a soft spot for the old girl. A pity I didn't see so much of her at the end, after I moved out to St Furseys.'

'No. I'm sorry about that.'

The two men looked ahead to where Leon's ex-wife, Jacqui, in an elegant black hat, was walking with their curly-haired teenage daughter Anna. A mask of make-up disguised her expression.

'Stuff happens. At least she didn't bring the boyfriend to the funeral. And I still have Anna every other weekend. But it's not the same. I envy you and Suzie and the kids.'

Nick looked round. Suzie was chatting politely to some of Aunt Eleanor's elderly friends. Her own soft brown hair was hatless. She had opted not to wear funereal black. Instead, a two-piece dress of floating lavender and a lilac scarf gave a touch of half-mourning that was also celebratory.

'Sorry we couldn't bring Tom and Millie. They didn't really know Aunt Eleanor that well, and Tom's coming up to A-levels next term. He's just starting to panic. I only hope he hasn't left it too late.'

'That's teenage boys for you. We were the same, weren't we? Skating on very thin ice, I remember. Girls seem to get their act together better.'

They had reached the cars. It was still a jolt to see Leon go to a different one from Jacqui and Anna. He looked a small, rather tired man, greying sooner than his tall, black-haired brother.

He called over his shoulder to Nick, 'See you back at the house, then. I thought of hiring a hotel function room, but, well . . . She made me her executor, you know. And there are one or two things she wanted special people to have. You included. You might as well come to the house and take them with you.'

'Not the china dogs off the mantelpiece, I hope.'

'All in good time. The statutory ham sandwiches and cheese and pineapple on sticks first. But I think your boot will be big enough.'

'What was all that about?' Suzie folded her skirt as she climbed into the car beside Nick.

'Search me. Something about Eleanor's things. She had a pretty little desk in the bay window, but I don't think that would fit in the boot. Do you have any use for a treadle sewing machine?'

'It might be more interesting than the table we've got in the hall.'

They drew up in front of Aunt Eleanor's house. It stood high above the road. Rock plants in purple, pink and white tumbled down the terraces of its steep garden.

'It was a big house to live in alone. She never married?'

'You met her. You know what she was like. Always an independent-minded lady. I don't think there were many men who could keep up with her.'

As they climbed the steps, Nick ran his architect's eye over the detached house. He tried to stop himself calculating its value. He didn't think Aunt Eleanor was the sort who would leave all her estate to a cats' home. But you never knew. More realistically, she might think Christian Aid had more need of her money than her nieces and nephews.

The house was filling up with her family and friends. Mourners, Nick decided, was the wrong word. There was a lively hum of chatter and jokes. Aunt Eleanor had been an active member of the Methodist Church. There had been about her funeral a confident assurance that this was not the end of her story.

Nick felt her loss more keenly. He hadn't seen her more than a couple of times a year, but he would miss her penetrating interest in him. She had been a perceptive old bird.

When the food on the buffet table had been halved – there always seemed to be too many sandwiches at a funeral spread – Leon called for silence.

'The will still has to go to probate, but while you're all here, you might like to know where you stand.'

He read out a list of bequests. Nick drew a quick breath when he heard his share. Aunt Eleanor, efficient as ever, had died after only a week's illness. There had been no nursing home fees to eat up her savings. He had been partly right, though. Christian Aid had got a sizeable sum. But even so . . . Suzie shot him a smile.

Leon held up his hand to still the outbreak of chatter. 'Besides the money, she drew up a list of her favourite pieces, and who she would like to have them. I've had them valued for the tax people. So despite the legal niceties, if no one has any objection, you might as well take them with you now. That way, if you're not over the moon about what she's given you, there'll be a chance for some horse-trading before you leave.'

The cherrywood desk went to Aunt Eleanor's god-daughter, who turned pink with pleasure. The sewing machine was left to a close friend.

'Nick, you get the portrait of Great-grandfather Sollie on the stairs. She thought it ought to stay with a man in the family.'

Nick started, then grinned. Suzie looked at him questioningly. He squeezed her arm.

'Right up your street. You're a nutter for family history. Great-grandad Sol is mine.'

He pulled her out of the crowd into the hall. The stairs climbed to a landing with a window edged in stained glass. Above this turn in the stairs hung a huge photograph in a plain wooden frame. A man in an oilskin smock leaned against a fishing boat. His crinkled, weather-beaten face looked out, rather fiercely, from under a sou'wester.

'That's the nearest we've got to fame in the family. Sollie Margerson. Lifeboat coxswain. At *his* funeral, there was a procession of lifeboatmen half a mile long. They came from all along the coast to give him a send-off.'

Suzie stared at it in silence. She turned to him accusingly. 'Why did you never tell me about him before?'

Nick looked at her indignant face. His eyes creased with laughter. 'You've filled every free moment for the last three years chasing up your own family history. I shudder to think what would happen if I let you start on mine.'

He saw her lips compress, determination harden in her hazel eyes.

'*You* may not be interested, but what about the children? Sollie Margerson's their ancestor, too. They have a right to know his story.'

Nick spread his hands in surrender. 'Here, give me a hand, then.'

Together they lifted the heavy picture down from its hook. Where it had hung, the rectangle of wallpaper showed startlingly fresh columns of twining green leaves on a white background.

'It makes everything around it look suddenly dirty, doesn't it?' said Suzie.

TWO

'Right, where would you like it?'

Nick stood at the foot of the stairs in their own, more modern, house in a West Country town 100 miles from Aunt Eleanor's house. The sepia photograph, in its large frame, rested on the bottom step.

Suzie looked into the sitting room and shook her head. 'There isn't a big enough space of wall free in there. It'll have to be the staircase again.'

'Righty-ho. I think I've got some picture hangers in the shed.' He started to carry the picture upstairs.

'Hold on. You're getting cobwebs on that suit. Let me give the thing a proper clean down first, while you go and get changed.'

She led the way into the kitchen. Nick laid the picture on the table while she found a duster. She wiped the glass and rubbed the fly-spots away. He left her dusting the frame and spraying furniture polish on it.

'He hasn't looked that smart in years,' Nick told her when he came back in jeans and sweater. 'I suspect Aunt Eleanor's eyesight was failing.'

The wood shone. He was about to pick up the photograph again when the front door opened.

Nick never quite got over the shock of surprise whenever he saw his son. It was like looking at his younger self in the mirror. The same shock of waving black hair. The same vivid blue eyes. Now he had turned eighteen, Tom could match him for height.

'Hey, what have you brought back? Captain Birdseye?'

'Great-grandfather Solomon Margerson . . . well, your great-great-grandfather.'

'Did he really own that boat he's leaning against?'

'Search me. All I know is that he was a famous lifeboatman on the east coast. It looks as though he had a day job as a fisherman.'

'You mean I've got nautical genes, as well as agricultural

labourers and lords of the manor? Cool, man.' Tom crinkled his eyes into a smile for Suzie. 'Hey, Mum, why aren't you following up Dad's people, as well as your own? This is different.'

A shadow of annoyance passed over Suzie's face. 'I'm sorry if my side isn't heroic enough for you two. When you start, you've no idea who you're going to turn up. You just have to take what's there. But yes, I can find out more about Great-grandfather Margerson, if you want.'

An unexpected thought struck Nick. Could she be jealous? He hadn't even tried to find his own family history, while she had spent years on hers. And here he was, presenting her with a ready-made hero. That picture of the lifeboatman would hang on the wall, where she would have to pass it every day.

He parted the soft brown hair and dropped a kiss on the back of her neck. 'I've been following your family trail long enough to know the risks. I bet we've got some skeletons in our cupboard, too.'

Suzie recovered her smile. 'Skeletons score brownie points with family historians. We all love a good scandal. It makes up for generations of ag labs with nothing remarkable about them . . . Now, if you two will get out of the way, I'd like to clean the cobwebs off the back.'

'You're not seriously thinking of hanging that in the hall, are you?'

A cool voice came from the kitchen doorway. The three of them turned. Millie's languid, fourteen-year-old form dangled her school bag just above the floor. Her lank fair hair drooped across her face. Her shirt hung half out of her grey school skirt.

'Hi, Millie,' Nick smiled. 'Had a good day?'

'Double chemistry? You're joking.' She walked across to inspect the photograph. 'That guy has seriously scary eyebrows.'

She's right, Nick thought. Under the brim of his sou'wester, Sollie Margerson's eyes were surmounted by a thatch of bushy growth. The piercing gaze beneath them held the onlooker.

Suzie turned the picture over. Brown paper had been pasted over the back of the photograph. A film of cobwebs coated it. She started to wipe them away.

'Hang on,' said Tom. 'There's writing on it.'

They all leaned over to read the faded ink at the base of the frame.

Solomon Margerson. Skipper of the Ellen Maud, *St Furseys. 1921.*

Suzie lifted her head. 'St Furseys? Isn't that where Leon's gone to live?'

'You're right,' Nick said. 'Now that I come to think of it, he did say something about going back to the family's old hunting grounds.'

'So?' Tom flashed his mischievous grin at all of them. 'When do we get a seaside holiday to chase up Captain Birdseye and the *Ellen Maud*?'

Suzie emerged triumphantly from the study, waving a sheaf of papers. Nick turned down the page of the gardening catalogue he'd been studying. There were some beguiling new colours for gladioli. He was planning the late summer display in the flower bed facing the patio window. But clearly, he was going to have to look interested in her latest find.

'I've been through all the censuses,' she said. 'From 1901 right back to 1841. I can get the 1911 too, if you like, but I'll have to pay for it. But it's the earlier ones that are most interesting, because we know what Sollie was doing in the twentieth century.'

She dropped the printouts in his lap. 'Look, this is 1901. He was twenty-three then, so he must have been born in 1877 or '78. And here's his father, Benjamin Margerson, also a fisherman. But before that . . .' Another shuffle. 'Here, 1851, Alfred Margerson, gardener. Born in Cambridge. What do you suppose brought a gardener from the Fens to St Furseys, to breed a line of seamen?'

The tabulated census returns danced before Nick's eyes. So much information to make sense of. Names of parents and children, addresses, ages, occupations, where born. He knew he ought to be responding more enthusiastically. Suzie was obviously pleased with her discoveries. He supposed a good deal of the pleasure of family history lay in the process of detection, not just the results. He had missed out on that side.

'Fascinating,' he told her, not entirely truthfully. He read the sheets more carefully. 'I wonder why it calls some of the early ones *mariners*, not *fishermen*. Is there a difference?'

She shrugged. 'Maybe they used their boats for other things besides fishing.'

'Such as?'

'How would I know? My West Country ancestors didn't live that far from the sea, but as far as I know, none of them were sailors. At least . . . I did have a great-uncle who was in the Royal Navy. He was shipwrecked off the Isles of Scilly and drowned. He's on my great-great-grandparents' grave-stone. That's not the same as making your living with your own boat. But I did have boatmen in the South-east. They made their living from something called hovelling. Taking supplies out to ships in the Channel.'

'Could have been pirates.'

Millie had that unsettling way of gliding up on them unnoticed.

Suzie turned to her daughter, her long brown hair swinging as she moved, curly where Millie's hung straight. 'I don't expect the skeletons in Dad's cupboard to be that colourful.'

'Well, smugglers, then.'

'It's possible. In the nineteenth century there'd be plenty of people on the coast with a hand in it. But we'll never know, unless he was caught. When the census enumerator asks someone for their occupation, they're hardly going to say "smuggler", are they?'

'*Brandy for the parson, baccy for the clerk.*' Nick dredged the words of Kipling's poem from his childhood memories.

'*Laces for a lady, letters for a spy.*'

'*And watch the wall, my darling, while the Gentlemen go by*,' Millie finished, surprising him. It was not the first time he had underestimated her.

'I used to be terrified of *Treasure Island*,' he told her. 'I wouldn't let my mum read that bit where Blind Pew comes tap-tapping with his stick on the road up to the inn.'

'You two are letting your imaginations run away with you,' Suzie scolded them. 'They'll have been perfectly ordinary fishermen, or maybe they carried small cargoes along the coast.'

She sat down, with an air of satisfaction, and turned on the television. It was a historical drama, which might be watchable. But Nick's heart sank when he realized it was yet another costume romp about Henry VIII's tempestuous marital affairs. Were there no other interesting monarchs?

He got up. The study was free now. There was, of course, no reason why he and Suzie shouldn't have their own computers. There was a spare room upstairs, which could serve as a second study, and still sleep guests. They had just never got around to it. He liked to keep as much of his architect's work as possible at his office in town. It was Suzie who spent long hours in front of the screen, researching family history.

But she had stirred a spark of curiosity. And then there was that framed photograph, newly hung over the landing. Sollie Margerson, fisherman and lifeboat coxswain. A man so respected, his funeral procession stretched for half a mile.

He opened up Google and typed in *Solomon Margerson*. It was worth a try.

There were more results than he had expected. 143. He clicked the first one.

Suddenly he found himself looking at the very same photograph he'd just hung upstairs. Solomon Margerson, in his oilskin smock and sou'wester, leaning against the *Ellen Maud* with a proprietorial air. Millie was right about those magnificent eyebrows.

He studied the page more attentively. It was from the St Furseys Local History and Maritime Museum. He'd never heard of it. But then, why should he? His family had moved away from the east coast two generations before he'd been born. He vaguely remembered a seaside holiday when he was small, but they hadn't been back since. They'd lost the connection with St Furseys when his grandparents died.

There were more photographs. Thumbnail icons too small to distinguish details. He clicked one.

Great-grandfather again, this time with his partner, Morgan Tully.

The next one showed the lifeboat crew on the slipway in 1928, after they had been awarded medals for rescuing the crew of the SS *Ithaki*.

A gala dinner, celebrating more medals. Solomon and Morgan with a ten-foot shark. Solomon and his wife Enid with . . .

He stared at the family group in joyful surprise. There was the older couple, Sollie easily recognizable by his eyebrows. Nick's great-grandmother, with her hair moulded to her head in the fashion of the 1930s. From the caption, that younger woman was his grandmother Nell, now long dead. And she was holding in her arms a chubby toddler who could only be Nick's father, Ellis Fewings.

He pushed back the chair and almost ran next door to the sitting room. It was his turn to experience the thrill of discovery.

'You'll never guess what I've found! Twenty-seven photographs of Great-grandfather Sollie, and one of them's even got my dad in it.'

Suzie and Millie crowded into the study to look. Even Tom heard the excitement, and came bounding down the stairs to find out why. He leaned over their shoulders and whistled.

'Fame at last! Come on, Dad. We really do have to go and check this place out now.'

Nick was clicking on more pictures, bringing up images of the flint-faced cottages of St Furseys in the 1800s.

'Well, Aunt Eleanor was good for more than I expected. It would be appropriate to spend some of her legacy on her father. Especially as it was her idea to leave me his picture. And it's nearly Easter. I'll give Leon a ring. He'll probably be glad of company, now Jacqui's left him. I don't know how big his cottage is, but I should think he could put us up for a few days.'

'I bet they were pirates,' murmured Millie. 'Never mind about that lifeboat stuff. That could be just a cover. With those eyebrows, he's got to be at least the captain of a smugglers' gang.'

'Don't be silly,' said Suzie. 'He was a hero.'

THREE

Suzie peered through the windscreen at the almost flat landscape. Only the merest ripples of wooded ridges disturbed the level expanse of fields and marshland.

'It's . . . big. I mean, it's a different sort of bigness from the West Country. No hills. Just miles and miles with nothing to interrupt it, except what people have built. And so much sky.'

'Good for philosophers. All that infinity to contemplate.'

Nick glanced sideways at her, enjoying the rosy flush of anticipation in her cheeks. This trip had been a good idea of Tom's. He noted with pleasure that Suzie had stowed her new laptop in the well by her feet. She wouldn't trust it in the boot. It had been his birthday present to her, two weeks ago. 'So you won't have to be parted from your beloved family history records in St Furseys,' he had teased her. She had hugged him hard.

Maybe he would get more access to the computer in the study now.

The evening sun winked on the long drainage ditches and a wind furrowed the tall reeds.

'It's beautiful,' Suzie said. 'Still, I'm not sure I'd like to live here. It's so . . . exposed.'

'Creepy,' said Millie's voice from the back. 'Like *Great Expectations*. When Magwitch lies in wait for Pip in the marshes. I'd keep away from churchyards, if I were you.'

'Can't promise,' Suzie called back to her. 'Gravestone inscriptions can come up with unexpected stories. Like my Great-uncle Richard, drowned in the Scillies.'

'Does Uncle Leon have a boat?' Tom asked.

'No idea,' Nick said. 'I've never asked him.'

The car sped along the causeway between the ditches. He could feel it was glad to be out on the level, with its load of four people and their luggage for a week.

'Pack plenty of woollies and gloves,' Suzie had ordered the children. 'It's likely to be a lot colder on the east coast than it is here in the west at Easter.'

If she felt a stranger without her West Country hills, Nick was experiencing an odd sense of homecoming. It wasn't logical. If anything, he'd been more interested in his father's Northern origins. He'd never lived here. He could only remember one holiday at St Furseys, when he must have been about five. Yet the broad skies and the watery landscape spoke to him. He felt a surge of excitement at the brightness in the air which spoke of the sea ahead.

A bank of shingle rose in front of them. Then the road swung right and they were heading for the little village just along the coast.

The sea glittered on their left, flecked with pink from the sunset behind them.

'It's not completely flat,' said Millie. 'There are cliffs on the other side of that dinky little village.'

'That dinky little village is St Furseys,' said Nick. 'And yes, we may not have cliffs the size of those on the Bristol Channel, but the geography here's not entirely predictable.'

'What's with the *we*?' Tom asked. 'One family photograph, and suddenly you're identifying with your North Sea fishermen genes. And all these years you've been teasing Mum about being a family history nut.'

'Point taken.' He smiled at Suzie. 'I guess I owe her an apology.'

'He's been trying to persuade me it would do Tom good to have a break before his exams,' Suzie told the children. 'Or that Leon will be feeling a bit low on his own, and we ought to go and cheer him up. But the truth is, he's been bitten by the bug.'

'You're still the researcher,' Nick tried to argue. 'I'm just your chauffeur. Those pictures I found on the website were just serendipity.'

'We'll see.'

They were spinning along the embankment towards St Furseys. The flint-faced cottages crouched above the dunes. There was no breakwater jutting out from the shingle beach. The sea was gentle now, just long swells running in on the wind. But Nick could imagine how the gales would howl in from the North Sea in winter. How the breakers would crash on this beach. How the fury of the storm would fling debris far inland across the marshes. And in weather like that, there would be men who did not crouch indoors by the fire, but who set off out into those gigantic waves to save lives. Men like his great-grandfather.

The car was entering the narrow main street. Suzie took out the sketch map Leon had sent them. Nick turned left towards the beach, bumping over cobblestones. He would be glad to arrive now.

'Rogues Roost!' said Suzie suddenly, pointing.

A low cottage, its walls glinting black with split flint stones, stood slightly apart from the others, almost on the edge of the beach.

'Rogues Roost?' hooted Millie from the rear. 'A bit twee, isn't it? I'd have expected something better from Uncle Leon.'

'I expect it already had the name when he bought it. Too much hassle to change it. Anyway, I think it's rather fun. More individual than sixteen Beach Street.'

Nick braked, but left the engine running. 'I can't park here. There's hardly room for anyone to get past me.'

'Does it matter?' asked Millie, opening her door. 'It's the last house in the road.'

'Let's unload, anyway.' Suzie joined Millie on the narrow pavement.

They were hardly out of the car before Leon appeared on the doorstep. He wore a rust-coloured canvas smock, smeared with paint. With his thinning hair rumpled he looked, Nick was glad to see, more relaxed than in his dark suit at Aunt Eleanor's funeral.

Next moment, there was a girl standing beside him. She was a little shorter than Millie. Short black curls clustered round her face.

'Anna!' cried Suzie. 'I didn't know you were going to be here. That's great.'

'Surprise!' Anna waved her arms in the air and struck an exaggerated pose.

Leon put his arm round his daughter. 'Thought it might be nice for the two girls to meet up. And Jacqui OK'ed it.'

Millie had stopped in front of the low wooden gate. The girls eyed each other across a small cottage garden, bright with daffodils and forget-me-nots. Nick watched the defensive hunching of Millie's shoulders. Leon should have said, given her time to get used to the idea of staying with her cousin. They had met on family occasions, of course, but they didn't really know each other that well.

'Going to be a houseful, then,' he said. 'How many rooms have you got?'

'Enough. I've put you and Suzie in my room. Millie can share with Anna. And there's a shoebox that goes under the name of the spare room that Tom can have. Though, by the look of him, I can't swear he won't have to sleep with his knees bent.'

'What about you?' Nick hoped his brother wasn't going to have to bed down on the living-room sofa.

'I'm fine. I've converted the loft into a studio. Put in skylights. Wonderful light from the sea. I've got a couch up there. It's like a coastguard's lookout post.'

'When they still *had* coastguards on the coast, and not at some windowless communications centre miles away. Real people, with real telescopes, looking at real ships.'

'True enough. They tell us it's more efficient. Can't see it, myself. You can't replace local knowledge, can you?'

He led the way indoors.

The cottage was simply furnished. Leon appeared to have walked away from his marriage, taking little from the family home with him. The furniture left behind had, Nick suspected, been mostly Jacqui's taste, anyway. Highly polished mahogany and walnut, with florid Victorian carving. Here, the mood was plain, Shaker-style – or just homely pieces from local second-hand shops, such as real fishermen's families living here might have used. Natural light wood, or painted a singing blue that lifted the spirits, like the forget-me-nots outside. Some of Leon's paintings brightened the white walls. Seascapes or beach scenes mostly.

'Not bad,' said Nick, examining a vista of beached fishing boats. 'I may have underestimated your sales potential.'

'Should be able to flog a few to tourists in the summer. Holiday souvenirs. Or solving the Christmas present problem ahead of time.'

'Enough to make a viable income?'

'I wish. No, I'm keeping my hand in with graphic design. Got some part-time work for a firm over in Murchington, ten miles from here. It pays the bills, just. This lot –' he waved his hand around the walls – 'is jam on the cake, sorry, bread. Getting paid for doing what I love.'

'Can't be bad.'

He caught the look on Anna's heart-shaped face, the child who had lost her father, and decided against saying, 'You should have done this years ago.'

He thought of his own successful architect's practice, the glass and chrome office in the cathedral city, the spacious house on the outskirts, set in his beloved large garden. Would he have had the courage to give that up?

But it didn't apply to him, of course. The thought shocked him. He and Suzie had had their occasional ups and downs, but nothing remotely terminal. He still loved her dearly. He glanced across the small, crowded room. Suzie was looking particularly young and feminine today. A flowered blue-and-white skirt, softly pleated. A white polo-necked jumper, which set off the roses in her cheeks. Light brown hair fell almost to her shoulders, just faintly curling at the ends.

Poor old Millie, lanky and pale. It was a pity she hadn't inherited her mother's looks.

'Tea first? Or do you want to take your stuff upstairs?'

'Tea would be marvellous,' said Nick gratefully. 'Milk, no sugar. But what about the car? I'm blocking most of the street.'

'It'll be OK while you drink your tea. Then I'll show you where to put it round the corner.'

They sat around the scrubbed kitchen table, nursing mugs. Nick noticed that eighteen-year-old Tom was unusually quiet. His eyes had gone past the family, out to the sparkling sea beyond the window. They must take a walk along the beach as soon as they were settled in, while the light lasted.

'So,' Leon was saying, 'you've been bitten by the family history bug? I know Suzie's been an addict for years.'

'Well, I suppose it's about time. It's not everyone who's got a local hero on their family tree. I thought I owed it to Great-grandfather Solomon, now that I have to pass him every day on the stairs. I want to find out more about him, the folk he came from, all this.' He gestured around him to include the fisherman's cottage, the sea, the masts of sailing boats at their moorings in what he assumed must be a creek a little further along.

'Millie's determined we'll discover pirates,' Suzie put in.

'Or at the very least, smugglers. I tell her she's just being romantic. But I suppose it's possible . . . the smugglers, I mean.'

'Nothing in the least romantic about smugglers.' Leon's face changed. 'And they're not just in the past. There's not a lot on this coast, but it still happens. There was a nasty case last year, not far from here. Local Customs boat went out after drug smugglers. Tried to board them. One officer got caught between the boats and crushed to death. Not entirely by accident, either. In the shock, the drug runners got away.'

'Yuck,' said Millie.

There was silence around the table.

Then Suzie said, with an attempt to lighten the mood, 'But it wasn't like that in the old days, was it? Everyone was in on it. *Brandy for the parson, baccy for the clerk.*'

'And you know what follows?' said Leon. '*Them that asks no questions isn't told a lie. Watch the wall, my darling, while the Gentlemen go by.* If you think it was all a jolly community romp, like *Whisky Galore*, I'm afraid you're the one being romantic, Suzie. They had ways of silencing inconvenient witnesses. They still have.'

FOUR

'I love the sound of the waves on shingle,' Suzie said.

They were strolling along the beach in the quiet of evening. The sea swung gently against the shelving shore. There was the gravelly slide of pebbles dragged down with the undertow.

The sun had gone, but an oddly cold pink-and-gold light lingered in the wide sky. Nick hunched deeper into his thick wool jacket.

'You were right about bringing gloves. I reckon it's ten degrees colder than at home.'

'They're two different countries, aren't they? East and west? I hardly recognize anything here. We have fishing villages at home, but they tend to be tucked away in coves or river estuaries, with stone breakwaters. There doesn't seem to be anything to protect St Furseys from the wind and the sea except that muddy creek. It's all so open.'

'There's no granite around here,' said Nick. 'They'll have been hard put to get big enough stones for the corners of their church towers.'

'Listen to the architect,' Tom teased him.

'Men have made a living fishing here for centuries,' said Leon. 'They seem to manage. In fact, living in the path of storms does have its up side. Well, it does if you've got a stout boat you know how to handle, and nerves of steel.'

'What do you mean?'

'I mean there have been plenty of wrecks on those sandbanks out there. And they didn't always have a lifeboat service. So the fishermen would race out in their own boats to see who could get there first.'

'And save the people on board?'

'Yes, they'd do that, of course. But there's not much money in picking people out of the water. The real prize was the salvage. The first one to get a line aboard and save the ship. There was *real* money in salvage. That's what the owners will pay you for, not saving the crew. And if you couldn't save the ship, you'd take what you could, and flog it back to them later.'

'So what's new?' said Tom, kicking his feet through the stones. 'When was business ever interested in the workers?'

'You think that's what the Margersons did before Grandad Solomon's time?' Nick asked his brother.

'You showed me the census returns, Suzie. They were all fishermen, weren't they? Right back to 1841.'

'Actually it was 1851. Don't you remember? The first one was a gardener from Cambridge. I'm still trying to work out what brought him here. But after that they were fishermen, or "mariners", whatever that meant. Seamen of some sort.'

'Old Sollie was certainly a lifeboatman,' Nick agreed. 'We've got the account of how they all came to his funeral. So how long before that did St Furseys get its own lifeboat?'

'Ah, that's the sort of thing I'm hoping you genealogical detectives will turn up,' Leon laughed. 'First stop the local museum, I should think. It's not bad for a place this size. Local History and Maritime. You'll enjoy it.'

'And if we want parish records or newspaper reports?' Suzie had swung out of her reverie into research mode.

'You might have to go to Murchington for that. I'm not the best person to advise you. They should be able to tell you at the museum.'

'Where's the lifeboat nowadays?' Nick asked.

'Gone. At least, the big one. They have a fast inflatable at the mouth of the creek.'

Nick looked back. Light was draining from the sky above the village harbour. In the greyer light, the two girls were some distance behind their parents and Tom. There seemed to be a rather large gap between them. Anna was walking close to the edge of the waves. Her head was bent, looking down at the tideline, as though she was beach-combing among the pebbles. Millie had come to a stop higher up the beach. She had her back to him, staring out to sea beyond the village.

The body language isn't good, Nick thought. *Why do we assume that because two kids are the same age they'll get on together? And Millie's got to sleep in the same room as Anna for a week. I hope it works out.*

He walked back to join her.

'OK, sweetheart? It makes a difference from being in town, doesn't it?'

'I like towns.'

'I'm glad you do, since we've brought you up in one. So do I, as a matter of fact. But I'm enjoying this.' He took a deep breath of air, tasting the tang of salt. 'I'd never really taken this roots thing seriously before. Not being from the West Country, where your mother's been doing all her detective work. I'm not complaining. It's taken us to some delightful spots. But suddenly . . . well, this is *mine*. And yours.'

If he had hoped to spark some shared enthusiasm he was disappointed. She didn't even look at him.

'There's a ship out there.'

He followed her gaze. On the far side of St Furseys he could just make out a grey shape hovering offshore. It was not as distant as the three container ships on the horizon, yet not close enough for details to be discernible. It was hard to judge how far away it was, across the expanse of greying water. He could detect no mast. A small motor cruiser, fairly close to land? Or a bigger vessel further out?

'So there is. Bet they're chillier than we are, out on the water.'

'It's not moving.'

'Moored for the night. Hove-to, or whatever the nautical phrase is.'

'Why don't they come into harbour, such as it is? They could have tied up and gone to the pub.'

'Perhaps they don't want to pay for a berth. I expect there are charges for mooring here. Or maybe they're out fishing.'

'I bet they're smugglers. Waiting to make a drop.'

'Don't be silly. Smugglers are hardly going to advertise their presence in daylight, are they?'

He regretted the word *silly* as soon as it was out of his mouth. Millie turned, with a scrunching of stones, and took off after the rest of the family. Her silvery padded coat had the curious effect of making her look thinner still inside it. He hurried after her.

'Sorry, sweetheart. I honestly don't know any more about smugglers than you do. You could be right.'

He didn't really believe it, but there was no point in arguing with her.

'Uncle Leon said they don't have coastguards on the coast any more. Who's going to bother if they *do* see them?'

'Her Majesty's Revenue and Customs?'

'Who are they?'

'Good question. I don't really know. I mean, I know it's their job to stop people smuggling goods into the country. But I've no idea how they do it, apart from us having to go through checks at airports and ferry terminals. I suppose they must have boats patrolling. Leon told us about that accident, when the Customs officer got killed.'

'It wasn't an accident.'

'No, I'm afraid not. So the Customs people do have ways of checking who comes in and out.'

'*All* of them? Little yachts and motor boats?'

'Well, I guess it must be difficult to make sure nothing slips through the net.'

'So it *could* be. That boat out there.' She nodded triumphantly over her shoulder.

Nick looked back. The grey smudge he had seen was lost in the twilight now.

'Yes, OK.' He took her arm companionably and squeezed it. He grinned down at her. 'You win. They could be smugglers.'

Her thin face smiled back at him, vindicated. Better to humour her.

FIVE

This morning, Leon was carrying his painting gear. Tom, with only a little prompting from Nick, offered to take the easel.

Leon led them through a warren of lanes, where fishermen's cottages crowded close on either side. Turning a corner, they were struck full in the face by the morning sun, making the vista of waves beyond the dunes glitter. Nick stopped and screwed up his eyes to focus more clearly on the view.

This little street ran out on to a slipway at the mouth of a creek. They could see the inshore lifeboat in its shed. A few empty boats were pulled up on the open beach. On another, two men were busy loading crab pots.

'It's early in the season yet,' said Leon. 'Come summer, this place will be packed out with flashy yachts. There are only a handful of real fishermen left.'

'Where's this museum, then?' Tom set down the easel and returned his hands deep into his pockets.

'You're standing in front of it.'

They all looked up, surprised. From the last cottage in the row, a wooden extension with large windows jutted out over the beach. Nick had assumed it would be a fish and chip café. Now he noticed a blue-and-white enamel plaque over the door of the cottage. ST FURSEYS LOCAL HISTORY AND MARITIME MUSEUM.

'This is it?'

'The real thing. They've taken over three of these cottages, to give you a feel of what it was like to live here. And they've built that deck out for more displays. I'll leave you to it, if you don't mind. This sunshine's too good to waste.'

'Can I come with you?' Anna asked him.

Nick caught the flash of surprise and annoyance that passed over his brother's face.

'I thought you might want to look at the museum with your cousins. You haven't been inside it yet.'

'Do I have to?' echoed Millie to Nick. 'You know I'm not really interested in this family history stuff.'

A quick look of complicity shot between the two girls. Nick remembered the distance of beach separating them last night. Whatever had happened between them in their bedroom, it had closed that gap. They were allies now.

He felt an unexpected lurch of disappointment. Now that he had got into this family history thing, he realized how much he wanted other people to share his enthusiasm. Particularly his own children. This was their history too. St Furseys was *his* contribution to their genes, to add to all the scores of human stories from the past which Suzie had given them.

To his surprise, Tom took his younger sister's arm firmly. His blue eyes danced at her under the fall of black hair, in the way people found hard to resist.

'Come on, kid. We may never see this place again. If the Fewings are famous here, I want to hear about it.'

'Not the Fewings,' Nick put in. 'These were the Margersons. My grandmother's folk.'

'Whatever. They're ours.'

He drew Millie with him back along the street and pushed open the museum door.

All four of them gasped with surprise, even Millie. In this first cottage, the dividing walls had been removed to leave an open space. To their right was the reception desk, to which a dark-haired woman came hurrying. Around the walls were glass-fronted screens, displaying the village's history. In the centre of the floor stood a three-dimensional model of St Furseys.

But what caught their eyes, on the wall directly facing them, was another huge framed photograph. The man with the bushy eyebrows, in oilskin smock and sou'wester, was unmistakable. This time, he was surrounded by his lifeboat crew. But he held the central place. His piercing eyes met theirs.

'Great-grandfather Sollie!' Tom gave a breathless laugh. 'He must have been quite a guy, mustn't he? They've given him the top spot.'

The woman from the desk came bustling up to them. She had some leaflets in her hand.

'There's a reduced rate for families.' She counted them quickly. Anna, Nick saw, had followed them in. 'That will be eight pounds. And three pounds for this young man.' She smiled flirtatiously at Tom.

There was something not quite English about her accent.

Nick produced his credit card and they went to the desk for tickets. She handed him the leaflets.

'You will find the plan in there. It is a good idea to start here, with the history. Then there is a typical fisherman's cottage on your right. Upstairs is wildlife and geology. There is a controversial scheme to stop coastal erosion, but there are others who think nature should be allowed to take its course. You will find all that up there. And out on our new deck –' she gestured to their left – 'you will find more photographs and a little tea room.'

That slight trace of a foreign accent was rather sexy. Nick considered the sleek black hair, drawn back severely from her olive-skinned face. Spanish? Latin American?

The woman was looking at the two girls. 'I don't know if the children would be interested, but we have a room in the cottage where they can dress up in fishermen's gear, or try their hand in the kitchen.'

Millie and Anna gave her the sort of withering look that only fourteen-year-old girls can deliver.

'Well . . . I will leave you to it. Please ask one of our helpers if there is anything you want to know.'

Nick's eyes met Suzie's. 'Where do you want to start?'

'It's your family. But we've got all morning. Why not do as she says and start here? When we've got the history straight, we can look at everything else. We won't know what's relevant until we see it . . . Though I don't think the geology's going to help much.'

The display boards began with the Neolithic. There had been communities living in causewayed villages in the marshes for thousands of years. Saxons had built the first church, replaced by Normans. St Furseys had been a busy little port in the day of sailing ships, when vessels needed to stop to take on fresh provisions or unload passengers. And as Leon had said, there had been a brisk business in salvaging wrecked ships' gear from the treacherous sands and selling replacement equipment to those which survived.

The decline began with the coming of steam ships, which powered past St Furseys, straight to London. More recently, factory ships and then EU quotas had devastated the fishing fleet. But the new demand for line-caught fish and sustainable catches meant that a handful of local boats survived. And the area was famous for its crabs.

They wandered through to the cottage next door, where the rooms were caught in a moment around the end of Victoria's reign. Nick tried to people them with what he remembered from the censuses of his own family. Benjamin the fisherman, Mollie his wife. Young Solomon, already helping his father in the boat. Sarah, Rose – or was it Lily? – Edmund . . . His memory ran out as he tried to recall their children.

'Did you bring what we've got on the Margersons?' he asked Suzie.

She patted her shoulder bag. 'It's all here.'

He should have known she would have come prepared. He took the sheets from her and traced back several decades. In a house like this, in a bedroom like the one he had just climbed up to, Mollie Margerson, and her mother and daughters, had given birth. Here, small children had died. Of diphtheria, typhoid, scarlet fever? Maybe he should order some death certificates to find out. And the men? How many of them had died in their beds? Or out there on that sea, which looked so deceptively inviting this sparkling spring morning? He realized that he didn't even know how Solomon Margerson had died. Only about that half-mile funeral procession.

There was an elderly volunteer sitting in the cottage kitchen. Presumably he was there to make sure no one stole anything. Nick wondered if there was CCTV in the other rooms. He didn't think so.

They had to pass through the entrance hall again to reach the wooden deck area. Nick turned aside to talk to the receptionist.

'That lifeboat coxswain, Sollie Margerson. He was my great-grandfather.'

'Really? How exciting. We get quite a lot of people coming here tracing their family history. We are planning to put some microfiche readers in the new extension, so that you can check the parish registers.'

'But you haven't got them yet?'

'No, I am sorry. There is a Record Office in Murchington. They will have them.'

Nick felt a lump of frustration in his throat. He realized

how much he had been hoping that this visit to the museum, on their first morning, would provide a step forward. It was a thrill to see Great-grandfather Sollie's fierce stare greeting everyone who came through the door. But it hadn't told him anything he didn't already know.

'I hear they gave him a great send-off at his funeral. Do you know how he died?'

The woman thought for a moment. 'No, I am afraid I don't. But there are more photographs and newspaper stories in the tea room. You might find something there.'

Again he was struck by the incongruity of this foreign woman – he was sure she was not English-born, with her too carefully enunciated words – spending her working days advising visitors about the history of such an essentially English village.

'Thank you. I guess we're all ready for a cup of coffee.'

He looked around for the others. Tom was still upstairs, studying the plans for the coastal erosion defences, and the arguments against it. Millie and Anna were giggling over a display of Victorian women's underwear. Suzie was in the doorway of the fisherman's cottage, trying to find an angle from which she could photograph as much as possible of the small living room-cum-kitchen.

'Coffee?'

'I'd love one.'

He rounded up the others and they climbed the wooden steps. Light flooded the modern extension. Its height enabled them to see far out over the shoreline.

'There's Leon.'

Suzie had spotted a figure seated at the side of the creek, with an easel and canvas in front of him. Leon, padded warmly against the cold wind, was enjoying himself, painting ships settling aslant on an ebbing tide. The sun glistened on wet mud and driftwood. Nick wouldn't have thought of painting mud himself, but he supposed Leon would see colours trapped in the slick surface that escaped his own eye.

He ordered coffee and doughnuts all round. The children were sprawled over the table. They had evidently had their fill of historical research.

But Suzie was still on her feet, studying the photos hung around the walls, and reading the captions and the framed newspaper articles.

'Nick!' she cried suddenly. 'Look at this.'

He set down the tray of coffee on the table and came hurrying over. She pointed silently.

> ### TRAGIC DEATH OF LIFEBOATMEN
> *Coxswain Solomon Margerson, 55, and Peter Sullivan, 18, were lost when the St Furseys lifeboat tragically capsized when going to the aid of the stricken SS* Caractacus *on Friday night.*

He read on, hardly breathing. A night of pounding storm. A vessel driven on the sandbanks. The lifeboat labouring through mountainous waves to reach them. Twenty passengers and crew taken on board and ferried to shore.

And then the second attempt to save more souls from the disintegrating vessel. One giant wave too many. The boat turning over. Men flung into the sea. No self-righting lifeboats in those days. On a falling tide, most of the lifeboatmen had struggled on to the emerging sandbank to wait for rescue in the morning. When daylight broke, only the coxswain and the teenage Peter were nowhere to be seen.

A fragment from a newspaper two days later told how their bodies had been washed up miles down the coast.

'One morning!' Suzie said incredulously. 'You've been researching one morning, and you find *this*.'

'You found it,' he pointed out.

Yet he had to try very hard to keep the smugness out of his smile. In years of searching, Suzie had never turned up a story as heroic as this about her own family.

'Kids,' he called. 'Come and look at this.'

SIX

Millie was leaning over the garden wall after supper. There was more cloud in the sky now. The sea was smudged with violet and grey. Her head was turned to stare south along the coast. The wind lifted strands of her not-quite-blonde hair, but Millie herself did not move.

'What are you looking at?' Nick joined her, trying to convey a tone of father–daughter companionship.

'Nothing.'

'Sorry. I didn't mean to interrupt your daydreams.'

'I wasn't daydreaming. I was looking.'

'Looking. Right. At nothing.'

'Because there's nothing there.'

'You've lost me.'

'That boat we saw last night, out at sea. It's not there.'

'So? Should it be? Boats come and go. That's the beauty of being beside the sea. It's always changing.'

'You said they might be hanging about because they were fishing.'

'Just a guess.'

'So why aren't they fishing tonight?'

'How would I know? Something good on the telly?'

She punched him. 'Dad! This could be serious. Fishing's something you have to do regularly, isn't it? If you want to make a living?'

'Some people just do it for fun.'

'I don't think they *were* fishing. I told you.'

'Smugglers, waiting for a dastardly assignation? Pull the other one.'

He tried to make his smile fond and friendly, not mocking. But Millie turned away with an exaggerated sigh and walked back to the house.

Nick decided it was better not to follow her. He lingered, savouring the low roar of the shingle with every wave, the shifting shades of twilight. It was amazing how long the light lingered over this wide sea.

The door opened behind him, letting out a flood of brighter light. Millie appeared again, with Anna, both wrapped up in coats and scarves. They headed down to the beach and started to walk towards the creek.

Nick straightened up. 'Hey, girls? Where are you off to?'

They turned and stared at him. Their faces were no more than pale blurs.

'For . . . a . . . walk,' said Millie, enunciating precisely, as though to a small child.

'It's getting dark.'

'So?'

He knew he was making a mistake. Millie was fourteen. She was frequently out in the evening with her friends. If it was safe enough in the city, though admittedly a quiet cathedral town, then surely here in a rural village there should be no danger.

'Be back by nine. I don't want to call the coastguards out to look for you.'

'Ha, ha.'

They trudged away through the pebbles.

Nick went back into the cottage. When he stepped into the warmth of the living room an unexpected shiver ran through him. He hadn't realized how cold he had got, watching the sea in the evening wind.

Suzie, Tom and Leon were sitting around a driftwood fire. Nick lowered himself into a spindly rocking chair.

Tom turned his face to him, flushed by the flames or some inner energy.

'Dad, you saw it, didn't you? That programme about wreckers?'

'Sorry. Remind me.'

'Last year. There was some woman who'd been researching stories about people using false lights to lure ships on to the rocks. So they could snatch the cargo. She said they used to beat any of the crew or passengers who looked like making it to shore, so that they drowned. No witnesses.'

'Tom. I saw it too,' Suzie protested. 'Didn't someone else say there wasn't any proof of that? It just makes for a more dramatic story about smugglers. *Jamaica Inn* and all that.'

'Yeah, but I've a nasty feeling it wasn't just about wreckers

in Cornwall. Wasn't there something about the sandbanks
off the east coast, too? You didn't need to wreck the ships
there deliberately. The sea was dangerous enough, anyway.
But they could still make sure no one stopped them getting
the salvage.'

'How can you say that?' Suzie argued. 'After what we found
today? Do you really think people change that much, just
because somebody buys them a proper lifeboat? If Solomon
Margerson gave his life to rescue people, surely his father
and grandfather would have been doing the same in their
fishing boats for generations before?'

Tom shrugged. 'Have it your way. I didn't mean to rain on
your party. I was just reminding you what she said.'

Nick stared into the shifting flames. He had only the haziest
memory of that television documentary. And what he did
remember was mostly to do with the Cornish wreckers, and
whether they really existed. St Furseys had meant nothing to
him then. He'd vaguely known that the portrait of Sollie in
his oilskins, hanging in his great-aunt's house, was of an old
relation. But he'd never asked just who he was or what he
did. He just remembered that family story about the length
of his funeral procession. He had had no reason to connect
him with that other part of the programme that Tom remembered, about this east coast.

It didn't fit. He was still glowing with pride about the story
Suzie had found. His great-grandfather paying the ultimate
price for his courage and heroism. Nick looked out of the
darkening window. He could hardly imagine himself doing
that in a terrifying storm. But then, he wasn't a seaman. He
hadn't been brought up to handle a boat in all weathers. He was
a soft-living architect.

But Suzie was right. It was unimaginable that the kind of
men who risked their lives like that would also take lives
away for loot.

'We'll go to Murchington in the morning. See what else
we can turn up.'

'Please yourself. But they were hardly going to tell their
story to the newspapers, were they? The wreckers?'

It was fully dark when the girls came back. As the door
opened, Nick felt a sudden relief. He must have been worrying
about them, subconsciously. Silly, really.

There was a faint smell of chips and vinegar about them, as they unwound their coats and scarves.

'I can tell where you've been,' Leon teased them. 'My cooking not up to the mark?'

'It's cold out there.' Anna grinned at him. 'We needed to keep our blood sugar levels up.'

'And our eyes open.'

The girls glanced at each other with secret knowing.

SEVEN

'I woke up wondering why I'd agreed to spend a day indoors in a Record Office search room.' Nick threw a rueful grin at Tom in the passenger seat beside him. Suzie and the girls were sharing the back seat. 'I expect you did, too. Then I heard the gravel hitting the window, and when I looked out I decided it might not be such a bad idea, after all.'

Behind them was a surly grey sea, white-crested waves crashing on the beach. Showers of rain were flung across the marshes horizontally, rather than falling from the sky. Nick had lived in Suzie's West Country long enough to miss the warm red cliffs, the villages tucked away in sheltered combes. Everything around St Furseys was exposed. Fine when you could enjoy the huge skies and the vista of fens glittering with water channels. But as the car sped over the straight road to Murchington, he wanted to be somewhere cosier and safer.

'Maybe I'm not so much of a Margerson as I was beginning to think,' he said, staring ahead now through a spatter of rain. 'Wrong genes. I certainly wouldn't want to be at sea on a day like this.'

'I suppose if you'd grown up with it, you'd take it for granted,' Tom said. 'I mean, what else was there?'

'Sobering thought. Just you and the sea. And you'd have to get your living from it somehow, no matter how scared you were.'

The town crouched low, as though it had shrunk in on itself against the wind. Few high rise buildings. Even the church boasted only a squat tower. But it felt good to be in amongst streets again. Nick could no longer feel the wind buffeting the car.

He found a car park. Suzie, resourceful as ever, had run off a street map of the town. It showed the Record Office next to the library on the central square. She led the way inside.

'Right, Tom. I want you to look up that newspaper report of Solomon's death and get a printout of it. Here's the date.

Eleventh of September 1932. And the one two days later, about finding his body. Then there ought to be a big one on his funeral a week or so later. There might even be an obituary. See what you can find.

'Millie. See that big cabinet over there? That's the card index of the same newspaper. I don't think they've computerized it yet. Look up Margerson and make a note of all the dates. Some of them will be the ones Tom's printing, but there are probably others. All those photos from St Furseys Museum, with Solomon getting medals for lifeboat rescues.

'Nick, you need to go through the microfiches of the parish registers. We've got a fair idea of the family from the censuses, but they only take them every ten years. There could be children who were born in between and died in infancy. And the censuses don't show the dates of weddings or burials.

'Anna, do you want to help?'

'That's what I've come for. It's my family too.'

'Well, if Nick starts with the marriage registers, he's going to be turning up some new surnames, from the women who married the Margersons. If you make a note of those, then you can feed them to the rest of us. That means we can widen our searches to include them as well.'

'You've got it all mapped out, haven't you?' Tom laughed. 'Like a military operation. You've missed your vocation, Mum.'

'What about you?' Millie protested. 'I suppose you're going to get a coffee from that machine outside and put your feet up, while we do all the work.'

'No. I'm going to tackle any other parish records I can find. Churchwardens' accounts. Accounts of the Overseers of the Poor. Any books or pamphlets they've got on the parish. It's a question of trawling to see what you can find. With five of us, we should get a lot done in a day.'

'Don't worry, Millie,' Nick smiled at her. 'We'll find somewhere good for lunch.'

'Italian,' Millie said at once. 'I just adore pasta.'

They spread out across the search room and settled down to work.

Nick spent a fascinating morning working on the parish registers. It brought a lump to his throat the first time he saw the shaky cross his great-great-grandmother had used to sign her name. Even on microfiche, he was looking at physical evidence of a real woman. As he delved further, he was surprised to find, however, that more women than men could sign their names. What did that mean? That the men did the hard, dangerous work out at sea, but the women were better able to manage the business?

As he already knew from the censuses, the Margersons had come to St Furseys in the mid-nineteenth century, with the gardener Alfred Margerson from Cambridge. He loaded the microfiches of earlier decades. No. There were definitely no Margersons in St Furseys before then. No evidence of an extended family to bring Alfred here.

But there was now a growing number of surnames from the Margerson marriages, and the parents of their wives. *Horniman*, *Duffield*, *Thompson*. His workload was increasing as he tried to follow them all back, unearthing yet more names on the way. There were quite a few marriages he couldn't find. The men must have taken brides from other villages or towns. Weddings were usually held in the bride's parish. He realized now how big a job it must have been for Suzie to trace so much of her own family. You'd have to trawl all the nearby parishes in the hope of turning up the marriage you were looking for. Or wasn't there a website she used? The IGI, that was it. But he had an idea it didn't cover every parish. Not St Furseys, evidently, or she'd have known a lot of his findings already.

Still, maybe they could check out some of these other names on Suzie's laptop computer.

Once, he heard a sudden cry of 'Yes!' from Suzie. He turned around, but she was thumbing eagerly through a leather-bound book. He thought of getting up and going over to look at what she had found, but he was realizing how short one day was to unravel this ever-proliferating family. He turned back to the microfiche reader, and moved his search from the marriage register to the baptismal one.

By the time they adjourned for lunch in a pleasant glass and chrome restaurant, they had amassed an impressive body of information. Suzie had been right about the newspaper. Millie had turned up a sheaf of articles, which Tom had located on the microfilm rolls and printed out. Anna had been relaying

new names to the others, until Nick had gone as far back as
he could in the marriage registers. Since then, she'd been
helping Millie at the card index. Not surprisingly, several of
the families who had intermarried with the Margersons had
also supplied crew for the St Furseys lifeboat. Hearing their
stories, Nick had a growing pride in his family's roll of honour.
He should have taken an interest in them long ago.

His own research results were mostly names and dates.
There were few personal details in the registers. *William
Margerson, Beach Street*, or *Elijah Thompson, senior*, presum-
ably to distinguish one man from another of the same name.
Philip, son of John Horniman, deceased. The baptism of a
baby who would never know his father. Was John Horniman
lost at sea? *18 March 1811: baptized Thomasin, daughter of
Robert Thompson; buried Margaret, wife of Robert Thompson*.
A bitter-sweet day.

But for the most part, it was the others who had found the
living stories. Millie, Anna and Tom had mostly come up with
newspaper tributes to the heroism of St Furseys' lifeboatmen.
Scores of rescues, in the wildest of conditions. Nick looked
up from his spaghetti carbonara at the gusting rain in the
street. He could hardly imagine what it must be like out at
sea in a small boat. And this wasn't a real storm. A century
ago, that could have been his fate. And Tom's.

He thought of eighteen-year-old Peter Sullivan, drowned
with Solomon Margerson. He looked up to see his son's face.
The same age.

Suzie had been surprisingly silent while the others shared
their discoveries. At last they were done, and their faces turned
to her.

'Go on, then. Spill the beans,' Tom encouraged her. 'What
have you found?'

'Quite a lot, as it happens. I went through the trade direc-
tories for the Murchington area. Alfred Margerson, the one
from Cambridge, wasn't just a gardener. He was also a licensed
victualler – in other words, a pub landlord. He had the Noah's
Ark, just outside St Furseys. Probably his wife actually ran
it. That was quite common. The man would have a day job,
like a fisherman or a gardener, but the pub had to be in his
name.

'But better than that – or worse, depending how you look

at it – there was this history of St Furseys compiled by one of its vicars. He says the Noah's Ark was a notorious haunt of smugglers. Near enough to the sea, and just a bit out of town, away from prying eyes.'

'Like the Admiral Benbow in *Treasure Island*!' exclaimed Millie.

'Spot on. But *this* . . .' She turned to another sheet of paper and gave an anxious glance at Nick. 'I'm not so sure you're going to like this one. It's a quotation from a G.B. Wilson. Seems to have been a writer of Victorian melodramas. Nobody reads him now.' She read aloud:

'*Tongues cannot frame adequate censure for the heartless rogues who would beat the hands of the desperate survivors as they clung to the wreckage, forcing them to relinquish their grip and sink into the raging ocean. What devils are these who would sacrifice the lives of innocent seafarers in their wicked lust to seize what belonged to them?*'

An awkward silence fell over the table. Everyone was looking at Nick. It was illogical, really. Everyone here shared the Margerson genes, except Suzie.

Nick swallowed. 'You said yourself this guy wrote melodramas. He made his living out of conjuring up dastardly villains. He wasn't there, was he? It doesn't mean what he wrote is true.'

'I told you,' said Tom. 'You saw that programme.'

'If it's any consolation,' Suzie offered, 'I've got boatmen on the Kent coast on my mother's side of the family. It was probably the same for them.'

They finished their meal more quietly.

'What now?' asked Nick.

'I'd set aside the whole day for the Record Office,' Suzie said. 'But you've all done fantastically well. I expect you're cross-eyed by now. Is there anything else you kids would like to do?'

'Go home,' said Anna promptly. 'We could play games on my dad's computer.'

Nick raised his eyebrows at his son. 'Tom?'

'Whatever. I did bring a couple of books for revision.'

'Wonders will never cease,' said Millie.

'Suzie?'

'I could get on the Internet. See if I can find some of those missing marriages in other parishes.'

'But we've got the registers right here.'

He could see the day slipping away from him. He desperately needed to stay and find something else positive, to take away the taste of Suzie's discovery.

'I think the kids have had enough.'

Nick ordered ice-creams and coffee. He didn't know what he wanted to do himself, now. The buzz of excitement had gone out of the day.

'Do you know where the Noah's Ark is . . . was? If the rain lets up, I could try and find it.'

EIGHT

By the time they were back at St Furseys the rain was no more than a spatter of spray on the windscreen.

All the same, Nick dressed himself warmly in a thick jacket and then a waterproof, with walking boots and scarf. He had thought of inviting Leon to go with him, but the distant greeting called down from the attic told him his brother was engrossed in artistic creation, or maybe the mortgage-paying graphic design.

He studied the sketch map Suzie had made for him from an old map of the village. The Noah's Ark was indeed oddly isolated from other habitations. It stood on the narrow coast road going south from the village, towards the line of cliffs Nick had seen in this otherwise flat landscape. Suzie had sketched an area around it and marked it 'Gardens'. Not, presumably, a park with flower beds. More likely market gardens.

Of course! He could see the connection now. Alfred Margerson could have come to work here, and supplemented his income as landlord with a spot of gardening. Or perhaps his wife ran the pub, as Suzie had suggested.

Had Alfred known its dark reputation before he took it over? Who had granted him the lease? Had they vetted Alfred to make sure he would be no threat to their contraband operations? Was he, indeed, a willing conspirator? Or had he taken the pub in all innocence, and then found a cutlass held to his throat and whispers of what would happen if he sang to the Revenue men?

Watch the wall, my darling, while the Gentlemen go by.

What had Beth Margerson thought? She'd been a local girl. Beth Duffield. He'd found the record of her marriage to Alfred this morning.

At the door of the cottage he was startled to find Millie and Anna, similarly dressed in woolly hats and scarves.

'Going somewhere?' he asked them. 'I thought you were computer bound.'

'Not if you're on the track of smugglers.'

'The Noah's Ark, you mean?'

'We're coming too.'

'There isn't a pub there now. It's just a house.'

'All the same, it was their headquarters, wasn't it? The smugglers?'

'So your mother says. She's photocopied that bit about it in the book.'

'And our great-something-grandfather was the landlord?'

'Apparently.'

'Great,' said Anna. 'Then we're going to see where he did his dastardly stuff.'

'Do you suppose it has all sorts of hidey-holes?' Millie suggested.

'And secret tunnels?'

'You're letting your imaginations run away with you. And even if it has, we won't be able to get inside to see them.'

'Couldn't you knock on the door and tell them who we are? They might let us in to look.'

Nick had been nursing a similar hope himself, though he wasn't going to tell them. He patted the bulge of the camera in his pocket.

'Come on, then. Let's see what they've done to it in the last century and a half.'

They crossed the creek by the bridge, then walked along the beach, to avoid traffic on the road. The big pebbles gave way to smaller shingle and more sand.

'I can't decide which is worse: turning my ankles over on the stones, or ploughing through the soft stuff,' Millie complained. 'It feels like endurance training for a marathon.'

'It's firmer lower down, where the tide's been.'

'Is it much further?' Anna asked.

Nick consulted Suzie's map. 'There's a gap between the village and the pub, but she hasn't put the scale on this. Still, they've built some new houses facing the sea since then. I'm sure those we've just passed wouldn't have been on this map. So we're probably further on towards the pub than it looks.'

'What's that? Where the trees are.'

Nick screwed up his eyes against the wind-blown sand and peered where Millie was pointing.

Dark fir trees clustered around a solitary house, set back from the road. It rose taller than the cottages in the village. The dark slates were slick with rain and the grey rendering on the walls was dark with damp too. There were no market gardens around it now. Two forlorn-looking cows moved among the salt-marsh grasses. A wire fence surrounded the house, but the growth inside looked almost as rough as that outside.

'Is it empty?' asked Anna. 'There don't seem to be any curtains in the windows.'

'It's hard to imagine it was once a place where you'd want to go for a crack round a log fire and a pint of beer.' Nick hunched his shoulders as he stared at it.

'Maybe they didn't *want* too many people dropping in for a booze-up,' Millie suggested.

'Well, we've come this far. Might as well take a closer look.'

They trudged up the beach on to the road. A drainage channel on the other side cut the house off like a moat. There was an unfenced pathway across it, barely wide enough for a vehicle. It led to outbuildings beyond the house, which might once have been stables. A rusty car lay abandoned beside the unsurfaced drive.

Nick fished out his camera. 'Not the ideal light. But if it comes out dark and gloomy, we can tell the others that's just what it looks like.'

He stepped on to the bridge and raised the viewfinder to his eye.

'What you doing? Did I give you permission to take a photograph of my house? Put that thing away!'

The shout almost made Nick drop the camera.

The figure that burst out of the fir trees was dressed in dirty garments, the colours of the landscape. Coarse trousers tied up with rope. A shapeless coat and a cape of sacking over his shoulders. Beneath an ancient sou'wester grey locks hung down. The sharp nose and pinched cheeks were red with cold. Purple fingers showed through ragged mittens. They were brandishing a rake.

'I'm sorry to disturb you,' Nick smiled gallantly. 'We were just interested in the history of your house. It used to be an inn, didn't it? The Noah's Ark.'

'What's that to you? It's no public house now, so you can get yourself off my land.'

Nick retreated to the road. 'My apologies. No offence meant. It's just that my ancestors used to live here, back in the 1850s. Alfred Margerson was his name. And his wife Beth. He was a gardener, and a publican too. I gather all the land round here used to be market gardens.'

He threw a glance around the wet meadows. It didn't look very convincing.

The man took another step towards them. His small, blood-shot eyes glared at them. Nick felt extremely glad that the rake wasn't a shotgun. The man's aggressive advance gave the unsettling feeling that he might have fired it. Maybe just a warning shot over their heads. If they were lucky.

A car sped past, spraying the three of them from the standing puddles. Anna shrieked and made a rude sign after it.

Millie was not so easily put off. 'They say the pub was used by smugglers. Have you found anything? Secret hidey-holes? Tunnels? Anything like that?'

The ragged man charged on to the bridge, rake levelled at them.

'You mind your own bloody business! It comes to some-thing when a man can't do a bit of work in his own garden without some busybodies coming asking questions they've no right to. Clear off, before I have the law on you.'

'Sorry. Only asking.'

They had backed into the middle of the road, out of reach of the weapon gripped in those purple hands.

'Well, then,' said Nick peaceably. 'We'll be going. Sorry to have disturbed you.'

'Car coming,' called Anna.

They hastened to the safety of the beach.

'Well, *he's* obviously got something to hide,' Millie exploded.

'He's still watching us,' murmured Anna. 'I think we should move.'

They turned to walk down to the sea, angling away from the house.

'There's a boat,' said Nick. 'Do you suppose it's his?'

A black-and-grey rowing boat lay upturned on a shingle bank above the reach of the tides.

'I bet *he's* a smuggler,' Millie declared. 'That's why he doesn't want anyone near the house. Those sheds are probably stuffed to the rafters with cocaine or something. Unless there are secret hiding places in the house.'

'Don't be silly,' said Nick. 'He's just some poor old misfit who can't cope with the rest of the human race. A modern smuggler's not going to be anything like that.'

'That's just why he'd be the perfect cover. Nobody's going to suspect him of drug running.'

Nick sighed. 'There's no answer to that, except that it's totally implausible . . . to anyone except a romantic fourteen-year-old.'

She flung a handful of wet sand at him.

The driftwood fire in the cottage burned clear, its pale blue flames almost without smoke. The salty wood crackled.

'So, you've met Ed Harries,' Leon laughed.

'If you can call being chased off by the wrong end of a garden rake "meeting", then yes.' Nick's answering grin was rueful.

'He's weird, but harmless. Well, if you keep out of range and upwind of him.'

'Then, if no one goes near him, he *could* be stashing drugs there.' Millie was obviously not going to let go of the idea. She was sitting in front of Nick, hunched on the rug. Her usually pale face was flushed by the flames and her eyes, when she turned them up to him, were sparkling.

Nick sighed and rumpled her hair. 'There's no convincing you, is there, poppet?'

She wriggled away from him. 'You never take me seriously.'

Leon turned to Suzie. 'You've done an impressive amount of research for one morning. I never thought you'd come up with anything like this much information. And our Alfred Margerson was really landlord of a pub at Ed Harries' place?'

'The Noah's Ark. Yes.'

'I never realized. I've got an old book on smuggling in these parts. I think I remember reading something about the Noah's Ark in that. But I had no idea where it was. And not a clue that it was once in our family. I shall have a whole new feeling about the house when I pass it in future.'

'You should paint a picture of it,' suggested Tom.

'Some hopes!' Millie exclaimed. 'If that man saw him, he'd run Uncle Leon down with a lawn mower, or shoot him, or something.'

'You're probably right,' Leon agreed.

'You said you had a book,' Suzie said. Her hazel eyes lit up with anticipation. 'What is it called?'

'*Shipmen and Smugglers: Bygone Days Along the Coast.*'

She frowned. 'I don't remember seeing that in the Record Office.'

'You might find a copy in Murchington library. It would probably be reference only, though. They're quite rare. I think mine was in a box of books that came my way after Dad died.'

'Can I see it?'

'If I can remember where I put it.'

He disappeared up the narrow stairs. They heard his footsteps overhead. It was some time before he emerged with a battered blue-covered volume in his hand and an expression of proud achievement.

'Still under the bed. I hadn't unpacked the box. Here you are.'

He handed it over to Suzie and threw a conspiratorial smile at Millie. 'You'll like this. It has wonderful tales of derring-do. Did you know there's said to be a cave here, with the entrance high up in the cliff? The smugglers could actually haul a lugger up there and hide it from the Customs officers. The boat would just disappear before the Revenue cutter got round the headland. It was a complete mystery to them where it had gone. And then there were tunnels leading from the back of the cave to goodness knows where.'

'See, I *told* you!' Millie sat bolt upright, her face blazing with triumph. 'I *said* there were hiding places and tunnels. But you never believe me.'

'Just one problem.' Tom leaned forward from the window seat. 'There aren't any cliffs at St Furseys. So it couldn't be here.'

'How big an area does this book cover?' Suzie asked.

'Quite a distance. The whole county coastline, I think. But you're wrong about the cliffs, Tom. As you've seen, this is one of the flattest counties in the country. But there's that rocky outcrop just south of here. You can see it from the beach. Not the grand sort of cliffs you get in the West Country, but I should think they're big enough for caves.'

'Haven't you been to see?' Anna demanded.

'Give me a chance. I've only been here a matter of weeks.'

There was a small silence, as everyone remembered the break-up of Leon's marriage.

Nick broke the tension. 'We could go and look, couldn't we? Tomorrow, if the weather's decent.'

'You're on,' said Tom with alacrity. 'I'd rather be stomping along the beach looking for smugglers' caves than sitting in front of a microfiche reader in the Record Office . . . No offence, Mum. You did a fantastic job organizing us. But . . .'

'Not your sort of holiday,' Suzie agreed. 'Still, it *was* chucking it down with rain and blowing a gale. What else would you have been doing?'

'I bet that's the sort of weather smugglers like,' Millie insisted. 'Nobody about to see what they're up to. And don't tell me I've got smugglers on the brain. They're real. Uncle Leon told us. They murdered a Customs officer only a few weeks ago, didn't they? And nobody's caught them yet.'

'True enough,' said Leon quietly.

The silence lengthened. It was shattered as a log on the fire cracked with an explosion of sparks.

NINE

The morning was fine but cold. Straight after breakfast Tom appeared, in a rather stylish navy-blue jacket and a scarf which set off the brighter blue of his eyes. He wasn't, Nick noticed, wearing gloves. Boys of Tom's age didn't seem to possess gloves.

'Right,' he said with enthusiasm. 'We're walking to these cliffs, are we, to look for a smugglers' cave? It can't be more than a couple of miles.'

'You're kidding!' protested Millie. 'That means four miles there and back, *plus* clambering around on the beach looking for it. Dad, we're going in the car, aren't we?' She swung round to appeal to Nick.

'What do you think, Leon? Is it too far to walk?'

'To Brandon Head? Not if you're keen. But Millie has a point. We'll want to do some exploring when we get there. And we'll have to watch out for the tide. I think it's low tide around midday, which would suit us. But we'll stop off at the harbour and check.'

'Can we all get into one car?' Suzie asked. 'There are six of us, if Leon's coming.'

'Tom and I can walk, can't we?' Leon nodded at his nephew. 'Or we could take both cars.'

'We'll walk,' Tom affirmed. 'If we step out, we'll be there in under an hour.'

'Right, then. We two will be off. You can't drive all the way to the cliffs, Nick. The road bends inland to avoid that headland. But there's plenty of flat grass where you can pull off the road near the bend. It's not too far from there.'

'I want to walk, too,' said Anna unexpectedly. She smiled up at her tall cousin.

'Since when did you discover the pleasures of hiking?' Leon asked her, with what Nick thought was a lack of tact.

'It's a lovely day.' Anna turned an innocent stare on her father.

Nick glanced at Millie. She was evidently fuming with indignation at Anna's betrayal.

'Oh, well. If *you're* going to walk . . .'

'You don't have to, love. I can drive you.'

'Tell you what, Nick,' said Suzie diplomatically. 'Why don't you and I drive out to the cliffs? Then anyone who wants to can get a lift back.'

'Done,' agreed Nick.

It took the girls a lot longer to get ready than Tom.

Leon's own car was garaged in an old boathouse, round the corner from the end of Beach Street. Nick had parked his on the sandy ground alongside. They all walked that way now, enjoying the sparkling run of the waves before the breeze.

It was only a short step past the boathouses to the creek, which the walkers must pass to take the coastal route south of the village. Nick had his ignition keys out when he changed his mind.

'Why don't we come along with you to check the tides? Just in case we need to change our plans. Suzie and I are in no hurry, since we've got wheels.'

They followed the footpath above the beach to the creosoted shed at the mouth of the creek, where the inshore rescue boat was kept. A white board on the side of the shed showed the tide table. Sailing boats were moored on both sides of the creek, as far as the bridge.

'Not more than half a dozen fishing boats left,' Leon commented. 'It's becoming more of a marina, with yachts and cabin cruisers in the summer.'

'There are some fairly classy numbers in already,' Tom said. 'I fancy that white yacht with the black trim.'

'What's going on?' asked Anna. 'Are there usually that many people round the harbour in April?'

At the side of the creek local people had gathered to watch what was happening there. Some of the nearer boats were leaning sideways on the mud, but at the mouth, there was still enough water for a grey-painted motor boat to come gliding in alongside a large cabin cruiser.

'HM Customs.' Tom read the lettering on the motor boat's side.

'Do you suppose the other boat's drug smugglers?' Millie cried. 'It might be the ones who killed that Customs officer, mightn't it?'

Leon frowned. 'I guess that's what everyone here is hoping.'

They joined the small crowd watching the two boats in almost silent hostility.

'It's different now,' Suzie murmured, as she pressed herself warmly against Nick. 'These locals aren't on the side of the smugglers.'

'Not if it's drugs. I wouldn't be so sure about cigarettes and booze.'

The cabin cruiser was equipped for rod fishing, with high rails in the bows. There was a Customs officer on board. Papers were being examined. Another officer appeared from below, shaking his head. The Fewings watched a third officer step across from the Customs vessel. Two of them disappeared into the cabin again.

Time dragged on. Nick thought of suggesting that they should be on their way, but the tense expectation in everyone's faces silenced him. A man had died, trapped between two boats like this. And if these really were drug runners, then thousands of other lives might be ruined by their hidden cargo. A search for the cave used by nineteenth-century smugglers of lace and brandy seemed petty by comparison.

It ended at last with a stiff handshake between the senior Customs officer and the captain of the cruiser. The crew of the strange boat secured its mooring to the landing stage. The Customs boat turned neatly and shot out of the harbour entrance on the ebbing tide.

'Well, *that* was a disappointment,' complained Millie. 'I'm chilled to the bone, and all for nothing.'

'You'll warm up walking,' Tom told her.

'You mean we're still going to walk all the way out there?'

'You were the one who was mad to find the smugglers' cave.'

'I'd rather find a cappuccino right now.'

Leon had left the group to consult the tide table outside the lifeboat shed. He came back and pulled a face.

'Low tide eleven thirty. We might still make it if we're quick. But we'll only just have got there before it starts to come in again. Should we put it off?'

'Two cars?'

'*Hello*. Leon, isn't it?' A genial voice interrupted their discussion.

Leon turned. He hesitated for a moment, then held out his hand. 'Dr Partridge. Good to see you. You've been watching this morning's drama too? This is my brother, by the way. Nick Fewings.'

Nick shook the hand the doctor offered. He was a big man, expensively dressed, Nick noticed, in casual clothes which yet gave the impression of being carefully chosen. A blue reefer jacket with brass buttons. A navy-blue yachting cap. Pigskin gloves.

'Dr Partridge is another refugee from urban pollution,' Leon explained. 'Semi-retired now. Isn't that right?'

'Malcolm, please. Yes. I do a couple of morning surgeries for the local GP. And a bit of locum work. That sort of thing. Keeps my hand in. And helps pay for the hobby.'

'Which is?' Nick asked.

Dr Partridge waved a hand towards the harbour. 'Boats, my boy. Never be tempted. Worse than horses for draining the bank balance. Still, it gives me a lot of fun.'

'Malcolm's commodore of the St Furseys Yacht Club,' Leon explained.

'That sounds very grand.'

'Oh, no. We're small yet. But the tide's swinging our way. Fewer fishing boats, more yachts. That's the way of the world. Can't turn back history. So why not enjoy it?'

He cast a glance over the assembled Fewings. 'Your family?' he asked Nick.

Belatedly, Nick made introductions. 'My wife, Suzie. Tom and Millie are ours, and Anna is Leon's daughter.'

'Didn't know you had children,' Dr Partridge said to the painter.

'No, well, Anna's just here for the week.' Leon's reply was curt.

'Ah. The fractured family. Another aspect of modern life. You interested in boats?' He had seen Tom gazing at the smart white-and-black yacht which had caught his interest earlier.

'I fancy that one.'

'You have good taste, young man. That's mine. The *Moonraker*. Have you ever sailed?'

'No.'

'How long are you here for? If the weather holds, we might be able to take a spin around the bay.'

'*Really?*'

Millie had heard the conversation. 'Do you often go out this time of year? What about the smugglers? Have you seen any?'

'Millie! Don't be daft. How would he know?' Anna laughed. 'They don't exactly fly the skull and crossbones.'

'That's pirates, silly. And anyway, why did the Customs people pull that other boat in? They must have thought it looked suspicious. What would they look for?' She appealed to Dr Partridge.

He smiled at her intensity. 'I really couldn't say. It's not as if they were hanging about offshore after dark, is it? By the look of her flag, she's Spanish. It might just be that they check any foreign boat. Still, you're right. Since that tragedy a few weeks ago, I've put an alert out to the Yacht Club to keep an eye out for any shipping acting suspiciously. Can't have too many eyes watching, can we? The Revenue and Customs wallahs can't be everywhere. Not that the east coast is notorious for drug running, mind you.'

'And you really would take us out on your yacht? So we could look too?'

He laughed. 'I'll talk about it with your parents. See what we can arrange.'

'Great! Dad, we *are* going to have that coffee, aren't we?'

Tom grinned at Anna. 'So much for a bracing walk along the coast to search for caves this morning.'

Millie tucked her hand into Nick's arm. He smiled down at her fondly. 'It's not a game, Millie. These are seriously dangerous people we're talking about.'

'I *know* that. That's why I want to catch them.'

In the warmth of the café, Millie stirred her cappuccino. 'If that old cave really *is* near St Furseys, perhaps the drug smugglers are using it.'

'Millie!' protested Tom. 'Get real.' He turned away from her to Leon. 'Your Dr Partridge. He did mean it, didn't he? He really would take us out in his yacht?'

'It's his favourite toy. I'm sure he'd like nothing better than to show it off.'

TEN

'So, if we can't do the headland at high tide, we've got a free afternoon,' Nick said. 'Any ideas?'

There was a pause. They had all been keyed up with the excitement of searching for a smugglers' cave. Now, with the afternoon tide rising, they would have to postpone their expedition until tomorrow.

'I've plenty of work to do in the studio,' Leon said. 'You folk feel free to go where you like.'

'I rather fancy curling up with that old book of yours,' Suzie said. 'We've got such a long list of surnames from the Record Office yesterday, there's a chance that some of them might get a mention in that sort of local history.'

'Mum, don't you think of *anything* but family history?' Millie exclaimed.

'It's what we came for . . . Sorry, Leon! And to catch up with you, of course . . . And, yes, I love turning a list of names and dates into colourful anecdotes about real people. *Your* people.'

'It's the places that get to me,' Nick told her. 'I've always enjoyed going round the villages at home with you, even though it's not my family we're chasing. But this really *is* mine. I can begin to imagine them, all living and working here, even if it scares me to think of setting out to sea in the sort of conditions they did. I think what I'd like to do now is to take my camera and all the addresses you've turned up from the censuses and registers. I could try and find as many of them as possible, and get pictures of them while this sunshine holds. With our combined efforts, we could put together an illustrated history of the Margersons and the related families as well.'

He caught the answering smile in her eyes. Suddenly, what had been her hobby, even obsession, had become something both of them could share.

'Tom?' He turned to his son. 'Do you fancy coming?'

'The thing that scares me at the moment is A-level Law.

I've got some catching up to do there. Don't get me wrong,
Dad. I'd love to come cave-hunting with you tomorrow. Unless
Dr Partridge comes up with the goods. But you're on your
own this afternoon.'

'Millie?'

'Boring. Watching you fiddling about with lenses and stuff.
And one fisherman's cottage looks much like another. Right,
Anna?'

'I suppose so.' Anna was looking at Tom regretfully. She
would, Nick felt with some concern, have gone anywhere he
did. Fortunately, Tom seemed impervious to the signals his
younger cousin was sending out.

'We'll do our own thing,' Millie said.

'What?' Suzie wanted to know.

Millie shrugged. 'Not sure. We'll find something.'

After lunch in a fish and chip shop, they decided to walk
out along the creek before they separated. The Spanish boat
was moored towards the end of it, where the water was deepest.
There was no sign of life on board.

'She looks fast,' said Tom.

'If she was really drug-running, she'd need to be,' Leon
told him. 'To outstrip the Customs vessels. I'm not sure if
even this one could match their cutters.'

He stared down at the gleaming rails, and the gear for deep-
sea angling. 'I don't know how thoroughly they check every
foreign boat coming into a little port like this. But Malcolm's
right about the Spanish connection. I gather there's quite a
trade in drugs coming in that way. They ship them across
from South America to North Africa, and then they make their
way north. There could well be Spanish boats involved on
the way. But you'd expect to find them in the English Channel
ports, not here.'

'We better bone up on foreign flags, then,' Tom said. 'North
African and the countries between here and there. So we can
spot any suspicious customers hanging around. I could get
them up on Leon's computer or Mum's laptop.'

'I could help you,' Anna said eagerly.

'That woman in the museum was Spanish, wasn't she?'
Millie broke in. 'Or South American. She might be in on it.'

'*Millie!*' Suzie was torn between exasperation and laughter.
'You'll be accusing Leon of being a drug baron next.'

'There's a ship out there now,' Leon said. 'Doesn't look like one of the local fishing boats.'

The sea breeze caught Suzie's brown curls and whipped them across her face as she turned. With a catch of his heart, Nick lifted them aside and smiled down at her.

The others were intent on the grey shape hovering some distance from the shore.

'It doesn't seem to be moving,' said Anna. 'Is it anchored there?'

'What would it want off St Furseys?' Tom asked. 'If it's not fishing.'

Leon shrugged. 'Could be anything. Marine biologists sending down divers? Mapping the seabed? Treasure hunting for wrecks?'

'There'll be plenty of those,' Nick said. 'From what we've read about those sandbanks.'

'Is it one of ours?' Millie peered across the waves. 'Can you see the flag?'

'I've got a pair of binoculars at home,' Leon said. 'You're welcome to borrow them.'

'Well.' Nick turned his back on the sea. 'No more drama today. The Customs people don't seem to be interested in that one. No sign of their cutter.'

'Just our luck,' mourned Millie. 'I really thought we were in on something exciting this morning. And we didn't even get to the cave.'

They parted at the bridge. Leon, Suzie and Tom were going back to the cottage for an afternoon's work. Nick came with them to get the list of addresses he wanted to find and photograph.

The two girls gave a casual wave and strolled off back along the creek. When Nick looked back, they had stopped on the waterfront. They were now facing each other, in animated discussion.

Nick spent a happy afternoon exploring the narrow streets of St Furseys. It was no surprise to find that some of his fishermen forefathers had lived in Beach Street, where Leon had his cottage. There were more in Middletown and Marsh End. Time and again his lens focused on the flint-starred walls of cottages, a line of herring gulls on the ridge of a slate roof, a vista of low houses leading to the masts in the creek. The shutter clicked. Memory was captured, to be relived with enjoyment, months hence, and hundreds of miles away.

Only Grays Court defeated him. It sounded like a rather grand house, only that didn't seem likely. He found Grays Street, running seaward from the main thoroughfare. Presumably the Court must have been somewhere near. He decided to drop into the museum for advice.

The Spanish-looking curator was at the reception desk.

'Hi,' said Nick. 'I came in a couple of days ago.'

'I remember.' Her dark brown eyes smiled up at him. 'You were looking for evidence of your family. Solomon Margerson, wasn't it? Our local hero.'

That intriguing lilt in her accent was really quite attractive.

'That's right. You've got a good memory. You must get lots of visitors on the family history trail.'

'Not all with such distinguished ancestors.'

She was making him feel better about his family already. In the discoveries about smugglers, and the hints that some might have been more ready to destroy lives than save them, the lifeboatman with his string of medals had got pushed into the background.

'You have a wonderful collection of photographs. I'm on a bit of a photographic safari myself. Trying to track down all the places where my family lived. I was doing pretty well locating them. And a surprising number of the houses still look much as they must have done centuries ago. St Furseys doesn't seem to have suffered too much from gentrification.'

'No. And we are working to keep it that way. You might like to read about our Conservation Society.' She pushed a leaflet towards him.

'Thanks. Keep up the good work. But I dropped in to see if you could help me with one puzzle. I've got a family on my list in Grays Court. But all I can find is Grays Street.'

'That's right. Grays Court would have been a little yard off it. Claud Gray used to own the Dolphin Inn in Grays Street. I would not be surprised if the Court was round behind that.'

She led him up the steps to the sunlight-filled gallery over-looking the sea. As well as photographs of weathered boatmen and stiffly-dressed Victorian businessmen with their families, there were old framed maps.

'Here you are. It is not marked here as Grays Court, but you can see there is a . . . how do you say? . . . an alley leading off the street to this very little square. It would probably have been a rather poor sort of housing. Several families crowded into the same building.'

'I suppose that's why it hasn't survived.'

'That is very likely. We think of cottages today as being the poorest sort of house people lived in. But it was mostly the better ones which have lasted, not the worst.'

'Well, thanks. It's cleared up that mystery. Even if I'm not going to get my photo.'

'Come in any time. I will be glad to help. It is what I am here for.' She flashed him a wide smile, showing large white teeth.

Her English was fluent, he noted, just a little too correct. He wondered again where she had come from, and what had brought her to St Furseys.

'Thanks. Yes. I'll probably be back for something.'

Nick left her and went out on to the street with a warm feeling that helped to counter the chill of the stiff sea breeze.

He pursued two more addresses, a little further from the centre of the village. When he found them, he felt a stab of disappointment. Perhaps they lay outside the conservation area. At any rate, they had been recently modernized. They had picture windows with what must be fabulous sea views. Their smart garages had natural wood doors which matched the window frames. One had even had wrought-iron balconies added. Nick winced at that.

Upmarket family homes? Or holiday cottages? Almost certainly the latter. St Furseys was too far off the beaten track to appeal to commuters, and there must be little employment round here nowadays, with the fishing fleet all but gone.

He strolled back to Leon's, picking up a bag of crumpets on the way, to toast over the fire.

There was the sound of laughter as he opened the door. He unwound his scarf and joined the party. The fire in the living room had been lit. Work seemed to be over for the afternoon. Suzie, Tom and Leon were sitting around it with mugs of tea.

Suzie turned a happy face to him. 'Had a profitable afternoon?'

'Great. Stacks of photos. I can show you this evening. I found nearly everything I was looking for. I'd been expecting to come up against some blanks. But St Furseys doesn't seem to have changed that much in the last two hundred years. Just spread outwards a bit. How about you?'

'Oh, I've been enjoying myself with Leon's book. Not too many of our surnames, I'm afraid. Lots of colourful stories, though. It's a matter of guesswork as to whether your family were involved.'

'Such as?'

Her face sobered. 'Well, there was one terrible one. In 1793, when William Pitt was Prime Minister, he got fed up with the smugglers round St Furseys getting the better of the Revenue officers. So he sent a detachment of redcoats, in January, when the boats were all pulled up on the beach for the winter. And he ordered them to burn the whole fleet.'

'He did *what*?'

'I know. It's dreadful, isn't it?'

Nick sat down heavily in an empty chair. 'It doesn't bear thinking about. What would they do for a living? The whole village must have been on its knees.'

'Wasn't there something that triggered it?' Leon asked. 'It's a while since I read the book. I can't remember all the details.'

'Yes, there was.' Suzie frowned. 'I think they'd been sending in soldiers before that, to help the Revenue officers find evidence against the smugglers. One night, Corporal Terence Staveley was out on his own, keeping watch on the shore. The boatmen took him by surprise. Apparently there was a fight, and the corporal was killed. They found his body on the beach next morning.'

Nick felt a chill close down on his righteous anger. It was happening again. The long arm of accusation reaching out over the years. He tried to shake it away. Suzie had said there was a shortage of surnames in the book. Surely she would have told him if there was evidence his ancestors had been involved. There was no proof. The fishing fleet was far larger in those days. It must have been only a handful of boatmen who were guilty. There was no reason to believe any of his family were among them.

But it left a sour taste in his mouth.

'And to crown it,' Suzie went on, 'six years later William

Pitt's appealing to the boatmen of St Furseys to man the British fleet against Napoleon.'

'And did they?'

'Apparently, yes. Tea or coffee?'

She got up and switched the kettle on to make him a drink.

'Thanks. I bought some crumpets at the bakers'. I thought we might toast them over Leon's wonderful fire. Are the girls upstairs? Shall I call them?'

'They're not back yet. Did you see them in your travels?'

'No. Not a hair of them.' He thought for a moment, remembering how he had criss-crossed the village's few streets. 'That's pretty odd, now I come to think of it. I've been all over the place looking for addresses. You'd think I might have bumped into them somewhere.'

'They'll be back soon,' Leon said, looking at the window. 'It's clouding over. We've had the sunshine for today. It'll be pretty chilly out there now.'

'We'll save some for them. Have you got a toasting fork?'

His brother picked an ornamental brass-handled fork from the fireplace. 'How's that for service?'

'I've never had crumpets toasted in front of an open fire,' Tom said. 'Do they taste better than in the toaster?'

'Of course they do,' said Leon. 'Where's your sense of romance?'

Suzie walked over to the window. She peered out at the lowering sky. 'I wonder where they've got to. Millie never did tell us what they were planning to do.'

'They'll be looking for smugglers,' said Tom.

The adults turned to stare at him. Nick's arm was still stretched out towards the fire, a crumpet speared on the toasting fork.

Tom laughed uncertainly. 'Look, guys, they didn't actually say so. But Millie hasn't thought about anything else since you put the idea into her head. I can't think what else would keep her out in the cold as long as this.'

'And Anna,' said Leon heavily. 'She'd jump at anything to bring a little excitement into her young life.'

'But where would they go,' asked Suzie, 'if they're not in the village?'

'That cave?'

'No. They must have heard us saying there was no point

in looking for it with the tide coming in.' Leon was beginning to look alarmed.

Nick fought to stay calm, but fear was growing. 'The Noah's Ark? Millie was convinced there had to be smugglers' hideyholes there. And even that mad old guy was in on it.'

'Ring her mobile,' said Suzie.

Nick tried. The ring tone mocked him.

'She's not answering.'

Leon dialled Anna's number.

'It's switched off.'

ELEVEN

Nick fought to control the panic racing through his blood. There had to be a rational explanation which did not involve some catastrophe to Millie. Or to Anna, of course. His mind refused to function steadily.

'Millie's not daft.' Tom was looking from one adult to another. He was evidently trying to reassure the fear he could see in their faces. 'I know she may look far out sometimes, but that's just an act. She's really quite sharp. There's no way she and Anna would have gone off to explore that headland for caves with the tide coming in.'

It was odd that their teenage son should be trying to comfort them.

'What else, then?' Suzie's voice came sharply.

Nick tried to face his dread calmly, but too many dark possibilities presented themselves. 'That guy at the old pub was pretty scary. I wouldn't want to think they'd gone ferreting around in his outbuildings.'

'Shall we go and see?' Leon was reaching for his car keys.

'He wouldn't let us in, would he? Not without the police.'

'We ought to call them.' He saw Suzie's face was white and strained. Probably his was too.

They were all hesitating. Nick knew it was because ringing the police would be an admission that they were not overreacting. That the girls' absence was serious. He couldn't bring himself to face that openly yet.

'It's only half past four. They could be in a café somewhere having tea.'

Of course. Now that he'd framed the words, it was such a simple explanation. He breathed more easily.

'They should have rung and told us,' Suzie said.

'Girls!' Leon tried an unsuccessful laugh. 'They don't think, do they? Wait till they're parents themselves.'

Suddenly it seemed easy to believe that Millie and Anna were somewhere safe and warm, nursing mugs of frothy coffee or hot chocolate. Exchanging girl talk. Ignoring the possibility of boring, over-anxious parents worrying about where they were.

Suzie's laugh was only a little less shaky than Leon's. 'Half past four? And we only left them at two. The police would think we were being ridiculous if we reported them missing.'

'How about those crumpets?' Tom said.

They returned to the fire. Leon fetched plates and butter, while Nick wielded the toasting fork in front of the crackling logs.

But the conversation flagged. They were all listening for footsteps on the path, for the rattle of the front door. For girlish voices complaining about the cold. For the phone to ring.

Each of them nursed the possibilities they would rather not speak about.

Tom tried to lighten the mood. 'Leon was right, Dad. They do taste different done on the fire. Especially the burnt bits.'

Nick started. He had barely tasted the crumpet he was eating. It might have been cardboard.

The minute hand of the clock on the mantelpiece climbed toward the vertical.

It was Tom who broke the silence again. 'It's my fault. I should never have mentioned modern smugglers this morning. That other ship outside the harbour. If they thought it *was* connected to drug runners . . .'

'There's no way the girls could get out to it,' Leon countered briskly.

'No, but if they saw someone from there come ashore . . . If the girls followed him . . . or them . . .'

'Look,' said Nick. 'This is St Furseys. A picture-postcard fishing village in a nineteenth-century time warp. It's not gangland. The girls might *think* it's full of drug smugglers. But it's hardly likely, is it? I'm just worried about what trouble they might get themselves into, following a wild goose chase into the wrong places.'

'Drug smugglers are real,' Leon told him. 'They've got to put the stuff ashore somewhere.'

By twenty past five, Suzie could stand it no longer. She startled Nick by leaping to her feet. 'I'm going to try ringing Millie again.' She fetched her mobile from her handbag and speed dialled. They hung on her answer.

'No. She's still not answering.' Her eyes challenged Nick. 'We can't just sit here, can we? They certainly should be back by now. We have to tell someone.'

'I'll do it,' said Leon.

He moved away to the landline phone and looked up the number of the police headquarters. Nick, Suzie and Tom listened while he explained the girls' absence to someone at the other end. How many miles away across the fens would that be, Nick wondered.

'Yes, that's right. Both fourteen years old. Medium height. One with short curly black hair, the other straight and blondish . . . What were they wearing?' He appealed to Suzie.

'Millie had a silvery padded jacket and, I think, black trousers. Anna's coat was pale blue, and didn't she have blue jeans? Oh, and Millie was wearing a white woolly cap. I don't think Anna had anything on her head, did she?'

'Roger that,' said Tom.

After a while, Leon put the phone down.

'They say it's not dark yet. And if neither of them is familiar with the locality, they might have misjudged how long it would take them to get home.'

'They haven't phoned to say,' Suzie objected.

'They're teenagers. Look, I'm not saying the police weren't taking it seriously. They're just telling us not to panic. They're putting out an alert to any cars in the area.'

'We can go and look for ourselves.' Nick was on his feet, reaching for his coat on the pegs by the door. 'We could start by checking the cafés in the village.'

'They'll mostly be closing by now,' Leon said, buttoning on his own coat.

'If they're not there, we'll drive along to those cliffs. Just in case.'

'We'd better be quick then. It won't be dark for a while, but the visibility's getting poorer.'

'I'm coming too,' Tom said, grabbing his scarf and jacket.

'Suzie, stay by the phone. I've got my mobile.' Nick gave her a fierce hug. 'Try not to worry. They're probably fine. They just won't have thought about what we'd be imagining.'

'I know.' She kissed him. 'I'm trying to be sensible.'

They were all striving to behave like mature, intelligent English people. They were not going to panic or get hysterical, even though nightmare scenarios were beginning to chase through Nick's brain. The pale drowned face of Millie under the waves. Millie in a pool of blood. Two frightened teenage girls locked in a dark barn or attic. He would not let himself think of the man or men who might have done that to them.

Leon took the waterfront restaurants. Tom set off at a loping run to cover the pubs and cafés in the High Street. It was left to Nick to comb the side streets.

It was a depressing search.

'No, love. We don't get that many visitors this time of year. I'd have noticed your two if they'd been in.'

Another shake of the head at the White Swan pub. 'Sorry. We closed after lunch.'

He passed a couple of tea shops, already shut. He could feel his tension rising. Daylight was running out.

He remembered the museum at the end of Quay Lane. The girls had liked the sea views from its gallery cafeteria's huge windows.

Nick felt a little embarrassed to be going in again, so soon after his last query. He scolded himself that his personal feelings were unimportant now. But when he got there, the sign on the door said CLOSED.

He was turning away in frustration when he noticed that there was still a light on inside. He hammered on the wooden door. There was no answer. He moved to the small window. Yes, he could see the curator inside, tidying away something at her desk. He rapped sharply on the glass.

She looked up, startled. When she saw who it was she seemed to hesitate. Then she flashed him that wide, white smile and came to the door.

'Yes? Can I help you? I am afraid we are already closed.'

His face was too stiff with worry to respond to her smile.

'I know. But it's urgent. I'm afraid it's not family history this time. It's my daughter. And my niece. You might remember them from Monday. Millie's rather pale and thin. Long, straight hair, a sort of mousy blonde. Wearing a silver jacket. Anna's a bit chubbier. Curly black hair, cut short.'

'I remember them. A very pretty girl, the dark one.'

It hurt. Poor pale, vulnerable Millie. She knew she wasn't pretty. Too colourless, too sharply featured. Suzie tried to comfort her that she would grow into a distinguished-looking woman. But Millie knew her mother was more attractive than she was. It seemed unfair to be reminded of that today, when anything might have happened to Millie.

'Have they been in today? For a coffee or something?'

The woman shook her sleek, dark head. 'I have not seen them. Is it important?'

'They haven't come home. We don't know where they are.'

Concern dragged her smile into suitably downturned lines. 'I am so sorry. Have you called the police?'

'Yes. They're not taking it too seriously yet. But they'll have to soon.'

He was in a hurry to go now. The museum had been his last hope. He had covered all the other possibilities.

Outside, he was alarmed to find how fast the spring daylight was going. He strode fast along the footpath to Leon's garage.

His brother was already there, car keys in hand. His eager, questioning look at Nick told that his own news was not good. They raised their eyebrows at each other and shook their heads.

Tom was their only hope now. It was several minutes more before he came at a fast trot down Beach Street to join them.

'Nope. One or two people remembered seeing them at the harbour this morning, with us. But not since then.'

'Suzie would have rung if they'd come home.' Nick double-checked that his mobile was switched on.

He rang her number, just in case. Suzie answered at once. He heard the hope in her breathless, 'Yes?'

'It's me, I'm afraid. No sign of them in the village.'

'Nothing's happened here, either, since you left. They haven't rung.'

The car sped along the winding coast road, raised up above meadows and reed beds, towards the cliffs. Leon was silent, grim-faced at the wheel. Nick looked out at the lowering rain clouds threatening to bring night on early.

He hit his hand violently on his knee. 'We've wasted too much time. We should have left Tom to check the cafés, while we came straight out here.'

'They're not little kids,' Tom said from the back seat. 'If they did go out there, which seems unlikely, and one of them got into trouble, the other one would have rung for help.'

'Millie's not answering her phone. She may have dropped it.'

The headland was rushing towards them. The cliffs were not high, compared to the coastal scenery of the South-west Nick was used to. But the total flatness of the land around them made them seem dramatic. Waves were crashing on the rocks at their base, a chilling white without sunlight.

Leon parked on the grass verge where the road swung sharply right to avoid the high ground. The men got out and set off for the rocks at a run.

As they drew near, Nick cupped his hands to his mouth and shouted, 'Millie! Anna!'

The wind whipped his words away.

A few strides in front of them, Tom stopped. 'Listen. Can you hear something?'

They waited, tense with hope.

A wail came back between the gusts of wind.

'Just a gull,' Leon said heavily. 'That wasn't human.'

The tufts of grass were giving way to slabs of soft rock, half hidden at first among the sand. Nick stumbled painfully over one. The sand was thinning out. The ledges were filling with sea-water pools. They jumped across them recklessly.

They were nearing the bigger rocks at the foot of the cliffs. Nick began to feel the mist of salt spray prickling his cheeks.

He stopped and shouted again, against the sound of the breakers. This time, not even the gulls answered.

Before long, they reached the line where the tide had swept in, covering the slabs they were running over. Nick's shoes were already full of water. It was useless to splash on. They hadn't even reached the tumble of rocks where the breakers crashed. There was no way they could get out there.

He looked up. The cliffs were close now. But their faces were ghostly pale, featureless, in the fading light.

'Can you see any sign of a cave?' he called to the others.

They stopped and studied the wall above them.

'It would have to have been pretty well hidden from most angles, wouldn't it?' Tom suggested. 'Otherwise, those old Revenue officers would have been on to it.'

'They might have known it was there,' Leon said, 'but not that you could get up to it. They wouldn't know about the men inside with ropes.'

'It all sounds pretty incredible,' Nick sighed. 'But that's not to say Millie and Anna wouldn't have believed it. If they came this afternoon, the tide would have been lower. They could have got further out on the point.'

It was not only the wind chilling him as he said this.

'Why don't we climb up on this headland?' Tom said. 'Look over.'

Nick felt a wave of astonishment and anger at himself that he hadn't thought of this. Terror for Millie was clouding his judgement. He couldn't think straight. How could Tom remain so detached and lucid? Millie was his sister, for heaven's sake.

Anna was Nick's niece, but he couldn't feel the same raw emotion over her loss. Not the way Leon must be feeling about her.

They sloshed their way back to the sand dunes.

'Where can we get up?' Nick demanded of Leon.

'How do I know? I've only been living here a few weeks.'

They scanned the headland in the gathering gloom. At the highest point, a grassy slope tilted away from the sea. It ran out into fields with fences and hedges lower down, before it met the road.

'There has to be a footpath,' Nick said. 'It must be a local beauty spot.'

'We could drive inland a bit and look for the signpost,' Leon agreed. 'It's probably quicker than charging cross country and running into difficulties.'

'I'll try the short cut,' Tom offered. 'You two look for the footpath.'

There was no gate in the fence where they were parked. Tom vaulted over. He turned to wave to them and then set off at a run. For a moment they watched him dodging around what must be patches of wet ground.

Then Leon and Nick sprang for the car doors. As they swung inland, Nick craned to scan the verge, searching for that longed-for brown finger post, which would point the easier path to the top.

They were almost behind the summit of Brandon Head, far from the beach, when he saw it. He shouted to Leon and the wheels skidded in the roadside gravel as he braked. There was a small, empty car park.

From this angle, the slope of the headland was indeed more

gradual. If Tom had found a way across the fields he would face a stiff climb. From here the path rose steadily, between fields of vegetables at first, towards open land at the highest point of the cliffs.

The two brothers forged up it. As they climbed, the air seemed to grow lighter around them. The sea was widening the higher they went. To their left lay the harbour of St Furseys, mockingly cheerful now with street lights. A light further out puzzled Nick, until he realized it must be the ship they had seen at anchor, now making its way in towards the breakwater.

But what he could not see yet, and would not until they reached the top, were the rocks at the foot of the cliffs. His lungs were bursting, but he forced himself on without slowing. He could hear Leon's laboured breathing beside him. Leon was older than he was. How good was his heart?

At last they were out on open grass, scattered with gorse bushes. The path ended at the concrete pyramid of a trig point.

They had hardly got there before Tom came pulling himself up from the more precipitous slope to their left. He made a face that was half laughter, half defeat.

'You were right. I kept having to change direction to find my way through hedges,' he panted. 'Any sign of them?'

They approached the lip of the cliff.

Nick had a dizzying view of white breakers smashing in spray on yellowish rocks. He searched, with a chill in his heart, for the pale smudge of Millie's silver jacket, the light blue of Anna's. Even in this light, they should be visible. If they were there. If they hadn't been swept out to sea by those relentless waves.

None of them said anything. But Nick and Leon drew back from the edge and looked at each other. *He's probably feeling the same as I am*, Nick thought. *He doesn't know whether not seeing them down there is good news or bad.*

Tom, however, had lain down on his stomach. He craned his head over the lip of rock and peered directly beneath him. At last he wriggled back and stood up, brushing the dirt and grass from his clothes.

'It's hard to say. I think I can pick out a shadow in the rock face. Might just be a shallow hollow, but it *could* be a cave entrance.'

'We didn't bring a rope,' Nick said.

'I've got one in the car.' Leon was poised to run. Then his shoulders sagged. 'No point, though. The girls won't have had one. I can't see either of them attempting to climb down this on their own.'

Nick drew out his mobile again and rang Suzie. There was still no news.

'That's it,' he told her. 'It's nearly dark. You have to ring the police again. They can't tell us it's not serious now.'

TWELVE

Grey light lingered where the sea met the sky, but night was advancing. As the car sped along the road, black shadows clotted the stand of firs in front of the former inn. No lights showed from the house.

Nick craned sideways. 'Shall we look?'

Leon slowed, frowning. 'We'd probably be wasting our time. It would need the police to make a proper search.'

All the same, Nick found his head turning to look through the rear window. What if Millie and Anna were there? What if they'd had some crazy idea of searching the outbuildings, and Ed Harries had caught them at it? What would a cantankerous halfwit like that do to them? He felt an almost uncontrollable urge to fling open the car door and jump out.

He tried to tell himself that Leon was right. The police could do it more effectively.

If they took the girls' disappearance seriously.

They were rushing towards the lights of St Furseys. Closer to, the houses showed like a gap-toothed smile. Too many dark spaces where cottages sold for second homes were shut up. How many genuine villagers were there left? How many would come out on a chilly spring evening to search for two girls they didn't know?

It was an enormous relief to find a police car already outside Leon's cottage.

Inside, Nick went straight past the officers to Suzie, and they hugged each other without words. Nick felt for Leon. At what stage would he ring Jacqui to tell her Anna was missing? Would his wife blame him for not looking after their daughter? Just three days away from home, and she was in danger.

He turned to the two constables, a tall, lean man with a long jaw and a smaller woman with ginger hair peeping out from under her cap. Behind their bright yellow jackets they both looked young. Too young, Nick thought indignantly. Surely this warranted a more experienced officer? An inspector, at least.

They introduced themselves. Constables Grafton and Diggory.

The brothers went over the situation again, hurriedly. Suzie had already briefed the police. The woman, Constable Diggory, took notes: the girls were unfamiliar with the area; this was their first visit to St Furseys; they had been excited by stories of drug smugglers, and of smugglers in the past; they might have connected it to the history of a cave on Brandon Head, or the old Noah's Ark pub, or to any unidentified ship seen off the coast. If they really *had* come across drug runners, they could be in serious danger. Or if they had got on the wrong side of that paranoid householder, Ed Harries.

Constable Diggory closed her notebook with a snap. 'I have to tell you, there's a much more mundane possibility. When girls their age go missing, it's usually because they've run away from home.'

'I've told you: there was no note,' Suzie protested. 'They don't seem to have taken anything except the clothes they were wearing.'

'No, but maybe they wanted to put you off the scent. Get you searching the neighbourhood, while they put some distance between you and themselves. Have there been any arguments lately? Anything else to upset them?'

'No,' said Nick and Suzie together.

Leon shook his head.

'It's all been rather fun, really,' Suzie added. 'We're here on the family history trail. And we roped the girls in to help as detectives. They seemed to be enjoying it.'

'Boyfriends, then? Could they have gone to meet up with someone?'

Suzie shook her head more slowly. 'I don't think there was anyone. Millie has a crowd of girlfriends she hangs out with. She has crushes on boys, from a distance, but she wasn't going out with any of them.' She appealed to Tom. 'That's right, isn't it? There's not someone she didn't tell us about?'

Tom shrugged. 'Not as far as I know.'

'And Anna?' The constable turned to Leon.

His face was stiff as he framed his curt answer. 'Anna has been living with my wife recently. I only see her about once a fortnight, for a weekend. This is the first time she's been to stay with me for any length of time since . . . since we broke up.'

'I think we need to contact your wife. It's possible the girls may have gone there.'

Leon gave a choking snort.

'We have to cover all the possibilities, sir. And we need to ask your wife the same questions. She may know something you don't. Have you told her yet that Anna's missing?'

'No.'

'I think you should.'

'Excuse me,' Leon muttered. He went upstairs to make that difficult phone call in private.

'I probably don't need to tell you,' Constable Diggory's freckled face turned back to Nick and Suzie, 'girls can meet unsavoury people on Internet chatrooms. They pretend to be attractive boys.'

'Millie knows about that.' Nick's curt answer shut off the subject.

The other constable, Grafton, was fidgeting. Nick felt a sudden rush of sympathy for him. The young man kept looking at the darkening window. It was evident he would rather be out there, organizing a search party. Sheds, boathouses, maybe even checking that ship they had seen. It was what Nick was yearning to do.

Meanwhile, this policewoman was pursuing family relationships, possible romances, parent-and-daughter quarrels. Millie hadn't gone missing of her own free will. Nick was sure of it.

They heard Leon's step, heavy on the stairs. It must have been a grim phone call. The older brother avoided the expectant gaze of the faces turned up to him.

'She doesn't know anything. It was a complete surprise to her. She'll call us if they show up.' His glare hardened on the police officers. 'And how are they supposed to have got away from St Furseys, anyway? Have you questioned the bus company? Has anyone seen them?'

Constable Diggory's own grey eyes grew steely. 'We left someone at HQ checking that.' She was keeping her voice level. 'It's routine for a missing persons enquiry.'

Missing persons. Was that what the girls were? An innocuous phrase. Not *kidnapped*, not *assaulted*. Not – he forced his mind to frame the word – *murdered*. It brought a physical shiver. He felt cold and sick.

'Well, what are we going to do?' His voice came out harsher than he meant it to. 'We can't just stand here. It's nearly dark.'

Constable Grafton was talking into his radio. He raised his face from the stiff collar of his fluorescent jacket. His eyes were eager now. 'I've called up reinforcements. Mr Fewings?' He turned to Leon. 'Do you have friends or neighbours who might turn out to help us? We ought to check the immediate area straight away.'

'I'm pretty new here, but I'll have a go.'

This time Leon used the phone downstairs. Nick listened to him somewhat awkwardly explaining the situation to people he didn't know very well. But there was deep gratitude in his voice at the unheard answers. 'Thank you! You've no idea how grateful I am. That's right: sixteen Beach Street. We'll see you soon, then.'

They went from house to house, questioning. Had anyone seen the girls? Did they have a shed or garage where someone might be hidden? Powerful police torches probed the shadows.

At one point, Nick exploded to Constable Grafton. 'This is a waste of time! If they were hiding away, it wouldn't be within a stone's throw of Beach Street.'

The young officer's face grew even longer than before. 'Not if they were hiding voluntarily, sir.'

As night fell, two more policemen arrived. One strode down the yellow-lit street with Constable Diggory. He held out a gloved hand.

'Sergeant Thompson. Sorry to hear about this, sir. It must be a worrying time for you.'

'Yes. Look, I know we were teasing Millie about being obsessed with drug smugglers. Hoping she'd catch them red-handed. But do you suppose . . . Is there a serious possibility that the girls might have stumbled on something they shouldn't?'

'Hard to say, sir. There's not a lot of drug running on this coast. And if the Revenue and Customs people haven't caught the latest culprits, I very much doubt that your girls would have done so. No, our best hope is that they've just run away. It's what usually happens, thank God. Some reason the parents may not even be aware of. I gather your brother's recently

broken up with his wife? Well, maybe their daughter's taken
it harder than she's let on. She might have persuaded your
Millie to do a runner with her. With any luck, they'll have
clearer heads in the morning and ring you.'

It all sounded so sensible, so reassuring. Just a cry for help
from Anna.

The search went on.

Nick saw shadowy figures moving along the streets, as
he was doing. Leon's friends and neighbours. Residents of
St Furseys. How much did his brother know about them? He'd
only been in the village a few weeks. How could he be sure
that one of them wasn't part of a smuggling chain, desperate
to cover up evidence of undercover criminality beneath a
respectable exterior? Or could one of them, outwardly innocent, be the sort of paedophile who preys on teenage girls?

Still, there are two of them, he argued with himself, as he
opened another garden gate and walked up to the front door.
They should be all right if they stick together.

But the thought of Millie's unanswered mobile sickened
him. How long before she picked it up? How long before the
battery ran out?

He failed to find a doorbell in the dark and knocked instead.
No one answered, though light showed through the curtains.

Constable Grafton was trying the house next door. Nick
had orders to call him if he found out anything interesting.

He knocked again.

He was just turning away when the door opened a crack.

'Yes?' It was a woman's voice, slightly quavering.

'It's about my daughter,' Nick said, trying to reassure her
that he was not himself a threat. 'And my niece. They've gone
missing. I wondered if you'd seen them. Two teenage girls.
One in a silver jacket and one in blue?'

The door opened wider. The woman was plump, elderly,
looking up at him through thick glasses. She wore bright pink
carpet slippers with pom-poms.

'Two girls, did you say? I might have. I was on my way
back on the bus from my sister's in Sandbeach this afternoon.
I think we did pass a couple of youngsters outside the village.'

Hope soared. 'What were they wearing?'

'I didn't take a lot of notice. But something lightish, like
you said.'

'Which direction is Sandbeach?'

'It's south of here.'

'Constable!'

Nick's eager cry brought the policeman leaping over the low hedge from the house next door. His melancholy face lit up as he heard the news.

'When was this, Mrs . . .?'

'Talbot. Bus gets back to St Furseys quarter to three. So it couldn't have been much before that, could it?'

'How far out of the village were they?'

'Now you're asking. I can't say as I remember properly.'

'This side of the headland? On the coast road?'

'Oh, yes. They were by the sea.'

'On the road or the beach?'

She was beginning to look flustered, almost frightened now. 'I don't remember. It was just two girls. Nothing special.'

'What were they doing? Walking? Standing still? Anything else?'

'Walking, I suppose. Well, it wasn't the sort of day for sitting on the beach, was it? This nasty cold wind.'

'Towards the village, or away from it?'

'I don't . . . Away. Yes, I'm pretty sure they were. Is it important? I won't have to go to court, will I?' Nick saw the panic behind the woman's thick lenses.

'I sincerely hope not,' said the constable. 'Thank you, Mrs Talbot. You've been very helpful.'

He reached for his radio. Before long, there was a knot of police officers round them. Leon came hurrying to join them.

It was Nick who put the possibility into words. 'They were on the coast road, going south. The next thing they'd come to would be the old pub where Ed Harries lives.'

THIRTEEN

Sergeant Thompson had gone back to his car. Nick could see him in earnest conversation on his radio. He got his own phone out and rang Suzie.

Leon joined him. The smaller man's hands were thrust into his pockets, his shoulders hunched. Nick put his mobile away with a stab of guilt. At least he and Suzie could share this pain together. Leon had the added burden of Jacqui's assumption that it must be his fault.

'They can't just go into Ed Harries' place mob-handed,' his brother said. 'It looks as if our sergeant needs clearance from higher up.'

'And I can't stop thinking what may be happening to the girls while we wait.'

The sergeant came over to join them. 'If we have your word for it that these girls had expressed an interest in searching Mr Harries' property, then Inspector Davis agrees we should take a look. But we'll need a search warrant. From what you say, we may get a warm welcome.'

'No problem with the warrant,' Leon said instantly. 'Dr Partridge is a JP. He'll do it.'

'Is that the nautical-looking gentleman who's helping the party on the foreshore?'

'That's him. He does like to look the part. But he'll be delighted to help you. He loves to be in the thick of things.'

The line of torches led them to where the search party was combing the beach. Pointless, Nick thought angrily. The tide's still rising. If there's anything to find, it will be at low tide.

He caught his breath. He could not bear to think what form that evidence might take.

As he, Leon and the sergeant neared them, the doctor was quickly visible. Leon was right about looking the part. Malcolm Partridge wore a shiny yellow waterproof, sea boots and his yachting cap. He looked, Nick thought, a little like those photographs of lifeboatmen in the museum, or the portrait of Sollie Margerson on the stairs at home. That was probably his intention.

He came striding up to them, concern on his usually genial face. 'Nothing to report, old chap? Still, no news is good news, don't they say? They'll turn up safe and sound, you'll see. You'll give the little madams a good bollocking for causing all this trouble.'

'If you wouldn't mind, sir,' the sergeant broke in. 'Mr Fewings tells me you're a magistrate.'

'You've got the right man here. How can I help you?'

'We'd like you to sign a search warrant, if you wouldn't mind. Firs Farm's the property. I gather it's on the coast road, on the way to Sandbeach.'

'Old Ed's place?' Malcolm Partridge broke into noisy laughter, which he quickly subdued. He looked from Leon to Nick in sudden interest. 'You think your girls are there?'

'It's a possibility,' Nick said. 'They were seen heading that way. And Millie had this idea that Harries might be connected with drug running. Yes, I know it sounds ridiculous, but you know what teenagers are like. She thought that might be the reason he won't allow anyone on his property. There's just a chance she might have persuaded Anna to go with her and check out his sheds.'

'Rather them than me. Ed's got a very short fuse.' Again, the laughter was wiped from his face as he considered the implications of what he had said. 'Sorry. Just like me to put my foot in it . . . Well, let's get on with it. Where's this warrant?' He turned to the sergeant.

'Detective Inspector Davis will be here any moment,' Sergeant Thompson said. 'She has it with her.'

Detective Inspector. A chill, that was more than the night air, went creeping up through Nick. With each increase in the rank of the officers involved this was growing more serious. It was what he had wanted from the beginning, but now he wished it wasn't happening. The fatherly sergeant in uniform was more reassuring.

Somebody somewhere had decided that this was more than a routine missing persons enquiry. Not just two teenagers running away from home. CID. Criminal Investigation Department. He did not want to name the crime they might be investigating.

* * *

Sergeant Thompson's 'moment' seemed to last an age. But at last DI Davis was there on the seafront with them, with a detective sergeant in tow. A woman about Nick's age, in a green Barbour, hatless in the breeze that was tugging at her untidy curls. She greeted Nick and Leon with brusque sympathy, and then went into a huddle with Dr Partridge in the light from her car.

'Thank you,' she said, straightening up. 'That should do it . . . Mr Fewings, both,' she addressed the brothers. 'I expect you'd like to be in on this with us, in case we find the girls there. But only on strict conditions. You are to stay with the police cars until I call you. You are not to approach Mr Harries. And you will obey any orders I, or another officer, give you, immediately and without question.'

'Understood,' Nick said.

'Right,' agreed Leon. 'Let's get on with it.'

They made for the cars. Three police vehicles were now lined up on the waterfront. The Fewings were steered towards the inspector's.

Someone else was standing there, hand resting determinedly on the open door. Tom. Nick registered a sense of shock. He had been so consumed by his fear for Millie that he had forgotten about his son.

Tom's face under the street lamps was unusually serious. 'I'm coming with you.'

'Who's he?' Inspector Davis turned to the brothers.

'My son, Tom,' Nick said.

He saw a moment of indecision in the inspector's face. Then she straightened her shoulders. 'Right. Get in Sergeant Thompson's car. And stay out of trouble. I don't want any have-a-go heroes, if Mr Harries proves less than welcoming. Leave that to the police.'

'I'll be on my best behaviour. Scout's honour.'

Nick threw him a warning look

At the last moment, Malcolm Partridge reappeared, the lamplight gleaming on his yellow oilskins. 'Thought you might be glad of a hand.' He started to climb into the second car.

This time the inspector did put her foot down. 'I'm very grateful to you for the warrant, sir, but I think we have enough manpower, thank you.'

Dr Partridge leaned towards her with a confident smile.

'But I know old Ed, you see. Treated him after he gave himself a nasty gash with his axe. He wouldn't normally go near the surgery, but he was bleeding like a pig. Saved two fingers for him. He had the grace to thank me for it. You might be glad of someone who can get on the right side of him.'

The inspector snapped, 'Very well, sir. Get in with Tom.'

The detective sergeant drove the lead car, with Inspector Davis, Leon and Nick. Six officers in all, thought Nick, plus three Fewings and Malcolm Partridge. And at the end of the dark road, a decrepit farmhouse, a paranoid householder, who might or might not have a firearm. Nick still couldn't believe Ed Harries was part of a drugs ring. But what the troubled man might do if he found two strange girls trespassing on his property was anyone's guess. The presence of the large, cheerful doctor, to whom Ed Harries might feel he owed a favour, was only the smallest comfort.

There was the sound of the wind rushing through the trees, the crash of waves on the shingle. It was fully night now, without stars, but when the police cars switched off their headlights, Nick could make out gradations of grey. The air was lighter over the sea, shading to impenetrable black under the stand of fir trees beside the road. No lamplight showed from the house beyond.

Inspector Davis and the detective sergeant went to the back of their car and took out heavy padded vests. Nick guessed the uniformed officers already wore theirs, bulking out their fluorescent jackets. He knew that stab-proof vests were routine these days. But bullet-proof ones were clumsier, impeding their movements. How well protected were they?

Against what?

'Do you think he has a gun?' he murmured to Leon.

'Wouldn't be surprised. If he's that suspicious of visitors.'

It was not a topic either of them wanted to pursue.

Hadn't Malcolm Partridge said something about an axe?

Just as Nick thought this, the doctor's loud, confident voice rang out from beside the second car. 'I'll come up with you. Friendly face, you know. You'll scare the pants off poor old Ed with those uniforms.'

'Thank you, sir. But I'd like you to stay right here until I call you.' The inspector's voice had taken on a hard edge.

'Oops! Have I put my foot in it again? Sorry, ma'am!' In the faint light from the open car door Nick saw him give her a mock salute.

His bantering tone set Nick's teeth on edge. This wasn't a joking matter. He resented the fact that, for the doctor, this was nothing but a bit of local excitement. He didn't know the girls. If he really cared, he wouldn't be making a jest of it.

He sympathized with the inspector.

The Fewings were left behind with Partridge and Constable Grafton. The doctor turned to the young officer.

'Got left out of the action, too, did you? While your girl colleague gets all the fun? Constable Diggory, did they call her? Good-looking wench. I rather like those ginger curls.'

'I'm back-up,' said the constable with dignity.

'And keeping an eye on awkward old codgers like me, probably. Of course, it's the latest psychology, isn't it? Putting women on the front line. Supposed to calm down the aggression. I'm an old-fashioned type, myself. Leave the women behind and go in hard. Politically incorrect, I'm afraid.'

Nick wished he would stop talking in that loud, jovial voice. He was straining to listen for sounds from the house. The bobbing torchlight showed that the police had almost reached the door. Were they still all together? Or had some fanned out, to be at hand in the shadows if anything went wrong?

Tom wandered off towards the fir trees. Constable Grafton made a movement, as though to stop him, and then stepped back and let him go. They could hear the cracking of twigs as Tom searched in the shadows. Nick was tempted to join him. The genial doctor was getting on his nerves.

A sudden burst of shouting brought even the voluble Malcolm to a halt. He took a few swift steps towards the house and then stopped. Nick could just make out the restraining hand of Constable Grafton on his arm.

'Leave it, sir. The inspector will deal with it.'

Tom's movements in the copse had gone silent.

Presently they heard swift steps coming down the overgrown drive towards them. A torch was switched on. The small frame of Constable Diggory was outlined behind it.

'Dr Partridge. If you'd like to come with me.'

Malcolm threw the others a triumphant smile. 'Delighted. Lead on, young lady.'

Nick ground his foot against the gravel in impatience as the torch led the pair back to the house. How long would he and Leon be left here, doing nothing? They could have been searching those sheds by now.

There were raised voices carried on the wind. A high screeching, wordless at this distance. That must be Ed Harries. A lower booming from the doctor.

Nick tensed, expecting a shot to ring out. Or cries of alarm from police officers under assault.

Tom reappeared, a tall shadow detaching itself from the trees. 'Sounds like he isn't in the mood for a house party.'

The shouts died. The sound of the wind and the waves took over. The four waiting by the cars breathed more easily.

'Are any of them armed?' Nick asked the constable.

'I shouldn't think so. There was no reason for it, was there?'

'Ed's just a sad, twisted misfit, from what I can gather,' Leon said. 'So long as you keep well out of his way.'

Nick sensed his brother turn his head to him. It was too dark to read the expression on his face.

It was Sergeant Thompson who came the second time, with a heavier tread. In the darkness, Nick sensed the smile of satisfaction in his voice.

'Right, gentlemen. All clear now. Mr Harries saw reason, after we'd put the handcuffs on and removed his axe.'

Will they be charging him? A sudden shock of guilt ran through Nick. *What if the girls aren't here, and we've brought this on him?* 'Just a sad, twisted misfit,' Leon had called him.

Sergeant Thompson was organizing them into search parties. 'Grafton, take those sheds on the right with Diggory. Young Tom, you can go along with them. Foster and I will sort out the ones at the back of the yard, and keep the good doctor out of the DI's hair. Messrs Fewings, if you'd care to join the inspector and her sergeant in the house?'

'Yes. Thank you!' He and Leon were starting up the drive, almost before the sergeant had finished speaking.

There were dim lights in the house now. More showed in the uncurtained windows before they got there. Nick could imagine vividly Ed Harries swearing at the police for wasting his electricity. It would not have surprised him to find the former inn still lit by flickering oil lamps.

Sergeant Thompson opened the door and called, 'Both Mr Fewings, ma'am.'

Then he stepped aside. 'Go on in. I'll get back to the barns. I wouldn't want Dr Partridge getting ahead of me.'

As they stepped into the living room, a stream of abuse met them. Ed Harries was handcuffed to the iron latch of a stout oak door. He had been sitting in a high-backed Windsor chair, but he sprang out of it at their appearance, lungeing as far as his restraints would let him.

'Bloody trespassing foreigners! You did this to me! You never had no business, poking your noses in here.'

His eyes were red-rimmed, glaring pale blue. Spittle flew from his mouth. It flecked the bristling stubble on his chin.

'A pity Dr Partridge didn't have his medical bag with him. A sedative would have come in handy.' Detective Sergeant Vine greeted them from an inner door.

In spite of himself, an inappropriate shiver of curiosity ran through Nick as he looked around. This was the house he had so wanted to enter when he saw it from the road. Where his great-great-great-grandfather had been landlord of the Noah's Ark inn. Where smugglers had reputedly brought their illegal cargoes, to distribute them across the neighbourhood. Had Revenue officers stood where this sergeant did? Had they combed through the rooms of the inn, as the police were now doing?

He looked around him at the dark panelled walls, the beamed ceilings, the small window panes. Sixteenth-century Tudor? Seventeenth-century Stuart? The interior seemed little changed, except that the bar had gone. A few items of cheap modern furniture stood haphazardly, as though they had been temporarily parked there. An uncomfortable-looking chair with wooden arms, stuffing leaking from its seat. A battered table, strewn with newspaper and dirty plates. A sinkful of crockery and pans, which would not bear closer inspection.

Inspector Davis had followed Vine into the room. She brought him back to the present with a shock. 'No sign of the girls yet, I'm afraid. It's a rambling place, but we're checking every possible hiding place and cupboard. We'll take the upstairs next. But you might like to cast a parental eye over the place too. Just in case the girls have been here and left any signs that you might recognize. It could be something quite trivial. A sweet wrapping. A bus ticket. Anything they might have had in their pockets that they could have dropped us as a clue. You said they haven't been answering their phones. But I expect it's too much to hope we might find those here. And please, don't disturb anything more than you have to. It's not a scene of crime yet, and I hope it won't be, but we'd better stay on the safe side.'

This is about Millie, not family history, Nick rebuked himself. *About Anna. Somewhere there may be two girls, shut up, terrified, maybe hurt, praying desperately for someone to come and find them.*

They moved through to a smaller room, piled with dilapidated cardboard boxes. DS Vine checked them, while Nick watched.

The walls had once been whitewashed, but were now curtained with dirty cobwebs. An unnamed smell came from a larger ceramic sink.

That beguiling inner voice again. Had this once been the stillroom, where the landlord's wife or her maid had done their dairy work or prepared preserves to feed the crowd of men in the bar next door?

Sergeant Vine sighed as he replaced the last empty box.

As they combed through the dirty, unloved rooms, the sense of the past seemed more real to Nick than the shocking present. He was getting tired. He had lost that sense of immediacy, the belief that he would find Millie, here and now. He was just going through the motions.

They came to the foot of the oak stairs. Leon was already there, arguing with the inspector.

'You said one of us might spot something. Something we'd recognize because we know the girls. Tom's in the sheds across the yard. But what about the barns? There's only Malcolm with your officers. He doesn't know Anna, or Millie.'

'Sergeant Thompson's a family man. He knows the sort of thing to look out for. But if you'd rather go with them, we've got your brother here.'

Leon hesitated. Then he threw an anxious look at Nick. 'All right. I'll go and double check the barns.'

Nick followed the two detective officers up the stairs. The broad banister rail felt greasy to the touch.

This had been a substantial house once. It was not the cosy, low-ceilinged pub Nick was used to in the West Country. The rooms were loftier, with moulded plaster on the ceilings, as if it might have been a home for minor gentry when it was first built.

No time to think about that now, or why Alfred Margerson had made that move from gardening in Cambridge to become the landlord here.

Yet images persisted. Had his great-great-great-grandmother Beth pictured herself as a fine lady, sweeping her skirts down these stairs? She would surely have swept and dusted and polished in a way this house had not seen for many years.

They searched one sad, neglected bedroom after another. The light bulbs were the lowest wattage possible. They dangled from the ceilings without shades, but the accumulation of dirt shrouded the little light they shed.

The officers opened sagging wardrobes, shone their torches into low cupboards in the roof space. Nick cast a searching eye all around: the floors, the heavy furniture, older than that in the bar. There was nothing that might have been dropped by Millie or Anna.

Sergeant Vine went downstairs to fetch a ladder, then climbed up to probe the loft. He re-emerged, rubbing cobwebs from his hair, looking downcast.

'Nothing up there. Do you want to have a look?'

He stood back, so that Nick could mount the ladder, and passed him a torch.

Nick put his head and shoulders through the hatch and swept the beam around. It was emptier than most of the rooms they had searched. Ed Harries hadn't bothered to come up here.

He clambered up. There was no roof insulation. The slates were cold above his stooped head. There was no boarding over the joists, either. He had to place his feet carefully, to avoid going through the ceiling below.

It did not take long. There was not the smallest sign that two teenage girls had been here. The dust lay undisturbed, except for the prints of DS Vine's shoes and his own.

He climbed down again, with a chill resignation, and shook his head. 'Another blank.'

'Then, unless the others have turned up something in the sheds, that's it, I'm afraid.' The inspector's crisp tone wrapped up the search and put it aside.

The sense of present horror came sweeping back over Nick like an incoming tide.

'If they're not here, and they were seen heading in this direction . . .'

'We're planning to search the shore off Brandon Head at first light. I've already alerted the coastguard.'

When the tide was falling again. When the waves had been crashing against the cliffs all night.

'Are you OK, sir?' The sergeant moved swiftly to Nick's side.

'Yes, thanks.' Nick passed a hand over his face and felt the cold sweat that had broken out.

'Sergeant, do you think you could organize a strong cup of tea?'

He allowed them to lead him down the stairs.

At the bottom he paused, seizing the newel post with fresh urgency. 'This was supposed to be a smugglers' inn. There must have been hiding places. Not just ordinary cupboards. Secret openings. We haven't looked properly. We might have missed something. In the panelling. The floorboards.'

Inspector Davis looked at him patiently. 'Mr Fewings. I know this is a tough time for any parent. And I can imagine Millie and Anna getting carried away with smuggling stories. But we're adults. This is the twenty-first century. Yes, we lifted the carpet in the parlour. And we did look for any suspicious cracks in the panelling. We're not amateurs, you know. But I don't think we need to go around putting our fingers into every knothole in the woodwork. This is not an Enid Blyton adventure book.'

Nick took the hot cup the sergeant handed him. It was, he was relieved to see, not one of Ed Harries', but the plastic cap from a Thermos. The world steadied a little as the sugary tea coursed through him.

The old man was still muttering to himself in the corner. 'Trespassing on my property, you are. I'll have the law on the lot of you.'

The inspector turned to him with a tight smile. 'We *are* the law, sir. I'm sorry you've been inconvenienced. I shall be making a report on this evening's disturbance. You'll be the first to be informed if we decide to bring charges.'

Again, Nick felt that sense of shame. The Fewings had

brought this on Ed Harries. If Millie hadn't had that colourful idea of modern smugglers here . . . If Nick himself hadn't insisted she might have come back . . .

Just a mentally unstable old man.

Yet what had Millie said? *'That's just why he'd be the perfect cover. Nobody is going to suspect him of drug running.'*

Nick looked at the inspector's face and couldn't bring himself to say it.

He was outside, in the chill, clean air. Tom was waiting for him, hands glumly in pockets. Leon came disconsolately from the barns to join them, followed by Sergeant Thompson and his constable. The bulky figure of Malcolm Partridge in his yellow oilskins loomed behind them. His now familiar voice boomed out.

'I hear you're going to search the Parson's Rocks in the morning. What's the drill for that?'

'It should be getting light around five.'

Nick had to go back and tell Suzie they had failed.

FOURTEEN

A sharp rap on the bedroom door woke Nick. He struggled to orientate himself.

'Thanks,' Suzie called beside him.

The bedside light sprang on, revealing an unfamiliar room. Leon's bedroom. No light showed yet from beyond the closed curtains. Yet Suzie was already on her feet and dressing herself warmly. He stared at her through a haze of bewilderment.

Then the truth hit him, cruelly sharp. Millie and Anna were missing. They had been gone all night. And with the falling tide, he must join the search over the tumbled rocks of the headland.

He felt sick. He had only had a couple of hours of fitful sleep.

'What are you doing?' he asked, as he saw Suzie pulling on her boots.

'I'm coming too.'

He passed his hand over his aching head. 'Someone's got to stay here. In case they ring Leon's home number. Or even turn up here themselves.'

There was still the faint, rose-coloured hope that the two girls would walk in the door, sheepish with embarrassment, confessing to some wildcat scheme they had thought better of in the cold light of morning.

He had an idea that this was what the police thought would happen, though they were still covering every eventuality.

He remembered the drive home after the search of the old inn. The inspector tight-lipped. Despite the axe, she would have some explaining to do if Ed Harries complained about the search. Nick felt that she no longer considered him and Leon to be reliable witnesses to Millie and Anna's state of mind.

Were they? Had he exaggerated Millie's obsession with smugglers?

'You went out yesterday. It's my turn,' Suzie challenged him.

He pulled his warmest jersey over his head and sighed. 'It's not like that, love. I know you want to help. We all want to be up and doing something. But if the girls come home, it's you they'll want.'

He wasn't sure that was true. He sensed a closer bond between Suzie and her handsome son than her daughter. Millie could be sulky, awkward, at the age when mother and daughter exasperate each other. The shine that sometimes kindled in Millie's pale eyes was usually for him. A cord whipped round his heart and tightened.

'It's because I'm a woman. You've got to be the one who has to be out there doing things.' Suzie's hazel eyes flashed. 'Women can be left at home. You've no idea what it's like, waiting and waiting for the phone to ring or the door to open, only it never does. Just all that time to imagine things.'

He hugged her. 'I never said it wasn't tough. But this morning's going to be physically demanding too. Clambering about over steep, wet rocks.'

He did not say what he wanted to shield her from finding.

Downstairs in the living room, Leon was pouring coffee for them and filling flasks.

'I should be doing that,' said Suzie. 'Would either of you like a cooked breakfast? It's going be cold out there.'

But neither of the men had an appetite. She made them toast, and set about organizing sandwiches. Common sense told Nick they would be glad of food later. He couldn't imagine it now.

Tom staggered in from the bathroom, yawning, and accepted Suzie's offer of bacon and egg.

Nick was grateful to her. He hadn't thought enough of what she must have suffered yesterday, while he and Leon were busy searching St Furseys and then the old inn. That desperate drive to do something, anything, that might possibly lead him to the girls.

The faintest grey light was filtering through the murk when Leon drew back the living-room curtains.

'Time to go,' he said quietly.

Despite the early hour, there were lights in some of the windows of the village. Men and women, in boots and stout clothing, were coming out to join the search for girls they had never known. Dr Partridge, Nick thought, was sure to be among them.

Once more they drove out along the narrow coast road, going south. Sea, land and sky were still a leaden grey. There was a little convoy of cars, their lights the only warmth. They passed the old Noah's Ark.

'There was a boat, wasn't there?' Tom leaned forward suddenly. 'You know, that afternoon when you and the girls walked out to here and you told us that mad old guy chased you off? Millie said you found it above the beach, and there were no other houses around, so it must be his. Did anybody search it last night?'

Leon pulled the car off the road and waved at the others to drive past.

The bleak grey-and-black boat lay inverted among the long dry grass of the highest dunes. They stood for a moment looking at it. Nick wasn't sure what he should imagine.

'Do you think there could really be something under it?' he asked Leon. It was not just the early morning cold which was making his lips stiff.

'Only one way to find out.'

The three of them heaved on the weighty hull. It rocked and tipped and then crashed over on to its keel.

A jumble of ropes, a plastic bucket, fishing twine.

They stared at it in silence. Then Tom went down on his hands and knees to do a fingertip search of the sand. The men watched him. That brief moment, that had been more fear than hope, had passed. One more blank door that had opened to reveal nothing.

Tom straightened up, dusting off his sandy hands. 'Nope. Not a hair of them. Literally.'

They drove on in silence.

By the time they reached Brandon Head the light was strengthening. Leon cut the headlamps. The grey of early morning was broken by the white of surf, still swinging against the lower rocks. Above them, the cliff bulked in shadow, the yellow and red streaks of its different strata not yet visible.

There was a small crowd of people on the jumble of rocks. Others had spread out along the beach, probing the receding tideline.

The three Fewings walked soberly across the grass and sand to join them.

'I wonder who's in charge,' Nick said. 'Can you see the inspector?'

'There's Sergeant Thompson.' Tom pointed.

The rocks were slippery, almost like clay. The tide had not long since left them. Tom's trainer skidded, plunging his leg into a pool left behind in a crevice. He swore. For once, Nick did not correct him.

He must have, he thought wryly, something of Malcolm Partridge himself. He had packed Wellingtons for this trip, perhaps with a nod of recognition to old Sollie Margerson's photo in his lifeboat outfit. He was glad of them now.

The fatherly Sergeant Thompson was talking to a man whose uniform Nick did not immediately recognize. Foul-weather gear of yellow overalls. A peaked cap with a hint of gold braid.

'Morning, gentlemen. I hope you managed to get some sleep. This is Dennis Gaiman, coastguard. He knows a sight more about this shore than I do. We'll be working with him to coordinate the search.'

The coastguard put out a large hand. He gave them a brief smile, which soon faded into an expression of grimmer sympathy. 'Sorry to hear about your girls. Sergeant Thompson tells me you thought they might have come out this way.'

'Yes. Looking for a smugglers' cave.'

He shook his head. 'There are a few fissures in the cliff. I don't know if you could really call them caves. There's no depth to them. We checked them first thing. It seemed the kind of place your girls might have taken shelter in, if they were cut off by the tide.'

'Are they above the high-water mark?' Nick's heart was in his mouth.

'Depends on the wind. Normally, I'd say yes. Last night?' His hand hovered in the balance. 'Touch and go. If they'd been there, they might have kept their heads above water. But we've found no sign of them.'

Another brief hope dashed. He must try not to imagine the girls trapped and helpless, a last wave crashing higher than the all the rest, sucking them out to sea, to be hurtled against rocks and left limp and lifeless in a rock pool.

He must take comfort from the fact that no one had found their bodies yet.

'But the smugglers' cave wasn't down here,' Tom was saying. 'It was higher up. There was a story that the smugglers used to haul a lugger up to it, when the Revenue men were after them.'

'Yes, I've heard that one. I never did believe it, myself. These cliffs are pretty unstable. And look around you. Would you want to bring a boat in under them through these rocks?'

Leon had walked away from them, desperate to begin the search. He called back, 'There's a gully here between the reefs. I reckon an experienced sailor could edge a boat in, if he was careful.'

They came across to join him. The water was nearing its shallowest now. Looking down from the rocks, Nick could just make out in the grey light the paler blur of a sandy bottom, scattered with dark pebbles.

Tom turned to look above them. 'We're just about at the point of the headland. It must have been somewhere around here that I looked over the edge and thought I saw something. A sort of shadow in the cliff face that could have been a cave entrance.' He tilted his head back to squint at the top of the headland. 'Trouble is, we're too close under. It's hard to be sure. What we really need is to get out to sea. If it's there, it should be plain enough from offshore.' He spun round on the coastguard. 'You must have a boat. You could take us out.'

Dennis Gaiman shook his head. 'Sorry, young man. Let's stay in the real world, shall we? For a start, your girls didn't have a boat, did they? And suppose that old fishermen's tale was true, who would there be up there in that cave to haul them up? We'll leave that one to the story books, I think. Now, if you'll excuse me, I've got work to do.'

Nick felt the rebuke, that the coastguard was more concerned about searching the seashore for Anna and Millie than their own family were.

But Tom would not give up. 'Dr Partridge said he'd take us out in his boat, didn't he?' he challenged Leon.

'And who's this, taking my name in vain? Young Tom, is it?'

He was back, as Nick had known he would be. Malcolm Partridge could not have had much more sleep than the rest of them. Yet he looked fresh and cheerful. His round face was reddened with exertion from scrambling over the rocks. He wore the same yellow oilskins and yachting cap as before. Not so very different from the coastguard.

'I'm just trying to think what was going through Millie's head,' Tom explained, urgent that they should believe him. 'She's brighter than she lets on. And she sometimes thinks sideways, when the rest of us only see what's in front of us.'

'Lateral thinking, eh? And how do I come into this?'

'She had this thing about the smugglers' cave. One they could pull a boat up to.'

'That old chestnut! Sorry to disappoint you. You'll hear that story told in places all along this coast. No reason St Furseys should be the right one – if it ever happened. Besides, the number of cliff falls we've had since then, I shouldn't think there'd be anything left of it, if there ever was one.'

'You must have sailed up and down this coast a good few times,' Leon said. 'Have you ever seen anything on this headland that could be it?'

'I'm out every weekend, unless there's a gale blowing. Evenings too, if I can. Can't say I've ever bothered to do a recce. But I should think I'd have noticed it, if there was anything there.' He cast his eyes upwards, as they had. 'Can't see anything from here. Can you?'

'I think there might be one,' Tom insisted. 'I just about caught a glimpse of it from above.'

'Well,' said Malcolm Partridge. 'And supposing I did take you out, and you saw a cave? How would that help you? You don't really think Millie and her friend would have fancied a bit of rock climbing? It's a pretty sheer face. And it can give way under your foot.'

Nick felt his own face fall. Even Tom was beginning to look doubtful. They had been snatching at a faint hope, any explanation other than the one the coastguard was clearly expecting. The terrible evidence that everyone on this headland was searching for.

He could put it off no longer. It was time to join that search.

It ended, as part of him had known it would, with nothing. Nick was beginning to feel that it would go on like this for ever. That every search would draw a blank. That there would

never be any news. That he and Suzie would spend the rest
of their lives not knowing what had become of Millie. Or
Leon of Anna. He watched his tall son standing on a high
rock outlined against the brightening sea. Leon had no other
child.

They drank the coffee and ate the bacon sandwiches Suzie
had prepared for them. He could not taste them.

It had been a long time since he had sat still. He became
aware, with surprise, that the sun had fully risen. The sky
above him was cloudless blue. Further out, the grey of the
waves was turning green. Beyond the searchers, the pink legs
of oystercatchers twinkled among the shallow ripples, while
their orange bills probed the seaweed. It was going to be a
fine day, with a promise of warmth.

A day he should have been sharing with Millie, on a family
holiday.

There was a cry from further along the beach, louder than
the gulls. Someone was running towards them.

He and Leon were on their feet. Nick felt sick with churning
emotions.

It was a woman in a blue parka, sensible-looking, older
than Suzie. She was waving something in her hand. Something
small, metallic. As he stumbled through the shingle, he saw
the eagerness in her face. He strained to see what she was
holding.

Sergeant Thompson was ahead of him. He took the object
from the woman. Nick reached them, panting, with Leon close
behind him.

A mobile phone. Silver, edged with blue. Millie's phone.
He did not need to examine it. He knew.

'She wasn't answering it.' He heard his own hollow voice.

The sergeant turned to him, concern on his face. 'It doesn't
tell us anything, sir, except that she was here. Or somewhere
along this stretch of coast. There's no need to assume the
worst. We haven't found your girls.'

There was no need for Nick to tell him their bodies could
be washed miles down the coast, to be cast up long afterwards, like Solomon Margerson.

Tom came leaping from his high perch on the rocks to join
them.

'Is it working?'

The sergeant tried. 'I'm afraid not. But you're right, young man. We'll get it back to HQ. See if any of our whizz-kids can pick something up of who she might have been talking to or texting yesterday. We'll check the phone company records.'

He slipped the phone into a polythene bag.

Nick felt an almost overwhelming urge to protest. To grab his arm and wrest it from him. That mobile was the only evidence he had of Millie since yesterday, the only link with what might have happened to her.

Instead, he had to watch the sergeant heading for the line of parked cars.

When he had gone, a heavy weight descended on Nick. At last he had some news to tell Suzie. It was a call he did not want to make.

A silence fell over those of the search party who had gathered round. They would all be wondering, as he was, whether another search of the beach, not just the rocks of the headland, might yield more evidence. Some moved off along the shingle, with fresh determination. But others were beginning to move away. Cars were starting, heading back to St Furseys. People picking up the threads of their own, less troubled, lives.

Nick got out his own mobile and dialled Suzie. Leon and the others moved aside to give him privacy.

It wasn't easy to hear Suzie's anguish. His own false optimism, intended to comfort her, sounded hollow, even to himself.

Someone else was coming towards him from the road. Inspector Davis, in her green Barbour. Thompson must have told her about the find.

She stood in front of him, without a smile of greeting.

'It seems you were right. About the girls and the cave. They did come here to look for it.'

'Then where are they?' he demanded.

She looked hard at him. 'I just hope the most obvious explanation isn't the right one. No reason why it should be. Millie could easily have dropped her phone climbing over the rocks. She and Anna could be anywhere by now.'

'It means one thing,' Leon cut in. 'They didn't run away, did they?'

'Unless they were planning to sleep in a cave,' said the inspector.

They looked at each other, absorbing the implications.
Tom had walked away and was staring out to sea.

'That ship!' he shouted. 'The one we saw yesterday, outside
the harbour. She's leaving.'

They followed his gaze. In the distance, a grey shape came
gliding out from the creek.

Tom spun round to the inspector, his eyes ablaze. 'Shouldn't
you be stopping and searching it? It was here last night. When
the girls went missing. And now it's going. They could be
aboard!'

'Tom,' ordered Inspector Davis. 'Leave it.'

FIFTEEN

Tom's mouth set in an obstinate line.

A curious crowd had gathered round them, many of those leaving drawn back by Tom's shout. Nick sensed the hush. Despite the inspector's brave words, he knew what they were thinking. Millie's mobile, washed up by the waves. What darker find would follow? Wary eyes looked at him and Leon. No one wanted to speak to them.

But two large men in yellow waterproofs had turned from where they were standing and were walking back across the beach towards them. The coastguard, Dennis Gaiman, and Malcolm Partridge. Gaiman was returning something to his inner breast pocket. A phone or a radio. Malcolm, as always, was in animated conversation with him. Something about their ease with each other told Nick they were old acquaintances.

The coastguard's strong voice bridged the gap between him and the Fewings. 'I've put out the word. We'll keep an eye out for a good few miles in either direction, though the currents usually take things south.'

For what? It chilled Nick to think. He looked along the line of detritus left by the tide. Bladderwrack, cuttlefish bones, plastic bags, drinks cans, a solitary shoe. His breath caught. No, it was too large to be Millie's or Anna's.

Malcolm Partridge's voice broke in on his thoughts. 'And I've got the yacht club on to it. The weather's changing. Most of them are just fair-weather sailors. Bit of sunshine might tempt them out. I've told them to keep their eyes peeled.'

Tom strode straight to the coastguard. There was none of that usual beguiling smile in his blue eyes. His belligerent manner told Nick his son was keyed up for another refusal and wasn't going to accept it easily.

'Have you checked that boat out there? The one that's leaving St Furseys? It was hanging around yesterday. What if they're drug runners and they've got Millie and Anna aboard? You have to search them before they get away.'

Dennis Gaiman halted. He was taller even than Tom, and

burlier. He looked down at the boy, with little sympathy in his face. He was clearly controlling his impatience, in an effort to remain professional.

'Look, Tom. Everyone knows how you're feeling. But we have to keep a level head here. That would be a job for Her Majesty's Customs, anyway. And they need to have a reason to search a vessel. They can't board everything that floats, you know.'

'They searched that Spanish boat in the harbour yesterday.'

'They'll have had . . . let's say, suspicions. And they were wrong. Or at least, they didn't find any evidence of contraband. Don't worry. If there are criminals along this coast, we're all as eager to catch them as you are. But I can assure you the *Cleopatra* is harmless. Marine archaeologists. From the local university, I believe. And I hardly think drug runners are going to be hanging about in broad daylight, for days on end. Do you?'

'How would I know?' Tom muttered. 'But isn't it a coincidence they're leaving now?'

'Leaving? Or just going off to the next square of their survey grid?'

Angry colour flooded Tom's cheeks, but he said no more.

The crowd was breaking up. Inspector Davis came up to them. 'The tide's turned. We'll leave a few people to check the beach and keep an eye open for anything fresh. I'm afraid there's nothing else we can do here.'

Nick was afraid that Tom was going to argue with her about still not having pursued the question of the smugglers' cave. The boy's chin was stiff with resentment. His black eyebrows frowned under the thatch of dark hair.

'I'm going back,' Nick told him. 'Mum's cut up about this. I need to be with her.'

'Sure,' said Tom. He swung round on Malcolm Partridge. 'Were you genuine about taking us out in your boat? Could you?'

The doctor's face lit up. 'To that survey ship? Like a shot. Anything to help. Whether I can get you aboard is another matter, but we could try, eh?'

His broad face was beaming, as if this was indeed just a children's adventure story, and not a life-and-death search for Tom's sister and his cousin.

Looking at the pair of them, Nick felt a great weariness. He knew it was a waste of time. For him, there was nothing left to do. He supposed there would be other searches, beyond the village. Not just on the beach. He should have asked Sergeant Thompson about that. But the police had gone, promising to keep him informed of any news, leaving only Constable Grafton with the beachcombers.

There was nothing left but to go back to Leon's cottage and share the burden of Suzie's grief.

Nick waited with some trepidation while Leon opened the door. Suzie sprang to her feet as she saw them. He was relieved to see that she was more composed then he had feared. They embraced long and silently.

'I'll put the kettle on. You must be frozen.'

'Actually, no,' he was surprised into saying. 'It's turning into rather a nice spring day. Blue sky and sunshine.'

They were talking of trivialities, skating over the surface of what really mattered.

'The police are going to check Millie's phone and the mobile company's log. See if they can pick up anything from her recent contacts.' Nick was sipping his coffee, reluctantly steering them back to more painful things.

'I've been ringing her friends back home, those I could get hold of. Nobody knows anything. They were all totally shocked.' She tugged nervously at her Aran cardigan.

He imagined her busy on the phone, desperate to do something, and all the while, fearful that Millie or Anna might, even as she talked, be trying to make the call home she so much longed for.

'Tom's got this mad idea that the girls might be aboard an archaeological survey boat that's working off St Furseys. Malcolm Partridge has agreed to take him out to it.'

Suzie's eyebrows rose, startled. 'You don't think that's possible? They could be on it? Why? What did the police say?'

'It was the coastguard who put the lid on it. They work pretty closely with the Customs folk. He made the point that drug runners are hardly going to hang about St Furseys, day after day, in full view.'

'What happens now?'

'We wait, I'm afraid. Or keep walking the beach, driving ourselves mad every time a wave washes up a bit of flotsam. There are still a few people there, keeping a watch. I think the police are searching outbuildings over a wider area. They're certainly not taking it for granted that the girls were washed out to sea.'

'People here are being so kind. The curator from the museum called in, on her way to work. Isabella da Souza.'

Leon turned from the window where he had been standing. 'Portuguese, then, not Spanish. I wondered about the accent. I'd never got around to finding out her name. What did she want?'

'Just to say she was sorry about . . . our trouble. To ask if there was any news, or anything she could do.'

'Did you tell her about finding Millie's phone?' Nick asked.

'I didn't know then. It was quite early.'

'Why? I thought the museum didn't open till ten.'

'This must have been about seven. Not that it matters. Perhaps she has admin to do before they open to the public.'

'It's only a small museum, run on a shoestring,' said Leon. 'Maybe she has to sweep and dust the place as well.'

'Has anyone else called?'

'No, just her.'

Tom came in. He brought a charge of teenage energy, where Nick and Leon had slumped into chairs, tired and defeated. He was keyed up, as though he still had a real hope of finding the girls.

'Malcolm said to meet him at the harbour in an hour's time.'

'Tom, you can't seriously think this is going to get anywhere? Going out to pester a perfectly innocent bunch of university archaeologists?'

'You don't *know* they're innocent. Do you think drug smugglers go around advertising the fact? And anyway, if we're out at sea, I can get a better look at where I think that cave is.'

Nick closed his eyes and sighed. 'Tom, you've got nearly as much of a one-track mind as Millie has. You've got obsessed with the idea that this is all about drug running. That Millie and Anna have got themselves entangled with some criminal gang.'

'Why else would they stay out all night?'

Nick found he did not want to answer that.

Suzie broke the silence. Her voice was shaky. 'Tom's right, in a way. Millie *was* obsessed with smuggling stories. I wish I'd never started it. It seemed such a harmless way to spend a family holiday, chasing up your ancestors.'

'It's not your fault.' Nick got up and put an arm around her. 'It was just a nasty coincidence that stories that could have involved my ancestors were uncomfortably close to what's happening here today.'

'I was reading that book again. The one Leon lent us. Trying to see if there was any clue I might have missed about what Millie and Anna could be doing. And I came upon that bit about the soldier. You know.' She picked up the old, blue-covered book from where it lay, face down, on the coffee table. '*10th October, 1792. Staveley, Private Terence, of the Cannock Militia, was found dead of head wounds on the North Beach at St Furseys. He had been set to watch for smugglers. It is believed he was attacked by a band of these notorious boatmen. There were signs that this gallant soldier had put up a determined fight, before being struck down.*'

'Millie's not a soldier, nor a Customs officer.'

'No, but those smugglers were *her* ancestors, too. At least, they probably were, if they were boatmen. She might think she had a responsibility to put things right. Private Staveley died, because of them.'

'And that Customs officer a few months ago. Killed when he tried to board a smugglers' boat,' Leon added. 'Anna would be the same. It's the age, isn't it? When they're idealistic and want to put the world to rights.'

'What would those people do . . . if the girls *did* discover something criminal, and they caught them?' Suzie's voice hardly rose above a whisper.

'That theory only works,' said Nick, 'if there *are* smugglers here in St Furseys. We're not in the South-west now, you know.'

Tom checked his watch. 'I'm going down the creek. Don't want to give the doctor a chance to change his mind.'

Nick looked across at his brother. 'Leon?'

The painter's face was drawn and tired. 'Count me out.'

'I'll come,' said Suzie, unexpectedly. 'If Leon's staying in.'

Nick got to his feet. 'It's crazy. Supposing the girls *were* on that boat, and it's pretty preposterous, there's not the slightest chance a crew of criminals would let us aboard.'

All the same, he reached for his coat and scarf, and pushed his feet into his boots. Anything rather than sit at home and imagine.

SIXTEEN

Suzie stared around her in a dazed wonder, as the three of them hurried along the path to the harbour. She began to unwind her knitted scarf.

'I can't believe the sun is shining. It's really warm. It seems . . . wrong.'

She looked, Nick thought with compassion, like an animal emerging from hibernation, blinking in the light. With a pang of remorse, he realized that he himself had been frantically busy in the waking hours since Millie and Anna went missing. All she could do was sit at home and wait.

Yet she was right. It felt a mockery that sunshine should be bathing the world this morning. Light sparkled on the gently running waves of the North Sea. There was only the occasional flash of a white horse thrown up by the breeze. Pure white pebbles shone out among the grey and brown shingle. The golden trumpets of daffodils rang for joy in tiny cottage gardens.

The earth should be in mourning.

'It'll be colder on the water,' he told her prosaically.

'You don't think he'll mind three of us coming?'

Tom, walking ahead of them, turned his head. 'Don't worry, Mum. He'll be pleased as Punch. He's the sort of guy who likes to show off to anyone who'll listen. Just so long as you admire his boat. A bit like Mr Toad.'

In spite of himself, Nick felt a smile twist his lips. Tom had summed up the extrovert doctor nicely.

'Still . . .' His spirits plummeted. 'I can't see that this is going to get us anywhere, Tom. You may be right about Millie having suspicions that this survey boat was up to no good. But it all sounds perfectly innocent to me. And even if she and Anna had some mad idea about following the crew when they came ashore, it wouldn't explain why they haven't come home. They'd only put themselves in danger if the people they were trailing *were* drug runners. If they're archaeology students, I should think the trail would lead straight to the nearest pub.'

'We went round the pubs yesterday. They'd have let us know if they saw Millie and Anna, wouldn't they?' Tom was like a dog who would not let go of a bone.

'And how is going out to their boat supposed to help?'

'Do you want to hang about all day and wait till they come back tonight?' Tom exploded. '*If* they come back.'

He stopped, looking out to sea. Nick and Suzie were forced to a halt behind him. The grey boat was no more than a smudge out to sea.

Was it possible the girls were on board?

Cold reason took over. Drug runners had already shown they would kill to escape capture. If the crew really *had* a motive to seize the girls, why would they keep them aboard?

The weight of weary despair descended on Nick.

Malcolm Partridge was waiting for them on the landing stage. The yellow oilskin coat had been supplemented by yellow trousers over his sea boots. He wore a blue life jacket round his neck. Nick, in his jersey and hiking jacket, felt underdressed.

'Do you think he'll let us help him sail her?' Tom was staring longingly at the moored yacht. She looked, to Nick's eyes, curiously naked. Bare masts. No sign of sails ready to be hoisted.

'Morning!' shouted the doctor, jovial as ever. Nick watched him make an effort to tone down his enthusiasm to a more sympathetic smile. 'No news then? How are you bearing up, Mrs Fewings? This is a bad business.'

Suzie made an incomprehensible murmur. Then she too made an effort. 'It was good of you to offer to take Tom out. Would you mind if we came too?'

'The more the merrier. No, belay that. It's not a joking matter, is it? But you're very welcome aboard my humble craft.'

He started to climb down the metal ladder fixed to the slime-covered woodwork. Nick waited for him to step sideways on to the spotless deck of the white-and-black yacht. But he carried on downwards.

Only then did Nick notice that tied to the stern of the yacht was a large black inflatable. Partridge stepped into it. He held up a hand to Tom, who had already started to descend after him.

'That one?' called Tom, taken by surprise.

'Welcome aboard the RIB. That's Rigid Inflatable Boat.' Malcolm guided Tom's step into it. 'She'll be much more efficient for this job. Out there and back in no time.'

From the wharf above, Nick registered the two powerful outboard motors bolted to the stern of the craft. Amidships was a console with a wheel, protected by a windshield.

'Right, Mrs Fewings, we'll have you next.'

Nick was last. He had expected the inflatable to feel precarious as he stepped into her. But with the weight of the other three, she seemed reassuringly stable. She was quite broad in the beam, with room – he cast a quick eye round to check – for perhaps a dozen people.

Tom had established himself in the bows. 'Nice one,' he called back to the owner. 'Those engines look seriously fast.'

The doctor glowed. 'Two hundred and fifty horsepower. Cruising speed thirty knots. But they'll do fifty knots at a push.'

'Wow!'

'Don't worry.' Malcolm turned gallantly to Suzie. 'I'm not aiming to break any speed records this morning. Come and take the seat beside me. You'll get a bit of protection from the wind.'

As Suzie settled herself in the upholstered seat behind the console, Nick was left to find his own place in the stern. Malcolm handed out more buoyancy jackets.

The roar of the engines shook Nick. He hadn't seen Malcolm press the starter. A second later, they were spinning round, sending the oily water eddying. They cleared the yacht and surged forward for the mouth of the creek.

He had been right about the cold. Once they were in open water, he watched Suzie huddle deeper into her jacket, and pull her scarf back up to her chin. He wished there were a third seat there, so that he could snuggle closer and add his warmth to hers. Malcolm Partridge had his face turned to her. He was enjoying his captive audience.

In the more exposed stern, Nick pulled up his collar and fished the beanie hat out of his pocket. The RIB might only be cruising at thirty knots, but it felt like a racing car.

Tom, on the other hand, had lifted his bare head to the wind that their speed whipped up as they forged out to sea. He was craning forward, not just because he was eager for the encounter ahead, but revelling, Nick could tell, in the sheer adventure of it. What it was to be young.

Nick was aware, above the noise of the twin engines, of occasional snatches of song. The doctor must be singing at the top of his voice for the sound to reach this far, competing with the rush of the wind and the smack of waves against the hull. The few phrases Nick caught sounded like 'A Life on the Ocean Wave'. Poor Suzie.

Tom gave a shout of alarm and reeled back. Water streamed from his black hair and his rueful face. The front of his jacket was soaked.

Nick heard the bellow of laughter from Malcolm Partridge, snug in his yellow oilskins behind the windshield. Tom was right, Nick thought. He *is* like Mr Toad. He can't really take in the seriousness of what this is all about. It's not his daughter.

Does he have a family?

Am I being serious? he thought, watching the green waves race past him and the widening walls of surf thrown up in their wake. *What am I doing here, when I know it's futile?*

The waves rose higher out here. Nick was increasingly fearful that the RIB was not as large nor as stable as it had seemed in the harbour. As they slammed over the mounting rollers of the North Sea, and skipped across the next trough, he thought how easy it would be for one of them to be flipped out into the sea. Should he fetch Tom back from the bows? He was wet with spray himself now. The sun did not seem to shine as warmly on the open water. Only Malcolm seemed to be enjoying himself.

Behind the tilted bows Nick had lost sight of the survey boat. The giddying moments on top of the next wave were not enough for him to steady his line of sight on where he thought it should be.

He worked his way forward, grabbing at scant handholds.

'How do you know where to steer?' he shouted at Malcolm.

'Compass, old boy.' The big doctor pointed at the dashboard in front of him. 'Took a bearing before we started.'

Nick looked up through the spattered windshield and was startled to find that the survey boat was suddenly there. Alarmingly close ahead. A workaday sort of vessel, blue-grey, with a sizeable forecastle.

Malcolm slowed the engines. The RIB glided in under the other boat's side. Curious heads were craning over the rail to stare down at them. Mostly young people, Nick noticed.

An older man with a ginger beard came pushing through them. His eyes blazed.

'What the hell do you think you're playing at? Can't you see the dive flag?'

Nick followed his gesticulating hand. The man was indicating a flag, white near the stays, with its outer half blue, notched in a chevron shape. It had meant nothing to him. Presumably the commodore of the Yacht Club should have recognized it.

He felt a stab of alarm run through him. There could be divers beneath them. Girls, boys, not much older than his own children. Lifelines connecting them to the surface.

'Sorry, old chap.' Malcolm Partridge did not sound at all chastened. 'Didn't mean to interfere. Just interested in what you were doing out here.'

'Is that any of your bloody business?'

'No offence meant. Perfectly friendly question.'

A small dark woman appeared beside the bearded man. She laid a restraining hand on his arm. Her delicate brown face smiled down at them politely, if not with warmth.

'We're an archaeological survey unit, if you must know. We're scanning the seabed to see if we can locate wrecks. If we come across anything promising, we send down divers to check. As it happens, we don't have anyone in the water at the moment. But you didn't know that, did you? The reason we fly the flag is to warn other boats off.'

'Sorry, ma'am. Point taken. We did come in gently.'

'Then you can be equally considerate about clearing off gently.' The ginger-haired man was not yet mollified.

Malcolm had a hide like a rhinoceros. 'Should have introduced myself. Dr Malcolm Partridge. Commodore of the St Furseys Yacht Club. Not just idle curiosity that brought us out here, I'm afraid. Though I'd love to hear more about what you're doing. Thing is, there are a couple of girls missing. I've got their parents with me. Well, the parent of one of them; the other one's their niece.'

Nick felt the stares of everyone on the survey ship turn on him and Suzie. Malcolm was doing it again, he thought resentfully. Raising his own importance by association with their grief.

'I'm sorry to hear it. But what does that have to do with us?' The man was made awkward now by Suzie and Nick's presence.

'Would you mind if we came on board? Difficult to do this sort of thing by a shouting match.'

Nick saw the struggle in the man's face. But the woman with him signalled to one of the young men. A rope ladder was dropped over the side.

Malcolm gestured to Nick. 'You go first. Then you can help Suzie up.'

It was not easy to transfer from the rocking inflatable to the higher deck. He wondered if Suzie would refuse to try. But she came after him, biting her lip with the effort, while Tom held the ladder below. Malcolm followed, bringing a mooring rope. Without asking permission, he secured the RIB to the survey ship.

Nick should have known that Tom would not be left behind. As Malcolm began to explain their mission, the boy came scrambling up to join them.

'. . . Found her mobile on the beach this morning. We're all worried as hell, as you can imagine. Got people out combing the tideline. Searching other places along the coast. I've alerted the Yacht Club, and the coastguards are on to it. Anything you can do . . . Flotsam. Something unusual on the shore . . .'

'We'll keep our eyes open.' The woman's eyes were sympathetic on Suzie. 'But I don't really think we can be of much help. We're quite far out from the shore.'

Nick watched Suzie's embarrassment. The woman was right. It sounded thin. Would the archaeologists guess that it was only an excuse?

'Since we're here,' Malcolm was saying, 'would you mind letting us in on to what might be under us? Miss, Mrs . . .?'

'Dr Kapoor,' said the woman, a little more frostily. 'And that's Professor Dancey.'

'Pleased to meet you.'

The professor clearly did not share the pleasure, but he found his reluctant hand enveloped in Partridge's.

'This is a working boat. We only have money for two weeks' surveying. So if you'll forgive me . . .'

'Go ahead. Don't mind us. It's just that I've got a bit of a passion for maritime history. All those wrecks down there. Some of them are the deathbeds of local men.'

Suzie nudged Nick's side. When he looked round at her, she was silently indicating for him to turn his eyes further. It took him a moment to realize why.

Tom had disappeared.

They exchanged alarmed glances.

Malcolm's next words jolted Nick's attention back to the conversation. 'Take my friend Nick Fewings here. He's a direct descendant of Solomon Margerson, lost overboard from the St Furseys lifeboat when it was trying to rescue the crew of the SS *Caractacus* last century. When his body was washed up days afterwards, they gave him a corking funeral.'

In an instant, the attitude of Professor Dancey changed. 'The *Caractacus*? Do you know where she went down? Was it here?'

'Oh, somewhere between the shore and the Sands.' Partridge waved an expansive hand. 'Must have been hereabouts, or they'd have called out the Sandbeach boat instead.'

'Get me those charts.' The professor signalled to one of his young team. 'Do you know how big she was?'

'Sorry. You'll have to ask at the museum. They've got a record of that sort of thing.'

Suzie's voice surprised them. 'She was a small liner. About two thousand tons, I think.'

'How do you know that, Mrs Fewings?' Dr Kapoor asked.

Suzie blushed. 'In normal life, I'm a bit of a family history nut. And he was Nick's great-grandfather.' Her breath caught. 'I know it sounds ridiculous to be talking about that today. That's not why I'm here . . .'

There was a muffled shout from the cabin below. The archaeology student who had gone for the charts reappeared, grasping Tom by the collar.

'Found him rummaging about below decks. Won't say what he was looking for.'

The circle of archaeologists and visitors widened, all staring at the defiant Tom.

'Sorry. Just curious,' he mumbled. 'Never been on a survey boat before. Just wanted to see what you did. What equipment you use . . .'

'That's not what it looked like. Opening every locker.'

The ferocious glint had returned to Professor Dancey's eyes. 'I rather think you've outstayed your welcome. As I said, we're on a tight budget and time is money. If you'll excuse me . . .'

He stood aside pointedly from the rope ladder. There was nothing left but to climb down into the RIB. Tom took his place in the bows in sullen silence.

Nick sighed. This had never been anything more than a teenage fantasy.

As Malcolm swung the boat away from the survey ship, Nick stared down through the grey-green depths. He had forgotten about Sollie Margerson. It was sobering to think that his heroic story, which had existed for them only as a photograph and a newspaper cutting, had been stark reality that night. Here, or close by. The *Caractacus* had sunk in a wild storm. Some passengers had been rescued. Many perished. And two lifeboatmen had been catapulted from their boat. How long had Sollie struggled in these waters, buoyed up by his cork life jacket, before the huge waves overwhelmed him?

He prayed that Sollie's two teenage descendants had not lost that same struggle here.

SEVENTEEN

Tom was craning over the black rim of the inflatable, peering intently at the rapidly approaching shore. His attention was not on the village of St Furseys, but over to his left. Port, Tom corrected himself; that's what the nautical doctor would call it.

Nick was filled with apprehension when he looked that way. The falling tide had revealed a murderous tumble of yellow rocks below Brandon Head. How many hidden pools might remain unsearched? How long before the sea washed in again to smother them?

He saw Tom scramble to his feet and make his swaying way to the open wheelhouse amidships. He seemed to be arguing with Dr Partridge, pointing at those cliffs. Nick rose and moved cautiously forward to listen.

The sullenness had gone from Tom's face. The intense blue eyes were eager. He wore a grin of triumph.

'Look! Can you see it? I told you. There *is* a cave.'

'Your eyes must be sharper than mine, old chap. Spray on the windshield makes it difficult. Can't say I can see it myself.'

Suzie was peering ahead, through the spume cast up by their progress. 'He's right. There could be something there. At least, there's a semicircular patch that looks darker than the rest.' She turned to greet Nick. 'What do you think?'

There wasn't room for anyone else behind the console. Nick braced himself on the side of the wheelhouse and concentrated on the cliff. The bucking boat and the flying water made it difficult to see steadily. It was several minutes before he could convince himself that there might be a stain of shadow, just below the rim of the headland. A lifting wave snatched it from his view. When he was able to focus again, he was no longer sure. The angle was changing all the time as the RIB neared the harbour. Malcolm was probably right. It was only there if you wanted to see it.

His shoulders sagged. Whether there was or wasn't a cave high up on the cliff was irrelevant to finding Millie and Anna.

For a moment he'd been beguiled into thinking that Tom had made a significant discovery.

'Aren't you going to investigate?' Tom sounded incredulous.

'Tom,' Suzie intervened. 'Dr Partridge has already given up a morning to take us out to the survey boat, just because you had a wild idea the girls might be aboard. Don't you realize how embarrassing it was when they caught you searching the cabin?'

Malcolm Partridge roared with laughter. 'Don't you worry about that, Suzie. I may call you Suzie, mayn't I? What did you think I took Tom out there for? We were hardly going to ask them politely, "Are you, by any chance, holding two girls prisoner on your boat?" Had to get him aboard to look for them somehow. Even the fiery professor could hardly say no to two grieving parents, could he? And then, of course, once I got them on to marine archaeology . . .'

Nick saw the shock in Suzie's face he felt in his own. That this man could be so insensitive as to exploit their misery simply to get Tom aboard.

And yet . . . If Tom's crackbrained idea *had* been right . . . If the girls had been there . . . Maybe it needed someone like Malcolm Partridge to break through the barriers of police procedure and social convention. He was not a man who was easily embarrassed.

Nick went back to his seat in the stern. To his surprise, Tom joined him.

'It's there. Whatever he says,' the boy muttered.

'Could be,' Nick soothed him. 'I never got a clear look at it.'

'All he has to do is swing round in an arc that way. Just close enough to be sure.'

'Your mother's right. He's done us a big favour already.'

'Big deal. He got an audience, didn't he? That's what he likes. He'll be dining out on this for months. But he can't see that the cave could be important.'

'Even if it's there, we couldn't have got at it when we were out on the rocks.'

'No, but the smugglers could. You've forgotten they used to have men up there with ropes.'

Nick threw him a wry smile. 'You don't give up easily, do you?'

'Should I? Before we've found them?'

The argument died on Nick's lips. He looked back over their foaming wake, searching for a safer subject.

'He certainly doesn't stint himself, does he? Our doctor friend? Not just a spanking yacht, but an expensive speedboat as well. What did he say these engines could do flat out?'

'Fifty knots. I'd like to see that.'

'I'm glad he didn't push her that fast today. I don't think I'm dressed for it. You must have got soaked in the bows.'

'I'll dry.' Tom leaned over to study the pair of big 250-horsepower engines. 'Hey, what do you think would happen if you bolted another two engines on? This thing would take off like a rocket.'

Nick was glad to steer the conversation along this more cheerful path. Father and son studied the metal housing across the stern that held the outboards.

'You're right. There's room to bolt on a whole row of them. That would make it *seriously* fast. I suppose we should be grateful Malcolm's settled for two.'

'Speak for yourself.'

'Tom!' The doctor's shout interrupted them. He was looking back at them, beckoning Tom urgently to join him. The engine noise had dropped. 'Water's calmer here. Would you like to take a turn at the wheel before we hit the harbour?'

'Could I?' Tom sprang forward to join him.

Suzie slipped out of her seat to make room for him and came back to Nick.

'He's really kind, isn't he, behind all that bluster? Even though he can be a bit of a pain. Look at Tom. He's proud as Punch.'

They watched Malcolm guide Tom's hands on the wheel. He had eased the throttle. To Nick's relief the RIB coasted more gently over the waves, following a slightly erratic course. He watched his tall son, dark head proudly erect, gradually taking over the wheel from Dr Partridge as his confidence grew.

The image shifted. Solomon Margerson, at the wheel of the *Ellen Maud*. Benjamin Margerson before him. The line of fishermen who had guided their boats into St Furseys like this.

At least we have Tom, Nick thought. *Whatever happens, we still have Tom.*

*   *   *

At the last moment, Malcolm took over the wheel from Tom and guided their craft through the harbour entrance. Nick was relieved that experienced hands were steering them through the moored boats. The doctor brought them, not to the vertical ladder by the stern of his yacht, but to a flight of wooden steps. He held the RIB steady while they climbed out.

'Aren't you coming too?' Nick asked.

'No. Business to attend to, I'm afraid. Anyway, I prefer to keep this one in the boathouse at the end of my garden. Don't want to leave expensive outboards on view.'

'Then thank you for this morning. I'm not really surprised that it didn't produce anything. But it was good of you to try. And letting Tom steer the boat took his mind off things for a while.'

'To tell the truth, I enjoyed a bit of piracy on the high seas. Stand by to repel boarders!' His laughter faded, leaving his face creased with something like genuine concern. 'By the look of you, I should have given you the wheel, dear boy. Or your good lady. I fancy you're the ones who need a diversion. Try not to worry too much. *Ciao*.'

A burst of unnecessary speed sent the RIB shooting away from the steps to cut a tight arc and head out to open water. The moored craft rocked noisily, metal clanging on their masts.

'It said *Maximum Speed 5 Knots* at the entrance to the creek,' Suzie observed. 'You'd think he'd bother about his own yacht, if not about others.'

The white-and-black *Moonraker* was indeed bumping against the wharf.

'That must be why he's equipped her with such a good set of fenders,' Nick said, eyeing the black PVC cylinders suspended along her sides.

'I thought he was supposed to be the commodore of the Yacht Club.'

'Why do you always have to be so critical?' Tom burst out. 'He got us on board that survey ship, didn't he? And he let me steer the RIB. Wouldn't let me open her up, though. I'd like to see her do fifty knots.'

'You were cross with him because he wouldn't take us round to see if the cave really was there,' Suzie pointed out.

'Yeah, well. But it was. I saw it. At least, I'm pretty sure I did.'

They started to walk back along the uneven planking. Suddenly Suzie stumbled and would have fallen. Nick caught her back.

'Are you all right? Did you catch your foot on one of the boards?'

'No. I . . . My legs just seemed to give way. I'll be all right in a minute.'

She stood bent over, her hands braced on her thighs, her head hanging. After a few moments she tossed back her brown hair and smiled weakly at him. 'Sorry. It's just . . . I know how you feel now, having to keep busy, trying to convince yourself that it will do some good. Any hope, however far-fetched. But now we have to go home and face the truth. Nothing's changed.'

'They might be there,' Tom said.

'Don't be silly. Leon would have phoned us.'

They walked on in silence. Sunlight glinted on the mud at the landward end of the creek, revealing unexpected streaks of purple and red. Gulls circled on bright wings.

'Just for a moment, I thought he had,' Suzie said bitterly. 'A phone rang while we were on our way back, and, even though it wasn't mine, I thought it must be Leon. Crazy, wasn't it? It was Malcolm's, of course. That business he's had to get back to see to. Probably why he didn't want to make a diversion to the cliffs. But at the time, it seemed the girls were the only thing anyone could possibly be making a phone call about.'

Nick looked around, at the handful of holidaymakers strolling along the waterfront, at local people coming out of shops. 'I know. We think the world revolves around our particular tragedy. That the sun ought not to be shining, and other people enjoying themselves, or going about their normal business. The world's a cruel place.'

It was not far round the corner to Leon's cottage. The door was half open.

There were voices inside. Nick and Suzie stopped and looked at each other, at first with alarm, and then with incredulous hope. They burst through the door into the small living room. Anna was in her father's arms, and Leon's face was alight with joy. Millie, her face both wary and excited, swung round to greet them.

EIGHTEEN

Suzie crossed the few steps that separated them faster than Nick. Her arms were round her daughter, her brown hair mingling with Millie's fairer locks. Nick felt his heart turn over, seeing them together. Then he stepped in to claim his share.

He was aware of a slightly musty smell about Millie, unlike the fresh sweetness of childhood he remembered. He held her off from him, and tried to look steadily at her peaky face.

'Where have you been? Why didn't you ring us? I know you lost your phone, but you still had Anna's, didn't you? We kept trying to reach you, but it was always switched off.'

Millie looked over her shoulder to catch Anna's eye. Then she turned back to Nick. Her eyelids were lowered, her expression unreadable.

'I'm sorry. We got lost. We thought we'd go and explore those reed beds, only it got, like, really confusing. We couldn't find the way out. The reeds were so tall, we couldn't see where we were going and we sort of lost our sense of direction. If we put a foot out of line, we were up to our knees in mud. When it started to get dark, we thought the most sensible thing was to stay where we were and wait till morning.'

'You slept out there? But why didn't you ring us on Anna's phone?'

'I . . . lost mine too,' Anna murmured.

The adults stared at them.

Nick found his voice. He found himself choking with anger. 'Look, this doesn't begin to make sense. You took off after lunch, and it doesn't get properly dark till mid-evening. Do you want us to believe you were walking about for five hours? And Millie's phone was washed up on the beach, nowhere near the reed beds. Now Anna says she's lost hers too. There's a lot more to this than you're telling us. You went out to Brandon Head, didn't you? What the hell have you been up to?'

The girls exchanged scared glances.

'I'm really sorry, Dad. I know how you must be feeling.
But we can't tell you that.'

'Anna?'

The other girl shook her dark curls. She would not meet
her father's eye.

Suzie exploded. 'What do you mean, you can't tell us?
We're your parents, for heaven's sake! We've been frantic
with worry. We've had the police out, the coastguard. Half
the village has been searching for you.'

'Yeah, and we got Malcolm Partridge to take us to this
survey ship,' Tom burst in. 'The one you and Anna got so
suspicious about. In case you'd got yourselves kidnapped by
them. And he's got this fantastic RIB with two whacking great
outboards. We even managed to board the ship, and Malcolm
kept them talking while I searched the cabins to see if you
were there. And he let me steer the RIB on the way back.'

'Oh, great! You've obviously been having a whale of a time
without me.' Millie swung round indignantly on her brother.

'Wait till I tell you about the Noah's Ark and the axeman.'

'Shut up, both of you!' Suzie shouted.

She steered Millie to a chair by the unlit fire and sat her
down.

'You too.' She did the same to Anna.

'I'll put the kettle on, shall I?' Leon offered.

'Shouldn't you tell Jacqui that Anna is safe?' Nick suggested.

He caught the look of dismay and guilt on his brother's face.

'You're right. But what am I going to tell her? That Anna's
been missing all night, but I don't know where she's been?'

'It's the truth. Just say that they've only got in this minute.
You wanted to tell her straight away, and you'll get back to
her when you've got the full story.'

'She won't let me get away with that. She'll want to talk
to Anna.'

'So put her on the phone. Maybe Jacqui can screw some
sense out of her, if we can't.'

'Now,' Suzie was ordering the girls. 'We're not having any
more of this nonsense. You're only fourteen. You stayed out
all night. Half the county's emergency services have been
looking for you. When they found Millie's mobile on the
beach, we thought you'd *drowned*. Now you're going to tell
us what happened!'

The girls exchanged mute, unhappy looks.

'Mum. I'd tell you if I could. But I can't. It's . . . well, it's something important.'

'Too right, it's important. It's important that you tell us.' She swung round on Nick. 'Phone the police. They need to know they're back.'

Leon had gone to make yet another difficult phone call in private. Nick retreated to the double bedroom to contact Inspector Davis.

Even diminished by the phone, he heard the sharp suspicion in her voice when he told her about the girls' silence. 'How are they? Do they seem . . . affected by what happened?'

'It's hard to describe. Obstinate and excited at the same time.'

'Physically?'

'A bit dirty. They say they spent the night in the reed beds. There's mud on their jeans. But apart from that, they look OK.'

'It might be an idea to bring a police surgeon with me. Just in case.'

Sick thoughts raced through Nick's mind. He had been so overwhelmingly relieved to have the girls back. The darker possibilities of what might have happened to them had not yet begun to occur to him. He thought about them now.

Was it possible? Could they be so bright-eyed and keyed up if *that* had happened? Wouldn't they be collapsing in tears in their parents' arms?

Why wouldn't they *say*?

He came downstairs slowly. Leon was back in the room. Tom was making hot drinks for everybody.

The girls were still sitting where he had left them, either side of the fireplace. They looked more sullen now. He raised his eyebrows at Suzie. She shook her head in exasperation.

'You'll have to tell your story soon,' Nick said. 'The police are coming.'

He saw alarm sharpen Millie's pale face. 'It won't make any difference,' she muttered. Then, more passionately, 'Honestly, Dad. We're not just being difficult. We *can't* tell you.'

'Why not?'

'That's just it. We can't tell you why we can't tell you, without telling you, can we?'

The adults paused to digest this logic.

'Anna,' Leon said, breaking the silence. 'Your mother wants to talk to you.' He held out his phone.

'Do I have to?' the other girl said. Her lower lip trembled. 'She'll only go on at me, the way you're doing. And I can't. tell her any more than Millie can.'

'That's your problem. She's your mother. Not unnaturally, she's been frantic with worry. We all have. You can hardly blame her for wanting to know what happened to you.'

Anna took the phone reluctantly upstairs.

Nick felt the joy of the girls' homecoming crumbling around him.

'Well, if the police are coming, you'd better go and get a shower and put on some clean clothes,' Suzie ordered Millie. 'I don't know where you've been, but you smell.'

'*Yes*, Mum.' With a show of mock obedience, Millie got to her feet.

'No,' said Nick, suddenly remembering his conversation with the inspector. 'I don't think she should do that. Inspector Davis is –' he felt his cheeks flush – 'bringing a doctor with her. I think she wants him to examine the girls, for . . . Well, you know.'

Suzie's face went white.

'Millie! You would have told us, wouldn't you?'

There were bright spots in Millie's cheeks now. 'Oh, for heaven's sake, both of you! Leave me alone. I don't want any horrible doctor pawing me all over. I'm all *right*. And so is Anna. Nothing *happened*. Well, not like that.'

An enormous relief washed over Nick. He let himself sink into the nearest chair. 'Well. That's something. You'll have to explain to the inspector. Just tell her the whole story, if you won't tell us.'

'Dad. How many times do we have to tell you? We *can't*.'

'I doubt if Inspector Davis is going to take no for an answer.'

'She'll have to. Now, can I have that shower?'

'Yes, I suppose so,' Nick sighed.

'Hold on,' said Tom unexpectedly from the window sill, where he sat caressing his mug of tea. 'Better not. I know what she's saying, but there might be other forensic evidence on her. Where she's really been.'

Again, that wary start in Millie's face.

Before she could protest, Anna came back downstairs. She flashed a mutinous glance at her father.

'How was it?' Leon asked. 'Did you manage to put her mind at rest?'

'What do *you* think? She's threatening to jump into the car and fetch me home.'

There was silence in the room.

Leon shrugged his shoulders, struggling to hide the pain in his face. 'What did you expect, after last night? She blames me, of course, for not looking after you. I shall be sorry to lose you, though. It's not going to be often I get a whole week of your company from now on. I thought it was all set up for a great family holiday. Time with your cousins. All this fun with the family history . . .' His voice broke off. 'Well.' He tried to rally himself. 'Does anyone feel like lunch?'

Tom's hand alone shot up. 'Nothing like sea air for giving you an appetite. What have we got?'

Leon unearthed fish and chips from the freezer. Once the hot food was on the table, the girls, it seemed, were as ravenous as Tom. Nick, listlessly chewing his own food, was comforted to watch them wolf down theirs. Nothing very terrible could have happened to them, could it? He felt concern beginning to give way to anger. He held his tongue.

The adults had not yet finished eating when the police arrived.

Inspector Davis, zipped up in her green Barbour again, was a small woman, but a formidable presence. Nick sensed both girls stiffen warily, saw them throw fearful glances at each other. What was it they were so anxious to hide?

He rubbed his tired eyes. It made no sense.

The cottage living room was crowded. Six Fewings, the inspector, DS Vine and a tall woman Nick had not seen before.

Inspector Davis took a swift look round. 'Tom, would you mind?' Her face relaxed briefly into a smile for him. 'This may be difficult for the girls, and we seem to have a very full house.'

'So I'm in the way? I'm the only one who doesn't get to hear the big story?' His blue eyes flashed indignation.

'Tom!' Nick did not normally use such a commanding tone

to his eighteen-year-old son. 'Unless things change, we may not have a story.'

With a show of impatience, Tom took down his jacket from the peg and strode outside.

'Sorry about that. I didn't mean he had to leave the house.' Inspector Davis indicated the woman beside her. 'Dr Evans.'

The woman gave a small, self-conscious smile.

Nick felt a conflict of emotions. When the inspector had spoken on the phone about the need for a police surgeon, he had had a sudden horror that it might be Dr Partridge. Friendly though Malcolm was – perhaps too friendly? – the thought of him conducting an intimate examination of Millie and Anna had been sickening. He should have guessed that the inspector might have brought a woman. Yet even so . . . His fists clenched. His instincts still denied this could be necessary.

Inspector Davis fixed them with a look from which the polite smile had gone. 'I'm sorry to do this to you, but under the circumstances I'd like a medical examination of the girls, to see if there's any evidence of harm. I'm not just talking about sexual assault. If the girls are refusing to talk, we can only assume that they've been subject to some kind of threat.'

'No!' cried Anna and Millie in alarm. Again, that questioning look at each other.

Anna rushed on, 'It's not like that. Honestly. Nobody's threatening us. We just can't tell you.'

'We're not allowed to,' Millie put in. Then she shut her mouth with a gasp, as though she might already have said more than she should.

The inspector pounced. '*Who* won't allow you?'

'We *told* you. We can't say. But it's all right. Nothing happened to us . . . At least . . . Well, we're *OK*.'

Looking at their faces, Nick saw for the first time how the girls were buoyed up with self-importance. They knew something no one else in the room did. Alongside their evident nervousness of the small inspector, they were revelling in their secret.

'Where did you meet them?' The unexpected question came from Sergeant Vine, half-hidden near the door.

Millie swung round, instantly tense. 'Meet who?'

'The people, or person, who told you that you weren't allowed to tell.'

A mutinous silence.

'Always assuming you're not making the whole thing up, then either they did something to you, and swore you to secrecy, with threats of what would happen to you if you told. That's very common in cases of sexual abuse. Or else you stumbled upon something you weren't meant to see, and you were told it was important to keep it secret. Which one of those was it?'

Millie turned white. Then blood flooded back into her usually sallow cheeks. She turned helplessly to Anna.

The darker-haired girl set her lips and said nothing.

'Millie and Anna,' said the inspector more softly, 'we're not idiots. We have reason to believe a crime has been committed. If you don't tell us, you could be charged with obstructing the course of justice. I know this is difficult for you. With your parents' permission, I'd like to question you separately, and alone.' She raised her eyebrows at Nick, Suzie and Leon. 'It's sometimes easier to talk about these things to people you're not too close to. And I'd certainly like Dr Evans to take a look at you.'

'I keep telling you,' Millie burst out. 'That didn't happen. It wasn't *like* that.'

Suzie looked uncomfortable. 'Nick said they shouldn't take a shower before you came.'

The inspector's eyebrows rose further. Her look brightened on Nick. 'Thank you. Good thinking.'

He was aware of his own embarrassment. 'It wasn't just . . . *that*. The girls swear they weren't . . . you know. And I believe them. But I still thought you might be able to find where they'd been. It can't have been just the reed beds. But they wouldn't tell us that, either. And there was a strange sort of smell about Millie. Not just mud.' He turned questioningly to Leon.

His brother nodded. 'Can't quite put a name to it. Something stale. We wondered if they'd been kept somewhere, and you might be able to tell where.'

The sergeant studied the row of pegs by the door. 'Which of these coats are theirs?'

'The pale blue jacket and the silver,' Leon said.

'Would you mind if we took them away for examination? And their shoes?'

'I haven't *got* another jacket,' Millie exclaimed. 'What if I want to go out?'

'I'll lend you something,' Leon told her.

'And my shoes?'

'Millie,' Nick said sternly. 'We could stop this right now, if you'd just tell us where you've been.'

'Would you mind rolling your sleeve up?' The tall doctor spoke for the first time.

Instinctively, Millie caught her arms back to her body. She was holding the long sleeves of her pink sweater to cover her wrists. So, Nick realized with a start, was Anna with hers.

'Millie,' said the inspector. 'Let's do this the easy way, shall we?'

Reluctantly, Millie held out her arms. The doctor gently folded back the knitted cuffs.

Red marks circled the bony wrists. In a few places, the skin had been rubbed away, leaving sores.

The inspector's voice was slow and deadly. 'Do you still want to tell us nobody threatened you?'

NINETEEN

Through his own shock, Nick saw a squall of emotions pass over Millie's face. Her pale eyes widened, scared by the intensity of emotion in the adults around her. Then, as he watched, the shutters came down. She retreated behind the same mute obstinacy as Anna.

'Millie?' The inspector's voice rang sharply. 'I'm waiting for an explanation.'

This time Millie didn't even look at her cousin. She tugged the sleeves of her pink jumper back over her damaged wrists, and then thrust her hands under her armpits. Hunched, defensive, her face deliberately blank. She would not look at any of them.

Inspector Davis turned to the other girl. 'Anna. This nonsense has gone on long enough. Whatever your reasons may have been for keeping quiet, they're over now. You can't keep a thing like this secret. Someone has tied you up and imprisoned you overnight. One way or another, I intend to find out who that is. You can either cooperate, or you can obstruct the police. I would strongly advise you not to do the latter.'

Anna murmured something incomprehensible.

'I didn't hear that.'

'Sorry,' whispered Anna. A solitary tear rolled down a cheek plumper and rosier than Millie's.

Leon moved towards her, but the inspector stayed him with an outstretched hand.

'I'm waiting, Anna.'

The girl hung her dark head. No further sound came from her.

Nick's eyes went back to Millie. Her face was curtained behind the fall of her pale, straight hair. The sight of her scarred wrists burned his memory. He felt a rush of helpless rage towards whoever had done this to his fourteen-year-old daughter. It burst out as anger against Millie. He leaped to his feet, crashing the dirty crockery on the table.

'I've had enough of this!' he shouted at her. 'I don't know what you're playing at, but you're going to tell me who did this, RIGHT NOW!'

Millie burst into tears.

No one moved for a moment. Then Suzie went to her and put her arm round the shaking shoulders.

'There, love. Just tell us, and it will all be over.'

Millie hid her face against Suzie's cardigan and sobbed wordlessly. Anna was now weeping silently too.

Nick subsided into his chair, his sudden rage spent. He felt incredibly weary. Leon forced a smile of sympathy for him. Then the same grim look of defeat took over his own face.

The inspector let out a loud sigh. 'Well, we'd better get on with it. Dr Evans?'

They took Anna first. Inspector Davis and the doctor retreated with her to the privacy of the girls' bedroom. After a brief hesitation, Suzie followed. When the girl came down again, her colour was heightened and she was trembling. She went straight to Leon and hid herself in his arms. Still she said nothing.

Suzie led Millie upstairs. Nick's heart ached for his daughter. She looked so small, so defenceless. He had not been able to protect her from what had happened, and he could not protect her from this further indignity.

She seemed to be gone a long time.

At last the three women appeared, without Millie.

Suzie crossed the room to Nick. 'They're letting her have a shower now. They've taken some samples and photographs. They didn't find evidence of anything worse than being tied up.'

'Thank God for that.'

'But she's still not talking.'

The inspector handed the samples to her detective sergeant. She came across to Suzie, Nick and Leon. Her face was stony.

She's holding her rage under better control than I did, Nick thought.

'Unfortunately, I don't have time to waste hanging around for these two to make sense. When you rang to tell me they'd turned up, I called off the police hunt and the coastguards. Now it looks as if I shall have to reinstate that. And it's not a missing persons enquiry this time; it's definitely a crime we're investigating. It takes resources. Thousands of pounds. I'll leave the girls with you, for the time being. If you can't break their silence, then we may have to take them into head-quarters, and try a harsher approach. Respecting their legal rights, of course, and the fact that they're minors.' Her grim smile held no humour. 'This is no time for playing games.'

'We understand,' said Nick, through stiff lips. 'I'm sorry.'

Her face lightened unexpectedly. 'Teenagers. Who'd have 'em?'

The police were gone.

Nick heard Millie cross from the bathroom to the bedroom and shut the door.

'Can I go now, Dad?' Anna whispered to Leon.

He took his arms away from her. She followed Millie upstairs.

'I need a walk,' said Nick.

'Shall I . . .?' Suzie threw a questioning look at him. 'Or would you rather be alone?'

'You go,' Leon told her. 'I'll be here. I think what I need is a session in the studio, to soothe my frazzled nerves. Paint does what you tell it to . . . usually.'

'On second thoughts,' Suzie said, 'I'd better stay. Maybe when they've cooled off, the girls will see that it can't go on like this. Sooner or later, they're going to have to talk to us. I should be around.'

Nick gave her a grateful look. He would not be sorry to be on his own for an hour or two.

As he slipped his coat on, Leon said, 'I feel rotten about this. How long is it since our two families had a holiday together? And now this has to happen.'

'It must be worse for you. You've had a rough year already.'

He regretted the words as soon as they were spoken. A shadow passed over his brother's face. Jacqui's threat to come and fetch Anna lay unspoken between them.

It was good to step out into the balmy spring air. Nick lifted his face to the light breeze. No need for gloves or scarf today. The sea twinkled with points of sunlight. Deceptively innocent and inviting. You would not think it was the graveyard of so many ships, the death of so many crew and passengers.

He had no clear idea where he wanted to go.

The sea drew him. He wondered whether it was the blood of his Margerson ancestors and all the local fishermen families they had married into. Or just that he normally lived some distance from the coast. It was a rare pleasure to walk along the footpath and hear the little waves slapping against the stonework, the tinkle of swaying masts from the harbour, the hungry cries of gulls.

He came to the street end, just before the creek, where the cafeteria of the museum jutted out over the beach. It occurred to him that Suzie had said something about the curator calling in to ask if there was news of the girls. Da Souza? What was her name? Isabella da Souza. The sleek black hair. The just too precise English. Portuguese? Brazilian? Yes, that made sense.

He turned into the street of fishermen's cottages. For a moment, he hesitated outside the museum door, then pushed it open. A bell rang. There was no one at the reception desk.

Presently, he heard her steps coming down the wooden stairs. She gave him her professional smile of welcome. Then her expression changed, as she recognized who it was. She hurried towards him.

'Mr Fewings. I am so sorry. About your girls. Is there any news?'

'Yes.' He felt his face relax into a genuine smile, as it had not done for so long. 'Yes. They've turned up safe and sound.'

'These girls nowadays. They do not think about the parents, do they? Where have they been?'

Suddenly he found himself caught in a dilemma. Inspector Davis had left them without instructions about how much they could and could not tell other people about the girls' injuries. The rope marks on their arms. Their defiant silence.

'Oh,' he said, inventing rapidly. 'They seem to have got lost and bedded down for the night, and then found their way back this morning. They were glad to get home for fish and chips and a hot shower.'

He felt guilty about deceiving her. So many villagers had turned out to search for the girls. Mrs (Miss?) da Souza had cared enough to call at the house.

He waited for her answering smile of relief. Instead, she frowned and pressed him further. 'Your wife said they were

seen walking on the road to Brandon Head. There was a big
search there this morning. Is that where they went? Did they
spend the night there?'

'I can't tell you the exact spot, I'm afraid. I'm a stranger
here. At least, I came on holiday with my grandparents when
I was small. But that was a very long time ago. I don't
know the lie of the land like you locals. Can't put names
to places.'

He was covering up. However sympathetic she was, he
didn't want to tell this woman that his daughter had been
seized and tied up, that she was refusing to say where she
had been held, or by whom. Friendly and concerned though
Isabella da Souza was, the story would be all over the village
like wildfire. Even now, there were people in the cafeteria
above them, cups paused over saucers, conversation hushed,
listening.

'Were they in a cave? A shed? In some bushes?' The curator
was oddly persistent.

'Anyway,' he said, with a forced cheerfulness, brushing her
questions aside. 'I just wanted to let you know. It was good
of you to call in and ask Suzie this morning.'

'It was nothing. We are all concerned about your children.'

Nick escaped into the street. He passed his hand over the
thick waves of his hair and drew a deep breath of air that
smelled of both salt and seaweed. It had been a mistake. There
were too many questions he couldn't answer. Questions it was
natural for the good people of St Furseys to ask. He would
have to be careful.

He sauntered into the main village street. There were more
people about here. He grew nervous again. How long before
someone else approached him with unanswerable questions?

A little way down the road the line of shops was broken
by a low stone wall. Dark yew trees hung over it. There was
a glimpse of grass beyond. A tall grey tower, in which flints
glinted in the sunshine. The village church from which
St Furseys took its name.

The promise of peace and solitude within its walls beckoned.

Steps led up from the pavement, through iron gates. Some
of the grave slabs that flanked the path tilted at angles that
looked unstable. He paused to read the names beneath the

lichen. Here and there, one sparked a memory. *Horniman*, *Duffield*. Hadn't he come across these in the parish registers? Wives of one generation of Margersons or another? Some of the bodies beneath those slabs might also be his ancestors.

If he were Suzie, he would have found a bit of paper and copied the details, to follow them up later.

Instead, he walked on, into the cool interior of the church. St Furseys. He ought to know who this saint was, but he didn't.

He was struck by the light. He had been into many parish churches on Suzie's ancestor hunt. They were always dimmer than the day outside. Stained glass, Victorian or modern, in vibrant colours. Very occasionally, if you were lucky, the delicate greens and golds of medieval work.

In St Furseys, unusually, the great east window over the altar was of clear glass. He could not see the sea itself, but there was that unmistakable brightness that spoke of sky over water. Little white clouds skipped like lambs across a blue field.

He sat down in a pew and let his troubled mind still.

He and Suzie did not regularly go to church. The great festivals: Christmas, Easter. Occasional Sunday mornings, when the weather was not conducive to gardening. And then it was the modern and friendly Methodist church up the hill, not the sparsely attended parish church, where elderly parishioners greeted them politely, but the congregation did not hum with life and purpose.

Now he was glad to be alone with his thoughts.

After a while, his gaze steadied on the gold crucifix on the altar.

Help me, he prayed silently. *I don't know what's happening. I don't know what to do. Suzie and I want so much to help her, to protect her. But she won't let us in. Show us what to do. If she won't let us help her, can you?*

There was no obvious answer, but the peace deepened.

At last he sighed, feeling some of the tension flow out of him, and stood up. He looked around him with greater curiosity now. He should have persuaded Suzie to come. She would have noticed things he didn't, seen meaning in historical details that eluded his untrained eye. What he was good at was the architecture. It was, after all, his profession, even if he did favour the futuristic end of the spectrum. But the old craftsmen could always teach you something. Skills the world was beginning to value again.

This church now. Probably thirteenth or fourteenth century. Early Perpendicular. He strolled to the back and found a booklet on the church's history on a table at the back. Yes, he'd guessed right. Fourteenth century. But there had been a church here since the seventh century, when Fursey, an Irish hermit, had come to live among these heathen Angles 'for love of his Lord'. They had been attracted to him for his simple holiness and his visions of heaven and an icy hell. The medieval village had lost an older church to the encroaching sea, but they had managed to save their Norman font. The east window, he discovered, had been shattered by a German bomb in the Second World War. Of course, the east coast would have been vulnerable, the flat landscape behind lending itself to airbases. The unusual decision had been made not to replace the Victorian glass, but to leave the clear view of the heavens.

Leaflet in hand, he walked dutifully round the church, checking off the points of interest. The knapped flints of its walls, black or golden, the turret at more than head height, which was all that was left of the chancel screen and its rood loft, the fine west porch, with weathered carvings of angels.

He came at last to the Norman font, in a bay at the back of the church, just inside the door. You were entering the church here, in more than one sense. It looked oddly like a large stone bucket, devoid of ornament, capped by a wooden lid.

Suddenly he started. This must be the realization that had hit Suzie so often when he was with her on her searches. This very font was where they were baptized. The Margersons, the Hornimans, the Duffields. Dozens, perhaps even hundreds, of his forebears. Had some of them even been here in Norman times? A thousand years of his past. Here, in *this* font, *this* church. The lines stretched back from when his grandmother had been baptized here. A real woman, who had held Nick in her arms.

There was a larger table here, behind the font. Plans were spread out on it. Some restoration scheme? With an architect's curiosity he walked round the font to investigate.

They were not the plans for a building. He was looking at a map of the churchyard. It had been marked off into little rectangles, each with a letter and a number.

Graves. The plan of everyone who had been buried at St Furseys, or at least since the records began.

He could not remember seeing anything like this in any of Suzie's churches.

There was a spiral-bound file beside it. A typed list of names, dates. He had found the topographical equivalent of the burial registers he had searched in the Record Office. Not just *when* his family had died, but where they were buried.

His fingers went straight to the page with the Margersons. They were there: Solomon, Benjamin, their wives, their children. Leaping out of the page to greet him. He checked the reference numbers against the plan of the churchyard. The one he most wanted was on the south side, not far from the boundary wall.

He went outside and searched through grass several inches high until he found it.

Solomon Margerson
1877–1932
'Greater love hath no man than this'

A wave of reassurance, of pride, washed over him. He could hold his head high. Solomon Margerson had been carried to his last resting place here, a hero, attended by that enormous procession of his fellow lifeboatmen. Here, on this spot, his family had stood in silence, to honour his courage and mourn his loss.

There were other names below his. The dates were earlier. They must have been added to their father's tombstone after his death. Timothy Margerson, aged eleven. Vera Margerson, aged fourteen.

The world stopped for moment. Solomon's daughter.

How had she died?

How near had Millie come last night to a grave in a cemetery or a plaque at the crematorium? His quirky, vulnerable teenage daughter's life cut off unbearably short.

TWENTY

Nick turned into Beach Street. The glitter of the sea met him, as it did at so many street ends. It had been good to get out of the house, alone. Some of the peace of St Furseys church had seeped into his being, soothing the anxiety and the anger. But as he approached Leon's cottage, he felt a choking hand tightening around his throat again.

He paused at the door to steady himself. Millie was alive. She wasn't lying under the turf of the churchyard, like Vera Margerson. She was well. The marks on her wrists were minor injuries which would soon heal. What was still menacing was the untold story of who had done this to her, and why.

He drew a determined breath and opened the door.

Suzie was alone in the living room. She turned quickly at his entrance, her face expectant.

'Oh, it's you.'

'Who else?' Then, with an anxious look upstairs, 'What's the news?'

'Nothing,' she sighed. 'They're asleep. I don't know what went on last night, but once the excitement died down they were both knackered. They're sleeping like babies.'

'Lucky them. I don't know when I shall get a good night's sleep again.'

'They're young. They can't imagine all the things we can. The important thing is that they're home.'

'They may not be for much longer, unless they change their minds. Inspector Davis is banking on us to get the truth out of them. If we can't, she'll have them back to HQ in Murchington. I'm afraid she'll give them a harder time there than she did here.'

'*Why* won't they tell us?'

'As Millie pointed out, they can't tell us that without telling us the whole story.'

'She said they're "not allowed to".'

'That means someone still has a hold over them, even now they're free. That's what's upsetting me.'

'It doesn't bear thinking about. Nothing feels safe any more.'
She shuddered, and then looked up at him with a new concern.
'Did you see Tom in your travels?'

'No. Should I have?'

'I suppose not. Only he hasn't come back.'

Nick looked out of the window. The sunshine was dimming
behind a veil of cloud, but the sky held the promise of daylight
for several hours yet.

'It's still early. It was a bit juvenile of him to storm off like
that, just because the inspector wanted to lift some of the pres-
sure off Anna and Millie. It's not like Tom. He can usually
laugh things off.'

'That's what I mean. It's really getting to him, what
happened to Millie. Those two may make out like they're cat
and dog, but he was genuinely scared for her.'

'So he's gone for a long walk. What's the harm in that?
It's a nice day for it. Or was. The sun's going in now.'

'As long as it *is* just a long walk.'

'What are you trying to say?'

'The girls went out looking for smugglers. And look what
happened to them.'

'And you think that Tom . . .?'

'He would, wouldn't he? Try to crack this on his own?'

A cold fear invaded Nick. Not Tom as well. The girls had
escaped with nothing worse than rope burns on their wrists
and a threat sufficient to keep them silent. If Tom charged in
. . . Not a teenage girl, but a young man. A danger who would
not be silenced by a mere threat.

Suzie saw the change in his face. She got up and ran to
him. 'He'll be all right, won't he? Should we tell the police?'

He had a weary sense that the grim events of yesterday
were repeating themselves.

'It's early yet.' He held her close. 'Tom's not an idiot. He
can take care of himself.'

He wished he believed that.

Leon came down from the studio to join them for tea and toast.
After a while, the two girls emerged, sleepy-eyed and quiet.

Suzie made more tea for them. Nick held himself in check,
forbidding himself to leap in hard, in case the shutters came
down in Millie's face, as they had before.

When he could bear the uncomfortable silence no longer he said, 'Well, you've had a sleep on it. Inspector Davis is going to be ringing back pretty soon, to ask if we've made any progress. If I say no, you know what will happen.'

'They'll take us to the police station.'

'Only if you refuse to talk. It's your choice. It doesn't have to be like this. You needn't be afraid to tell us. Whatever it is, we're not going to be spreading it around the neighbourhood.'

'*They* will.'

'Who?'

'The police.'

'What do you mean?'

He was met with silence.

'Anna,' Leon tried. 'You must see that this can't go on. Whoever tied you up and threatened you is a criminal. They've got to be stopped.'

The girl sighed. 'No, Dad, you don't understand.'

The silence lengthened, the tension palpable now.

They all started at the loud rap on the front door.

Alarm paled Leon's face. 'Jacqui?'

Suzie went to open the door. Instead of the diminutive, elegant form of Leon's ex-wife, the bulky presence of Malcolm Partridge filled the doorway. He was stepping over the threshold, even before Suzie invited him in. His eager-to-please geniality swept the room.

'So, the wanderers return! Good to see you home, girls.' He swung round on Nick and Leon. 'Why didn't you ring me, my dear boys? We've all been frantic with worry. It wasn't until I bumped into our lovely Senhorita da Souza that I heard the good news.'

'I'm sorry.' Nick felt himself flush. 'We should have told you. You've been so good to us. Helping with the search, getting out your boat for us. But we were so overwhelmed to get them back, it drove everything else out of our minds. I apologize.'

'Not at all, dear boy. Perfectly understandable. And then you had the police to deal with.'

Nick looked at his brother. The inspector and her colleagues had arrived in an unmarked car. Leon shrugged.

'So what's the story?' Malcolm boomed. 'Where have you young lasses been all night?'

The girls avoided his eyes.

Partridge let out a loud guffaw. 'Serves me right, eh? Teach me to mind my own business. Well, we all have a family secret or two, what?'

Nick caught Suzie's look. She was eyeing the kettle questioningly. He shook his head. He did not feel he could bear the doctor's enthusiastic concern much longer.

For once, even the thick-skinned Malcolm seemed to take the hint.

'Well, all's well that ends well, they say. I'd better leave you to it. I've called off the Yacht Club lookout.' He ambled towards the door. 'No Tom, then?'

'He's gone for a walk,' Suzie told him, shepherding him on.

'Let's hope *he* can keep out of mischief. Maybe we'll think about that yacht trip, if this weather holds.'

'Thank you,' said Suzie. 'That's very kind of you.'

She closed the door behind him and leaned against it with a sigh, her eyes closed.

'That man!'

'Old Malcolm's all right,' Leon defended him. 'A little of him goes a long way, but he's got a good heart.'

'How did he know the police had been here?' Nick asked.

'Goodness knows. This is a village. People talk. There's not much they miss.'

'So what if they do know about the police coming back?' Suzie said. 'It's pretty obvious they'd want to know what happened to the girls.'

Millie and Anna looked up in sudden alarm.

'People won't think we talked to them, will they?' Millie cried.

'Why? It won't matter if they do, will it?'

'Because . . .'

'Because what?'

'We promised we wouldn't,' Anna said.

No matter how hard their parents pleaded, that was all they could get out of the girls.

The mist was thickening, shortening the promise of lingering light, when the door burst open. It was as though the still air had erupted into a tornado. Tom stood there panting. His already tall form seemed to have grown, so that Nick had the sense that he filled the small room with the force of his excitement. He had evidently been running. His face was warm and sweating, his chest heaving. His blue eyes blazed.

'You found it!' he cried, struggling for breath. 'You found the back door!'

He was shouting at the girls.

Millie and Anna recoiled, as though he had struck them. They shot each other terrified looks.

Tom threw himself down on a kitchen chair, facing them. Suzie silently filled a glass with water at the sink and put it in front of him. He gulped it down. Then he leaned forward across the table.

'I'm right, aren't I? That's where you've been.'

The girls looked now, not boldly defiant, but like young rabbits caught in the glare of a car's headlamps.

'I think you'd better explain, Tom,' Nick said quietly.

The boy sat back in his chair. He was enjoying the attention, his own certainty that he was right. He threw Nick a triumphant grin.

'It's what I was saying. About Millie not thinking in straight lines like most other people. Finding another angle to come at things. So I was walking along the beach towards Brandon Head when it struck me. We've been wasting all this time trying to decide if there really was a cave up on the cliff, that the smugglers used. And people kept saying how it wouldn't explain about Millie and Anna disappearing, even if there was, because they couldn't have climbed up or down to it. And that's when it hit me.' He struck his hand on the table. 'We've been looking in the wrong place all the time. The contraband got *in* that way. Hauled up from a ship in a gully between the rocks. Or even the whole boat hoisted up, when the Revenue men were chasing them, if you believe the old stories. But what about the men already *in* the cave? The ones who did the hauling? How did *they* get in?'

Suzie, Nick and Leon stared at him, then at each other.

'Well, I'll be blowed,' Leon exclaimed. 'None of us thought of that.'

'We were rather preoccupied with the girls disappearing,' Nick replied.

'Don't you remember?' Tom went on. 'There was all this

talk of tunnels. But where did the tunnels come out? Because that's where the local smugglers got *in*. They'd have to, wouldn't they?'

He was enjoying the fact that he was gripping his audience, the knowledge that he was several steps ahead of the adults. The two girls, Nick noticed, had huddled close to each other. There was no surprise in their faces, only fear.

'It would probably be in the Noah's Ark, wouldn't it?' Suzie said. 'It had the reputation for being a smugglers' inn.'

'Think about it.' Tom allowed her a teasing smile. 'When Dad and the girls were there, they looked for the market gardens. The ones Dad thought old what's-his-name Margerson . . .'

'Alfred,' supplied Nick.

'Right. The ones Alfred Margerson worked on when he came from Cambridge. And you couldn't find any sign of them, could you? Just a lot of flat, wet meadows and some soggy sheep. Well, you'd hardly dig a tunnel to the inn under there, would you? You'd be below sea level. Unless you put in pumps, you could be up to your neck in water. Or worse.'

'So?' said Nick.

'So there's only one place it could come out, given most of the country round here's almost a swamp. Brandon Head. The back door has to be there, as well as the front door. There's nowhere else it could be.' He swung around with a triumphant flourish.

Then his eyes came back to his sister's pale, anxious face. 'Well done, Millie. You were way ahead of the rest of us. So when it finally got through to me, I went to look.' He turned back to Nick and Leon. 'You two must have passed it. When we went to search the headland yesterday evening. I went up the short, steep way, from the beach. But you two drove round the back of the headland to find the footpath. What did you see when you got out of the car? It wasn't just heathland at the bottom, was it?'

Nick tried to cast his mind back. It seemed impossible that it was only yesterday. It was true, the land at the start of the path had been fenced off. It was only halfway up that it opened out into turf and gorse bushes. But lower down? Meadows, like those around the Noah's Ark? No!

'You're right!' He almost jumped out of his seat. 'Over on

our right. There were fields of vegetables, weren't there, Leon?' His own excitement was rising. 'So *that's* where Alfred did his gardening. The fields around the inn aren't drained, as they are in other places round here. But still . . .' He appealed to Tom again. 'What's the connection with the tunnel?'

'Those gardens look a bit like allotments, except that there are bigger patches of the same crop. And in some of them, there are sheds and things. I did wonder if there could be a hole in the floor of one of them, with a trapdoor. But then I saw it.' He was leaning towards Millie and Anna again, his eyes intent on their faces. 'At the back of one field, there's a really solid-looking door, set into the face of the hill. There are bushes hanging over it, so you'd hardly notice it, unless you were looking. I went to have a closer recce. And there was this whacking great padlock on it. And footprints in front of it. It was a bit churned up, but I wouldn't be surprised if the forensic lab find traces of the same mud on your shoes. Am I right?'

Millie broke from her chair. 'You mustn't tell them! It's not what you think. At least, it is and it isn't.' She shot an anguished appeal at Anna.

Her cousin sighed. 'We've got to tell them, Millie. Otherwise it'll just get worse. Only,' she challenged the rest of them, 'you've got to keep this to yourselves. He particularly said the police mustn't know. It's a matter of life and death.' Her dark eyes were round and brilliant.

'Who?' Nick broke in.

'He didn't tell us his name. Don't be daft,' Millie snapped.

'Go on, Anna,' Leon said levelly. 'Tell us everything.'

TWENTY-ONE

Anna darted an apologetic look at Millie. Nick sensed that she was relieved to be able to tell their story.

'Tom was right. It was Millie's idea. She said there had to be two ends to the smugglers' tunnel. And like you said, it was pretty certain to be above the water level. So there was only one place it could be. Well, more or less. There's quite a lot of Brandon Head. But we starting walking round it, and Millie got excited when she saw the market gardens. We didn't know who they belonged to, because we could see some other houses and farms dotted around. But it wasn't so far from the Noah's Ark, either. And we'd all been talking about our Alfred Margerson, and how funny it was, him being a gardener and then the landlord of a smugglers' pub. And his sons became boatmen. It all seemed to fit. So we did the same as Tom. We went to have a closer look, to see if we could find the entrance.'

'But Tom said that door was padlocked.'

Now the girls were beginning to kindle with remembered excitement.

'But it *wasn't*!' Millie cried. 'Not when *we* found it.'

The chill of terror clamped Nick's heart. 'You mean there was someone in there?'

'We didn't know that, did we? We just opened it a little way and crept inside to look.'

Nick could feel the sweat starting on his forehead.

'And . . .?' said Suzie. She looked as drawn as he felt.

'There were all these boxes,' Anna explained. 'Stacked up near the door, as though they were waiting for someone to take them away. Only it wasn't the sort of thing we were expecting. We'd more or less shut the door behind us, in case anyone came along and saw it open. So there wasn't much light. But the ones we could make out nearest the door looked like flat-pack furniture, and there were some cartons there with funny writing on them.'

'Arabic?' Tom's head went up eagerly. 'That could be North African, couldn't it?'

'I'm not sure,' said Anna. 'It was stencilled. Like capitals.'

'It fits,' said Nick. 'They're not shipping cocaine in neat little bags of white powder. They're hiding it in normal-looking cargoes. The sort of thing the Customs wouldn't open unless they had a reason to.'

'Cartons of food, yes,' Suzie said. 'But flat-pack furniture?'

'A decoy,' Nick told her. 'To provide cover for the other stuff.'

'Go on, Anna,' urged Leon.

'We were just trying to work out whether it meant anything important, and whether we dared break open one of the cartons and grab a couple of samples to take away –' Anna's voice faltered – 'when we heard footsteps. Sort of soft and squeaky.'

'Not at first, we didn't,' argued Millie. 'We saw a light in the tunnel, bobbing about on the walls.'

'Whatever. Anyway, someone was coming. Not through the outside door, but down the tunnel. I looked at Millie, to see if we should make a run for it. Only by then we were too far from the door.'

'I was wondering if we could hide behind the boxes and stuff.'

'And then he came round the corner and saw us. And there was this awful crash. He must have dropped the stuff he was carrying. He had this torch-thing on his head, like a potholer, so he could see us, but we couldn't see him. We were just petrified.'

'You should have run,' Suzie protested. 'One of you might have got away to raise the alarm. If there was only one of him.'

'We didn't know it was just him. There could have been a whole gang of them.'

'Anyway, there wasn't time to think,' Anna went on. 'He swore. And then he just flew at us. He got an arm round my neck, so he was choking me, and he had Millie by the waist.'

The ice crawled through Nick's veins. It didn't matter that Millie and Anna were safe in front of him. All he could see was what might have happened.

'Only then,' Millie said, 'his voice changed. And he said something really surprising. "Keep quiet." It wasn't just *what* he said. It was the way he said it. So low, he was almost whispering. As though our being there was a secret, and he was on our side, and he didn't want anyone else to hear us.'

'And he took his arm away from my throat,' Anna said, 'though he still didn't let go of us. First, he made us hand over our phones. And then he said, "I expect you're wondering what's going on here?" I was still too frightened to speak, so I just nodded. He said he'd have to swear us to secrecy. I thought Millie was going to argue, but we looked at each other. Well, we didn't have much choice, did we? And it doesn't count if you're forced to make a promise. So we did. And then he started to tell us what it was all about.'

'And it was sort of what we thought,' Millie broke in, 'only not exactly. They *are* running drugs. They haul them up from a boat into the cave at night, and then a van comes to take the stuff away, from this other end of the tunnel. That was why he was shifting the stuff down the tunnel to the door. Only *he's* not one of them.'

The girls looked at each other, alight with self-importance.

'He's with the SBS,' Anna said, almost whispering.

'Special Boat Service,' explained Millie.

'Thanks. I think we know what the letters stand for,' came Tom's dry comment. He moved away from the table to perch on the window sill.

Millie shot him a withering look and went on. 'They do undercover stuff, for the Customs people. And he was drafted in to get himself into this gang. He has to get enough evidence to convict them. Not just the bit players, but the big guys. So that's why it has to be a total secret. If it got out who he was, they'd kill him. You won't tell anyone else, will you?' she begged.

'Only the police,' Suzie said firmly. 'They have to know.'

'No!' cried Anna and Millie simultaneously.

Anna's face was creased with worry. 'He particularly said *not* to tell the police. They can't trust them. All sorts of local people are mixed up in this racket. He only knows a few of them so far. They could even have someone inside the police force. It's a matter of life or death for him.'

The adults looked at each other, assessing this startling information.

'It's possible,' Leon said slowly. 'I know the Customs people do sometimes call in the SBS. Those guys have really fast boats, and they need them. Some of these super craft the smugglers use nowadays can do speeds you wouldn't believe. And the SBS are trained in commando tactics. Not exactly standard practice when you join Her Majesty's Revenue and Customs.'

'And he thinks there's police involvement in the gang? Is that really possible?' But even as Nick asked, he knew the answer.

Leon shrugged. 'Is any organization a hundred per cent secure?'

'At least we have to tell Inspector Davis,' Suzie insisted. 'Once she's heard the girls' story, she'll understand the need for secrecy. And if we don't tell her, she'll just go on hammering away for an answer. Goodness knows what she's got her people doing. She might blow this whole investigation without meaning to.'

'Unless *she's* the mole,' said Tom.

'Don't be ridiculous,' Suzie cried.

'Why? Because she's a woman?'

'No. Because . . . because I can't believe she is.'

'We haven't *finished*!' Millie all but shouted. 'Will you just shut up and *listen*?'

The Fewings turned back to her in silence. Her pale blue eyes sparkled, now she had their attention.

'He was going to let us go then. We'd sworn to keep it a secret, now that we knew what he was up to. And it was getting late, but we could still be home before dark.'

'But you weren't,' Suzie said.

'That's what I'm *coming* to. There was another sound, of someone starting to open the door behind us. And this guy switches off his lamp and pulls a sort of black mask over his face. So we never did get to see what he looked like. And he pushes us behind the boxes. And then, there in the doorway, is this other really big man. And he starts to ask the first one if he's shifted all the stuff. He had a really horrible voice, sort of low and cold. Only then he saw us. That was awful. There wasn't much light, and he banged the door shut, so it went really dark. And he pulled a torch out of his pocket and shone it on us. Right in our faces.

'"I . . . *see*," he said. Like, totally icy. "And what are *they* doing here?"'

'So the SBS man explained that he'd just caught us.

'"Get rid of them," the big one says. "After dark, when the van's been. But don't hurt them." And I thought it was going to be all right, and they were just going to let us go.'

'They couldn't, could they?' Leon said quietly.

'No, 'cos the next thing he said was, "Just take them out to sea and drop them over. This time of year, they won't last long in that water. Nothing suspicious when they find the bodies come ashore, if they ever do. Unfortunate accident. Two holidaymakers washed off the rocks. Usual appeals to be careful of the tides."'

Nick felt his heart hammering in his chest.

'But you're still here,' Tom prompted.

'Well, we were terrified by now,' Millie said. 'I still kept hoping the SBS man could get us out of it. But would he do it, if it meant blowing his cover and losing the chance of nailing this whole drugs racket? Maybe even getting himself killed? I didn't know how hard these types are. After that it all got a bit confused. I still don't know what really happened. He tied us up and blindfolded us. Then he hustled us up the tunnel and pushed us in somewhere to wait.'

Anna could keep quiet no longer. 'We kept hearing footsteps go past. They must have been shifting the rest of the cargo. I don't know how much of it was cocaine, and how much really was whatever it said on the boxes, but it seemed to take forever. Then it all went quiet. The big man went away, and I was *so* glad, because he was really scary.'

'Did you get a look at the second man, before they blindfolded you?' Nick asked.

'Not really. He had his back to the door, and then he switched the torch on us. All I could see was that he was wearing dark clothes, black or dark blue. And he had a cap with a peak. When he saw us, he pulled it down really low over his eyes, and pulled a scarf up to cover his mouth. But we could still hear that slow, creepy voice. It was so *cold*. Well, after that it went quiet. They left us there for ages.'

'And all that time, we were out looking for you, around the town at first. Then we got the police to raid Ed Harries' place, in case you'd got into trouble there,' Leon told her.

'We searched the headland,' Nick said. 'Only it never

occurred to us to look for the other end of the tunnel. To think we must have passed that close to you.'

'We couldn't hear when the van came to fetch the cargo. We were too far away then. It seemed hours before anyone came back.' Anna's eyes were round. 'And then we didn't know who it was until he spoke. It was our SBS man again. Only we didn't know whether he was going to let us free, or really take us out to sea and drop us overboard.'

'He wouldn't have,' gasped Suzie. 'Surely?'

'He didn't say much,' Millie continued. 'Just made us walk in front of him back down the tunnel. And we kept stumbling, because we couldn't see where we were going and the rock was rough. And then suddenly we were out in the fresh air. We still had to keep walking. It was soft underfoot at first, and then we hit the road. And we kept on going.

'After a long time, we must have got somewhere. I think there was a sort of bridge. He took hold of our arms and steered us across it. Then we went on up a path. And I could sort of see that there was a light, but it wasn't very bright through the blindfold. He left us alone then, and there was some sort of argument going on in the distance. I couldn't hear what it was about. Anyway, in the end he pushed inside this house, or shed, or whatever it was. Probably a house, because there were a couple of steps up to the door. And he pushed us inside a room and locked us in.'

'That was really scary,' Anna said. 'Because all the time, he hardly said anything to us. And we still thought he might be holding us there while he got a boat. Because, otherwise, why didn't he just let us go?'

'We were there for the rest of the night,' Millie said. 'There wasn't even room to lie down. We managed to lift each other's blindfolds a bit. We didn't dare take them right off in case someone came back. But it was still too dark to see anything. It felt like there were lots of cardboard boxes, all piled higgledy-piggledy. There didn't even seem to be anything in them, not like the ones in the tunnel.'

'And there was this really awful smell. Like somebody hadn't emptied the bins for a month.'

'So that's why you smelled so whiffy when you came home,' Suzie observed.

'*Thanks*, Mum. Anyway, we were beginning to think that

maybe the SBS man wasn't coming back. We didn't think there'd be time now for him to take us out in the boat while it was still dark, like the other man said he had to.'

Anna's face looked pale with the memory. 'Only then we thought, perhaps he'd just leave us there. And we'd die anyway, and no one would ever find us.'

'We started to try and undo the knots on each other's wrists. And then we heard someone coming at last. So we pulled the blindfolds back down. We didn't know if it would be our SBS man, or the horrible big one who wanted us killed. Or it could have been the man we heard arguing when we arrived. The owner of the place, I suppose. Because when they were arguing, it sounded like a man.'

'But I think it *was* him,' Millie went on. 'The first one. Only we couldn't be sure, because he didn't say very much and his voice was sort of muffled. I think he must have put that ski mask thing on, in case our blindfolds slipped and we recognized him. He made us walk in front of him. Then he put us into a car and made us lie on the floor. And then he drove us off. When the car stopped, we had to get out. And we still couldn't see where we were, because of the blindfolds.'

'But we felt we were out of doors, and I could hear this rustling all around us,' Anna remembered. 'He made us walk for ages. And there were these leaves brushing past our faces. It was really hard to follow him without putting our feet in the mud.'

'Then he stopped. He told us to say we'd got lost in the marshes and had to spend the night there. But if the police wouldn't believe us and got tough, then we could say we'd been caught by a man with a ginger beard.'

'The archaeology professor?' Nick exclaimed. 'What was his name?'

'Dancey,' Suzie supplied.

'But it *wasn't*. I don't think either of the men who caught us had a beard,' protested Anna. 'And we were to say we'd got a glimpse of the car, and it was a dark blue 4x4, with some sort of logo on the side.'

'It fits,' Nick said. 'The university's archaeology unit. They're here doing a survey of the seabed, looking for wrecks.'

'Could it be them?' Suzie asked. 'I thought Tom was being ridiculous, taking us out to their boat to look for the girls.'

'But that's the point, isn't it?' Nick said. 'They weren't on the boat. And they never were in that Land Rover either. He wanted them to feed the police a red herring.'

'So why didn't you tell us this story?' Leon asked his daughter. 'Not even when the inspector pressed you?'

Anna blushed. 'Because it wasn't true. I'd sworn I wouldn't tell about the tunnel, but I didn't want to tell a lie and get somebody else in trouble. And the bit about the reeds *was* true, more or less.'

'We had a bit of an argument,' Millie admitted. 'But she won. But that was afterwards. He told us to be careful we didn't fall in the water, and . . . left us.'

'We waited quite a bit,' Anna said, 'to see if anyone else might be coming. When we found we were really alone, we set to work to get the blindfolds off. And we were in this really strange place. Reeds right over our heads, and a big pool full of water alongside us. We just couldn't see anything except reeds and water, wherever we looked.'

'So then we had another go at undoing the ropes round our wrists,' Millie went on. 'And it took forever. And then all we had to do was to walk out of this jungle. Only we didn't know which way to go.'

'So you didn't spend the night in the marshes?' Suzie asked.

'No. Luckily the sun was shining by then,' Anna said. 'And we figured out if it was morning the sun must be in the east, and that would be where the sea was.'

'Take a Smartie and go to the top of the class,' murmured Tom.

His cousin shot him an indignant look.

'So we started walking. And it was a *long* walk. He must have carted us right out into the sticks. I thought we might have come to a house where we could have phoned you to come and fetch us. But there wasn't anything. Just these endless reed beds. And the path was so overgrown, we had to fight our way through the reeds. It got really muddy.'

'And just when we were getting, like, really frustrated, we saw the church tower of St Furseys over the tops of the leaves,' Millie cried. 'So we headed straight for it. And when we got out of the reeds we just kept going till we were home.'

Suzie hugged her.

Nick frowned. 'It still doesn't explain quite a few things.

All right, this SBS character did let them go. But how's he going to explain what he's done now that the girls have showed up safe and sound? He can hardly say they must have swum ashore. The sea's at its coldest at the end of winter. You could die of hypothermia in five minutes.'

'You think that other man will kill him?' Anna asked in horror.

'I wish I knew what was going on.'

'So?' said Leon. 'What do we tell the police?'

TWENTY-TWO

' I 'm not talking to the police,' Millie declared. 'And that's flat.'

'Millie, you have to,' Nick said.

She turned to him. The look of obstinacy he knew so well tightened her facial muscles.

'He saved our lives. And if that other horrible man found out we told the police – and I bet he *would* find out – he'd kill him. As it is, when they know we're still alive, he'll have a job to explain why. He'll have to persuade him that we swore we wouldn't tell anyone, if that's possible.'

'It's not that simple,' Suzie tried to persuade her. 'You two deciding whether you will or won't talk. Inspector Davis isn't just going to close the file on this. She said that if you wouldn't tell us what happened of your own free will, she'd be back to make sure you did.'

Doubt crossed Millie's face. She looked at Anna. Her cousin's eyes registered the same alarm.

'If the police come back here and take us to the police station,' Anna said, 'people will see them. They'll *think* we talked, even if we didn't.'

'There's one way round that,' Nick said. 'You could go voluntarily.'

Millie digested this idea. 'You mean, we could drive there in your car? So nobody knew where we were going?'

'If your man was right about there being a possible spy in the police force, then that person would know you hadn't talked so far. The word's bound to be all over this area. So if we ask to talk to the inspector privately, it might be enough to keep your SBS man safe.'

'You're kidding. What happens if Anna and I drive up to police headquarters and ask for her? Everyone will guess what we've come for.'

'It needn't be the police station,' Suzie said. 'We could meet her anywhere. Off the record.'

'And you could get her to shut up about it? And not to
foul up his operation till he can catch them all?'
'For goodness' sake!' Leon broke in. 'These criminals nearly
drowned you. They've got to be caught.'
'Dad!' Millie pleaded to Nick. 'We promised.'
Nick and Suzie exchanged troubled looks.
'We can't just do nothing,' Suzie said. 'She could be on
her way here any moment. If only the girls will tell *her*, it
would be a start.'
'Where can we meet? Somewhere out of the way, that would
look innocent if we met anyone who recognized us.'
'Got it!' Suzie cried. 'After we'd been to the Record Office,
I trawled through the IGI looking for marriages of your folk
in other parishes. I remember one I came across. Benjamin
Margerson married Mollie Cook in Parwold, back, I think, in
the 1850s. If things had turned out differently, I might have
suggested going there anyway, to check out Mollie's background. Is it far?' She turned to Leon.
'About three miles, I think. A bit inland.'
'I'll ring the inspector,' Nick offered. 'Where shall we tell
her we'll be? Is there a tea shop? Or a pub that's open in the
afternoon?'
'Pass,' said Leon. 'I'm new around here.'
'The parish church,' Suzie said. 'That's the one place you
can be sure will be open.'
Nick dialled the inspector's number. He was tense, as they
all were. The afternoon was slipping away. Inspector Davis
could be on the road to St Furseys already. Any moment they
might hear her ring the doorbell. He pictured her standing on
the doorstep, in full view of anyone walking to the beach.
A crisp reply. 'Detective Inspector Davis.'
He fumbled for the words that would explain what they
wanted to do, and why it was necessary. Millie and Anna
would talk. But only to her, in confidence. No, he couldn't
explain their reason on the phone.
He felt the resistance at the other end. No detective sergeant.
No police witness to corroborate the interview.
At last he closed his phone with a sigh. 'She's not happy.
But she's agreed. She'll meet us at Parwold in half an hour.'
He looked around at the crowded room with a sense of

unreality. They would have to pretend to be setting out on another light-hearted family history quest. Another parish to add to the checklist. Photographs of cottages and the church. But this time a darker agenda.

The full realization of what the girls had told him was sinking in. Someone had ordered that Anna and Millie should be murdered. Dropped overboard into an icy sea, in which they had no chance of surviving. That someone, with the slow, cold voice – the ice was entering his own spine now – must be local. The man who oversaw the despatch of drugs from St Furseys to their next destination. Someone who might have eyes and ears anywhere in this village, or even the police headquarters.

He must know by now that Millie and Anna were alive. How long would he trust the girls to remain silent, before he decided to silence them himself?

Around him, everyone was hurrying to get ready. Suzie, he saw, had even got her family history file.

'To look authentic,' she told him, quickly. 'Got your camera?'

As if this were really an innocent outing.

'The girls are going in Leon's car,' she told him. 'Tom's coming with us.'

Her face changed to deeper concern. 'You look dreadful.'

He could not tell her his worst fears.

'Yes, I'm not too good,' he admitted.

'I'd better drive.'

Mist greyed the sea, reducing the waves to an oily sleekness. Leon got his car out of the garage and the girls got in.

'You're as worked up as Dad is,' Tom said to his mother. 'Let me do it.' He held out his hand for the car keys.

'I'm OK . . . Oh, well. All you have to do is follow Leon.'

'I'd worked that out.'

A burly man in a fisherman's jersey called up to them from the beach below. 'Glad to see you've got your girls back safe.'

'Yes, thank you,' Nick replied.

'I heard the police were round to see them.'

Nothing could stay secret for long in a village.

'That's right. Just winding up the search.'

'There's a lot of parents will be wanting to know what

happened to them. Thinking about their own kids, like.' The weather-beaten face was crinkled with curiosity.

'Yes, I'm sure. But they're OK.'

It wasn't true. But Nick dared not say more.

Suzie waved her plastic folder at him and forced a smile. 'Just off to look up some more family history. That's what we came here for.'

'Oh, yes? From round this way, are you?'

'My husband is. At least, his grandmother was.'

'Better watch out, if you're going far. Don't want to get caught if this fog gets worse.'

Was that a threat?

'We'll be careful. We're only going a few miles.'

Nick got in beside his son. 'He's right. I hope this doesn't get any thicker.'

'It's not a real fog. I can see a couple of hundred metres ahead.'

Tom frowned, concentrating on negotiating the turn from the hard packed sand in front of the garages on to Beach Street.

Leon led them to the High Street, then turned north along the main road. Presently he took a left turn on to a much smaller road, leading away from the sea.

Tall reeds rose on either side of them. Their spear-shaped leaves spiked the overhanging sky. Drainage ditches showed muddy brown, without the sun to make them sparkle. Nick thought of Millie and Anna, dumped out here in a watery wilderness, blindfolded, bound and frightened, to find their way home. It could, he told himself, have been much worse.

The road ran straight and level. They met no other cars. It was not long before the church tower of Parwold came into view. A small, crooked spire, roofed with wooden shingles. The cars drew up in front of it.

A straggle of cottages lined the only street. Some of them were smartly painted, with hanging baskets. A few cars stood outside.

'I was right to pick the church, wasn't I?' Suzie said, getting out. 'That big white house down there might have been a pub once, but it's not in business now.'

'Not even a post office,' said Nick, looking around. 'Let alone a tea shop.'

'Holiday cottages,' Leon growled. 'They're killing all the villages off. No shops, no school. Parwold's pretty near the sea, but a bit cheaper. And it's still got that olde worlde charm.'

'At least there's still a church. Let's go inside,' Suzie said.

Nick scanned the quiet street. 'I don't see the inspector's car, do you, Leon?'

They followed Suzie.

The church was much smaller than St Furseys. Old-fashioned box pews still occupied the back of the nave. Nearer the chancel, they had been cleared away to make room for modern chairs with upholstered seats. In front of each was an embroidered kneeler. In one corner, an Easter garden glowed with gold, white and purple flowers. A miniature stone had been rolled away from Christ's tomb.

'Someone still loves this place,' Leon said. 'What is it about churches? They always feel so peaceful. Even when there's no one in them.'

'Especially when no one's in them,' Nick agreed.

'*We're* here,' Millie said. 'How would you know it was peaceful, if there was nobody here?'

It was the first time either of the girls had spoken since they got out of Leon's car.

'I guess it must be all those hundreds of years of prayer,' Suzie said, looking up at the window above the altar. 'They sort of accumulate in the place. As though they were here for us now.'

She sat down in one of the box pews and folded her hands in her lap. After a moment's hesitation Nick and Leon did the same.

The children stood more awkwardly. Tom wandered to the tower behind them, where the bell ropes hung. Anna and Millie moved slowly forward and sat down on the more comfortable chairs.

For long moments there was utter stillness.

The sound of the heavy latch turning made them all jump. Nick tensed, fearing the inspector would not have kept her promise. That she would have brought DS Vine in tow.

But she was alone. A small woman with tousled hair, in that green Barbour she invariably wore.

They were all on their feet now. Inspector Davis, Nick observed, was tense too. He was aware that she was going beyond the boundaries of normal police procedure. Her job was to uncover crime, to bring the perpetrators to justice. The Fewings were asking her to cover it up. Even to hide the fact that she was meeting the girls again. It must go against all her instincts.

He turned to Millie and saw from her face how scared she was. She and Anna had only met the inspector once. And it had been a difficult encounter. How far could they trust her? How great would their responsibility be if she let them down, and made public what they were going to tell her?

He feared the obstinate set in his daughter's face, and even more in Anna's stubborn chin, that might tell him they had decided not to talk, after all.

No, he corrected himself. It was too late for them to hold back now. If the girls didn't tell the inspector the truth, *he* would.

A new suspicion rose up to haunt him. If what the girls had told them *was* the truth? If it wasn't just a story they'd cooked up to explain their absence.

But Anna had told Leon she wouldn't tell the lie the SBS man had fed them. That was why they'd refused to talk at first.

Was this dreadful business making him distrust his daughter and niece even about that?

'Right, where shall we start?' Inspector Davis looked around her. She smiled at the girls, in an attempt to reassure them. 'Suppose you and I make ourselves comfortable on those chairs in the corner by the Easter garden. Does one of you want to be present, to see fair play?' She appealed to the parents.

'I will,' Leon got in quickly, before Nick and Suzie could speak.

Nick felt a grateful relief. If the girls became difficult, it would not be up to him to make them see sense.

Then Tom said unexpectedly, 'I'll watch the door. Warn you if anyone's coming. Just so we can all pretend to look like innocent sightseers.' He went out to the porch.

Nick gave Suzie a half-hearted smile. 'That seems to let us off the hook. What do you want to do while they talk?'

She studied their surroundings. 'Well, it *is* a church. And you do have connections with the parish. We could do what Tom says. Behave like innocent students of family history, couldn't we? Do what we always do on these trips. Look for evidence.'

'I can't even remember who lived here.'

'Mollie Cook. Your great-great-grandmother. Mother of the lifeboatman Sollie Margerson.'

He passed a rueful hand over his forehead. 'I don't know how you remember it all. Especially now. It's not as if they were your relatives.'

She smiled at him and tucked her arm through his. '*Whither thou goest, I will go. Thy people shall be my people, and thy God my God.*' She caught his alarmed expression. 'Ruth, to her mother-in-law Naomi. It's in the Old Testament.'

Nick tried not to listen to Millie's voice, reluctant but clear, saying, 'And then we heard someone coming down the tunnel.'

He followed Suzie as she began to inspect the floor for inscribed grave slabs.

'Nothing,' said Suzie, ten minutes later. 'I didn't really expect there would be. If Mollie Cook married a fisherman, she's hardly likely to be one of the gentry, with a marble plaque on the wall or a tombstone inside the church. But you never know. I've had agricultural labourers who turned out to be descended from lords of the manor way back.'

'Mmm.' Nick could not take this search seriously. He knew that Suzie was so overjoyed to have Millie back that she was almost in holiday mood again. But fear still pressed heavily on him. That second man. The one who had wanted to dispose of the girls. Who was he? Was he local, in a village where people gossiped, and he would hear? What would he do when he got the news that the girls were still alive? He felt his throat clench in fear.

'We could look outside,' Suzie said. 'We're more likely to find Cooks there.'

He went with her, because it was easier to be led than to have to think for himself. A low murmur of voices still came from the corner of the church with the Easter garden. He did not want to listen to that story again.

Suzie paused before the door. There was the usual table, with leaflets about the church and its services, the parish magazine, information about the charities and missions the congregation supported.

'You ought to sign the visitors' book,' she said.

It lay open on the table. Entries in a variety of handwriting showed dates, names, addresses and comments. He began to fill in the next empty line methodically. '*11 April. Nick Fewings and family.*' Their home address. He paused over the comments column. Nothing came to mind.

'You could say what we've come for,' Suzie suggested. 'At least, what's supposed to be our reason. Looking for your Cook ancestors.'

He glanced further up the column. Several others had done the same. Half the population, it seemed, were into family history these days. One entry caught his eye. '*Love this quaint little church. Found some of my Cooks in the churchyard. Thank you.*'

He pointed it out to Suzie.

'Who is it?' she asked. 'They must be your relations.'

'Louise Cook Reindorf,' he read out. 'Lives in Chicago. Gosh. Do people come all the way across the Atlantic to poke around in English churchyards?'

'They certainly do. Here, I'll make a note of her contact details. You ought to write to her. She'll be thrilled to hear from you. And she might have found a lot of other stuff you don't know about.'

He made an effort to sound interested. He knew she was trying to divert him from his black thoughts.

'We've been tracing the family tree back. I hadn't thought about bringing the lines forward to people living today.'

'Neither did I with my family,' she replied. 'But they keep popping out of the woodwork. I've had all sorts of second cousins and such I never knew about contacting me because of something I posted on the Internet. It's a worldwide community. Your Louise may not know about Mollie's son, Solomon. She'll be bowled over when you tell her about his funeral and all the photos in the St Furseys museum.'

'Won't she have seen them already, if she's been here?'

'Maybe. But possibly not. If she was descended from one of Mollie's brothers, she might have missed out on the Margersons.'

She opened the porch door. They both checked in surprise to find Tom in the porch. Nick had forgotten that he had stationed himself there to warn them if anyone was coming.

Tom raised an enquiring eyebrow. 'Are they done?'

'Not yet. We thought we'd look around the churchyard.'

'It's pretty quiet out there. A family came out of one of the cottages, got into their car and drove off. Nothing suspicious. It doesn't look as if we were followed.'

'That sounds a bit cloak and dagger,' Suzie said.

'It's supposed to be, isn't it?'

Nick hesitated at the porch door. 'Do you think it's a good idea to hang around outside? What if someone *does* see us?'

'Looking at gravestones?' Suzie smiled. 'It's just what we want them to think we're doing . . . Whoever *they* are.' Her voice took on a more troubled tone. 'I keep trying to make myself forget that they're still out there. Convince myself it's all over. But it's not, is it?'

'No,' Nick said. 'I just hope the inspector can sort it.'

'Can she? If it's an SBS operation and they don't want the police in on it?'

'Somebody has to. And soon.'

This time he led the way, walking faster than necessary, to burn off the helpless anger within him.

The mist was dampening the gravestones, not quite rain. Slowly he steadied his breathing. He looked down the deserted village street. The occasional parked cars. Inspector Davis, he noticed, had left hers a little way from the church. She and the Fewings were not obviously together.

'Here's one,' Suzie called. 'And another one next to it.'

He joined her. These were early-twentieth-century Cooks. He racked his brains. 'Great-uncles and aunts? Second cousins three times removed?'

Suzie noted down the details. 'I'll sort them out later.'

He stood looking down at names which had become newly familiar. 'I didn't tell you, did I? After lunch, when I went off for a walk, I ended up in St Furseys church, to get out of the way of awkward questions. And they had this plan of the graves in the churchyard. I found Sollie's. But he wasn't alone. There were two children. One of them was a fourteen-year-old girl. He would have been still alive when she died.'

In the silence, Suzie slid her warm hand into his cold one. 'I know. It doesn't bear thinking about, does it? Measles, TB, scarlet fever. You really didn't know if your children would grow up. We take so much for granted.'

'Not any more,' he said.

She held his hand tightly.

'They've finished.' Tom's voice called to them from the porch.

Nick and Suzie hurried back to the church. They met Inspector Davis inside, striding between the box pews towards the door. The girls were following her at a little distance, whispering together, with Leon behind them.

'Bloody SBS! They seem to think we're a lot of straw-chewing yokels. And, of course, they're the intrepid Royal Marines, loyal to Queen and country. Doesn't it occur to them that there could be a mole in the SBS, just as easily as in the police?'

'I suppose because you *are* local,' Nick said, trying to be fair, 'there's more likelihood that someone here could be involved. Or related to someone who is.' The intricate web of his own relationships, reaching out into places he hadn't expected, came sharply clear in his mind.

She rounded on him. 'Don't *you* start. They're your daughters. This isn't *brandy for the parson, baccy for the clerk* stuff. I've got a major drugs racket on my patch. A double kidnapping. Conspiracy to murder. I could throw the book at them. And this guy, who doesn't even have a name, wants me to keep stumm?'

'What are you going to do?' Nick asked in sudden alarm. 'We don't want to put the girls in any more danger than they already are.' He hoped he had kept his voice low enough for Millie and Anna not to hear.

Inspector Davis was trying to control her anger.

'I'm going to be making some colourful phone calls. Someone's ears are going to burn for this.'

'Will you go ahead and arrest the gang?' Suzie asked. 'The ones this man knows about? To protect the girls?'

The smaller woman glared at them. 'Too right, I will. If it's up to me. I'm not playing games with kids' lives.'

TWENTY-THREE

The Fewings left the church first. Outwardly, a family shaken, but trying to get back to normal and enjoy the rest of their holiday. It was agreed that Inspector Davis would wait, while the shadows deepened, and leave later.

Outside, the mist deadened everything. There were few lights on in Parwold's only street. Even those lit windows were smudged by moisture. No footfalls sounded. No voices called. Only the mournful cry of a curlew circled in the cloud overhead.

'It's like a ghost village,' said Suzie. 'Let's go.'

This time, the girls piled into the back of Nick's car. Tom shrugged his shoulders and got into Leon's.

When Nick turned the ignition key, he had a nightmare moment when he thought the engine was not going to fire. They would be trapped here, in this unreal world, while the fog closed in inexorably around them.

The starter roared. He gunned the accelerator too hard, just to be sure of the power under his foot. The spell was broken. They could go.

Nick led the way. The route back to St Furseys was short and simple. He could not get lost.

He would not have been surprised to find that the thick mist was only around Parwold, like a magic fence screening them from hostile eyes. But the murk persisted when they left the straggle of cottages behind. He drove on with dipped headlights. It was just enough to show the narrow road and the deep drainage ditch running along the left-hand side. He knew there was one on the other side of the road as well. He would have to watch his steering. Beyond, unseen in the gloom, stretched the ranks of head-high reeds, through which Millie and Anna had had to stumble.

As soon as they were clear of the village, the girls' indignation broke out.

'You said it would be all right if we told her,' Millie protested. 'It wouldn't go any further. It would just get her off our backs. And now she wants to blow the whole thing and go charging in and arrest them. We *promised*.'

'You said yourselves,' Suzie pointed out, 'a promise made under duress doesn't count.'

'But we would have sworn to keep it secret, anyway, once we heard who he was and what he was doing, and why it's a matter of life and death. *His* life.'

'If it's genuine, the inspector will find that out. Her bosses will order her not to take it any further.'

'*If* it's genuine? Do you think we're making this up?' Millie's shout expressed her outrage.

'I didn't say that. The question is, was *he* telling you the truth?'

'Don't be silly, Mum. He let us go. If he was one of them, he'd just have gone ahead and drowned us.'

'Shut up, Millie,' said Anna quietly.

'Sorry.' Suzie turned round to her niece. 'Let's talk of something else. Have you got any idea what you'd like to do tomorrow?'

'What *is* there to do,' said Millie, 'out here in the sticks?'

'Fancy a boat ride along the coast? Or a fishing trip?' Nick suggested.

'Slimy mackerel? No, thank you,' Millie retorted.

'I don't think I'm into killing things,' Anna said.

'Well, then.' Suzie was racking her brains. 'I think there's a Museum of Rural Life a few miles away. You know, reed-cutting and that sort of thing. Demonstrations of thatching. Basketwork. A cottage to show how people lived.'

'Reeds! I can't wait,' said her daughter.

Nick's hands tightened on the wheel. 'Look out. There's something up ahead.'

Through the fog he was beginning to make out the flashing lights of emergency vehicles. He slowed the car still further and crept forward. Leon's dipped headlights followed him.

An accident. It had to be. But he felt his muscles tensing. The sense of menace was closing in. Here in this car were precious parts of his life. His wife, his daughter, Leon's only child. He felt a cold horror that the scene emerging in his headlights was not all that it seemed to be. That figure in the yellow fluorescent jacket waving at him to stop.

He had a sudden urge to stamp on the accelerator and shoot

through the crowded scene ahead to safety, no matter what carnage he left behind.

The habits of a lifetime held him back. He braked and wound down the window.

'Trouble?' he asked, his voice surprisingly level, though his mouth was dry.

'There's been an accident, sir. There's a vehicle overturned in the ditch. If you wouldn't mind waiting while the ambulance gets clear.'

'Someone's hurt?'

'I can't tell you any more details, sir. If you'd just be patient.'

'Of course.'

The girls behind him were silenced. In the glow of the lights ahead Nick could just make out two figures who appeared to be carrying a stretcher. The ambulance doors closed. The vehicle disappeared towards the main road.

The way ahead was clearer now, though two police cars were still parked near the overturned vehicle. Nick could see little of that. Wheels showed forlornly above the right-hand ditch. Most of the bodywork was hidden.

The policeman was back at the window.

'It's a pretty tight fit, but I think you can get past if you're careful. Just watch you don't end up in the other ditch. Otherwise, I'm afraid it's a ten-mile detour the other way.'

'I think I can do it. We're only going to St Furseys.'

'Right you are, sir. Thank you.'

They crept past the police cars. In the mirror, Nick saw Anna twist sideways to stare through her window.

'It looks like a Land Rover, or something.'

'Poor beggar. Those ditches are pretty deep. And they're full of water.'

'Don't,' Suzie said.

'But how did it come to end up like that anyway? This road's narrow, but it's dead straight. And it's a bit early in the evening for the driver to be that drunk.'

'Who knows? Nodded off? Tried to pass another vehicle and misjudged it?'

'There wasn't another vehicle. Except for the police and the ambulance.'

'They might have taken a statement from the other driver and let him go. Or her.'

'Will you two just shut up?' came Millie's plaintive cry.
'Can't we talk about something cheerful?'

'What with one thing and another, I haven't done any food
shopping today,' Leon said when they got home. 'And the
freezer's running a bit low.'

'Let's go out for a pub meal,' Nick offered. 'Our treat.'

Even the short walk through the fog-draped streets of St
Furseys made it good to arrive at the lights of the White Swan.

The bar was crowded, but the adjacent room was set out
with tables laid for supper. A couple had occupied the corner
table. The rest were free. For a few moments, the Fewings
seemed to fill the space as they shed outer clothing and hung
their jackets on the backs of their chairs.

'I'll get the drinks in,' Leon said. 'What are you having?'

He threaded his way through the press of bodies to the bar.
Nick watched him through the gaps in the wooden screen that
separated the bar from the dining room. He thought it was
his own mood that was casting a gloom over the evening.
Then, slowly, it was borne in on him. The customers thronging
the bar, locals by the look of them, were not exchanging jokes
and cheery gossip in the way typical of a village pub. They
were talking, certainly. But the mood seemed tense, earnest.
Sometimes a newcomer would come in jauntily, ready for an
evening's relaxation. The sombre faces turned to him, words
were exchanged. The expression on the new arrival's face
changed.

Presently the crowd parted to let Leon through, carrying a
tray of drinks. Something of the concern Nick had been seeing
showed in his brother's face.

'Bad news from that accident, I'm afraid. It was a St Furseys
man in that Land Rover. He was taken to hospital seriously
injured. Nobody's quite sure whether he's alive or dead.'

'Did you know him?' Nick asked.

'Only by sight. Kevin Cook. Runs boat trips for tourists in
the summer. I've seen him getting his boat ready for the season
when I've been down painting on the waterfront.'

'Cook?' Suzie asked. 'Did you say his name was Cook?'

'Yes. Why?'

Suzie explained about the churchyard at Parwold. 'You may
not have known him, but he's almost certainly a relation.'

Nick tried to take this information in. His family was growing, in ways he hadn't expected. He had concentrated too much on the past. It hadn't occurred to him that they would still be here today: Margersons, Cooks, Hornimans, Duffields, all sharing his genes.

Did it matter? Just because they were genetically linked, did that make them as important to him as his friends who were unrelated?

A man was dead, or possibly dying. He didn't have to be a cousin for Nick to feel compassion.

'Does he have a family?' Suzie was asking.

'Apparently he was engaged.'

'Poor girl.'

'He was a popular character, by all accounts. A regular here. People seem pretty cut up about it. The landlord got a bit short with me when I started asking questions. You'd have thought it was my fault.'

'Private grief,' Nick said. 'They won't want strangers intruding.'

Strangers. Would it make any difference if those men – and it was mostly men – next door knew that he and Leon were closer to Kevin Cook than they imagined?

He picked up the menu. 'Have you all decided what you're eating?'

'You don't think,' Millie said, turning over the corner of her menu card, 'he could have been the man in the cave? The young one working for the *you-know-what*?'

The rest of the family stilled, looking at her. Then Suzie turned to cast an anxious glance at the couple in the corner. She lowered her voice to a whisper.

'Why ever do you think that?'

Millie raised her grey-blue eyes, unnaturally large and bright. 'Because he took a huge risk to let us go free. And now he's dead, or as good as.'

Slowly, her logic worked its way into Nick's brain.

'It makes sense. I couldn't see why the driver would go off a perfectly straight road. The mist wasn't *that* thick.'

'You think someone made him crash?' Leon asked.

'The Ice-Man,' Millie said. 'The big one with the creepy voice.'

Anna swallowed a mouthful of mineral water. 'You said

those men in the bar looked at you as if it was your fault, Dad. Maybe it was. Mine and Millie's.'

'They wouldn't know about that, would they?' Tom objected. 'I thought those goings on in the cave were all top secret.'

Suzie pushed the salt cellar in circles over the table. *'Watch the wall, my darling, while the Gentlemen go by.* We always said drug running wasn't like brandy and tobacco and silk in the old days. But what if people in St Furseys didn't know what they're smuggling today? Just that Kevin Cook was up to something after dark. Maybe they thought it was just duty-free booze and ciggies, or something. It must be hard to get work here in the winter. And he was apparently saving up to get married. They might have turned a blind eye.'

'So how would they connect his accident to Millie and Anna,' Leon asked, 'if they didn't know what went on last night?'

Anna shrugged. 'All right. You win. I don't have an answer to that one.'

All the same, Nick could see men eyeing them through the bars of the screen. His sense of menace persisted.

'Are we planning to put in a food order before closing time?' Tom wanted to know.

It was Nick's turn to make his way to the bar.

The crowd parted to let him through. He felt people were drawing away from him. It didn't make sense. Many of these were men and, now he saw, an occasional woman, who had turned out last night and in the early morning to search for Millie and Anna. Had there been some point at which they discovered the girls were not just innocent holidaymakers caught out by the tide, or lost in an unfamiliar landscape? Had they ventured too far into the village's secret? Or did these people just resent the fact that the girls hadn't made public where they spent last night?

He put on a determined smile and relayed their food order to a young woman at a side counter.

'Thanks. Where are you sitting?'

She seemed as pleasant as any bar assistant. He felt no wave of hostility from her.

There would be undercurrents in the village. Some would know what others did not. The men who sailed with Kevin Cook. Who understood, better than most, the movements of shipping off this coast. It was odd to think that these would probably be the same mariners who manned the St Furseys inshore lifeboat.

Hell. Was he starting to doubt even Sollie Margerson now?

Someone caught his eye, sitting at a table in the corner of the bar. A flash of ginger hair. He struggled for her name. Constable Diggory. She had been the first policewoman to answer his appeal to find the girls. She had been with the party who raided Ed Harries' home.

So, she was a local girl, out of uniform and enjoying an evening off in the pub. Or had been, until she heard the news.

Anna's words came back to him. '*He particularly said not to tell the police. They can't trust them. All sorts of local people are mixed up in this racket.*'

Diggory had seen him watching her and stood up. It was only politeness to move towards her. She looked up at him. Blue eyes in a freckled face showed concern.

'I'm glad you got your girls back. Must have been a bad night for you. Where had they been all night?'

He went through the routine he had practised before. 'They got lost in the marshes. Then they were afraid of falling into one of those drains in the bad light. So they did what they thought was the sensible thing and stayed where they were.'

'And they didn't phone you?'

'Millie dropped hers on the beach. Someone found it this morning. And Anna's battery ran out.'

'Kids! I hope you gave them a good talking to.'

'And so did your inspector.'

'So. Case closed?' she said.

'Of course. All's well that ends well. They're back safe and sound.'

She stared at him hard. He was not sure how convincing he sounded.

As he walked back to the dining room, he had a feeling he was picking his way across a spider's web he could not see. He had uncovered just the edge of a network of relationships, interweaving families in St Furseys and the neighbouring villages. How thick were those blood ties?

Were they stronger than ties of law and order?

Did it make sense that the local boatman Kevin Cook could really be an undercover SBS agent?

The family were talking in low voices as Nick approached. He sensed the sudden stillness when they heard him coming. Leon had his back to Nick. He stopped in mid-sentence. Then he turned, and his face relaxed as he saw his brother.

Nick slid into his seat beside Suzie. 'You may not realize it, but you look like a bunch of conspirators. It comes to something when we're acting as though we're the guilty party, instead of the victims.'

'It's not about us,' Millie said. 'It's him. The man in the cave. Kevin whatever-his-name-is.'

'Cook,' said Suzie.

'Right. Kevin Cook. He saved our lives. We've got to protect him. If it's not too late.'

'If Kevin Cook *was* our SBS man,' Anna added.

Millie jerked round towards her. 'What do you mean? He's got to be, hasn't he? You think it's just a coincidence he ended up upside down in a ditch the day after?'

'I just thought we shouldn't jump to conclusions.'

'Do you think Inspector Davis knows about this?' Nick said slowly. 'I mean, would she make the connection? No reason a detective inspector would get to hear about every traffic accident.'

'Should we phone her?' Leon asked.

'Wouldn't do any harm. She might want to question him. If she hasn't been told by her bosses to back off.'

'If he's still alive,' Suzie said quietly.

'Don't!' exclaimed Millie.

'Sorry, love. He's probably OK. Nobody in the bar seems to have heard about him dying, have they? They're just waiting for news, the same as we are.'

Nick was getting his phone out. He should have thought of this much sooner. The marked police cars at the scene, the uniformed officers, had lulled him into believing that anyone at police HQ would know about it. Now he saw his mistake.

At the last moment, he hesitated. Was he being overdramatic? Had the girls really heard a man order them to be killed? Could he even trust that the story they'd told their parents was the true one? He could never fathom the workings of Millie's mind. At times she was brilliantly logical. At others, she could be as devious as a labyrinth.

But Anna was made of simpler stuff. She hadn't been able to carry out the lie the man had told her to.

Was even *that* true?

And was it the man lying in Murchington Hospital who had spun this web of deceit for them? Had he got to the centre of it yet?

But true or false, the inspector needed to hear it. He dialled her mobile.

He was just putting his phone to his ear when the pub door opened. A party of young people erupted into the already crowded space. They looked around at the occupied tables of the bar, and then at the largely empty dining room. They headed through the gap in the wooden screen to join the Fewings.

Nick shut off his phone. The group of newcomers subsided noisily into seats, occupying another three tables. Only now Nick saw there were two older people with them. A woman and a man. He saw Tom stiffen, heard his indrawn breath, just as the same realization hit him too. A delicate-featured woman of Indian extraction, and a man with a curling red beard.

'It's them,' Tom muttered. 'Those archaeologists.'

Nick felt the same guilt and embarrassment. The people who had caught Tom rummaging in the cabin of their survey ship. He hoped the recognition wouldn't be mutual. But as a family group, the Fewings were hard to miss. Suzie, Nick, Leon and, worst of all, Tom. They had all been aboard. They had been ordered off ignominiously.

But Millie and Anna hadn't. They were staring at the table opposite, then at each other.

'It's the man with the ginger beard!' Millie hissed. 'The one we were supposed to say had taken us in his Land Rover.'

'That doesn't mean anything,' Suzie said. 'It was just a story. Your man in the tunnel must have seen this group around the harbour. I bet the whole village has been talking about them, and what they're doing with their ship. Of course he'd want to shift the suspicion to strangers, to take the heat away from local people.'

Millie glowered. 'That man with the beard should be grateful to us. If it hadn't been for Anna, I'd have done what the SBS man asked us to, and shopped him. Why not, if it was going to help bust this drugs ring? He must have had a good reason for asking us to do it.'

Poor, romantic Millie. Whoever the man was who had caught her in the tunnel, he had won her loyalty. Wasn't that the sort of thing that happened? Hostages bonding with their kidnappers?

Nick's phone rang.

'Inspector Davis. You were trying to ring me. Anything new?'

He glanced at the occupied tables. Too close.

'Just a minute,' he murmured. 'I can't talk here.'

With a brief apology to the others, he made his way outside. The street lamps were misty yellow globes, the only things visible in the fogbound street.

'Sorry. I was in a crowded pub. Yes, as it happens, there is something you ought to know . . .'

He told her about the accident on the by-road. About Kevin Cook. About Millie's fear that this was retribution for the man who had freed them. And of the fear that was stalking him worse than ever for his daughter and niece.

At the other end, she gave little away. He couldn't tell how seriously she was taking this theory.

'And I've got news for you,' she said when he had finished. 'You're not going to like this . . .'

He listened to her, stunned.

The waitress was serving food when he got back. Suzie raised her eyebrows to him, but he shook his head.

'Later,' he said in a low voice. 'There's something you all need to know.'

'Is it about the man in hospital?' Millie said. 'Is he dead?'

'Hush,' Suzie said, glancing behind her. 'Let's talk about something else.'

The professor's voice came from the next table, close to Nick's shoulder, unnecessarily loud. 'I do hope the landlord will count his cutlery after these people have gone. Not to mention those rather valuable copper warming pans on the wall.'

There were snorts of laughter from the students.

Not even Tom did justice to the food.

Out in the quiet street, Nick drew them away from the pub door. He tried to keep his voice down, though rage was burning him.

'The answer is no, she hadn't heard about the accident. And yes, she's going to go straight to the hospital. But that's not all. She's been on to her Chief Constable, and to the Revenue and Customs. She even got through to the Special Boat Service themselves. And nobody's telling her to shut up, to back off from fouling up their secret operation. Because there isn't one. Whoever it was who caught you in the tunnel, Millie and Anna, he's not in the SBS.'

TWENTY-FOUR

'**B**ut . . .!'

In the indistinct light Nick couldn't see Millie's face clearly. But he could imagine her expression struggling between denial and outrage.

'Don't you see?' she said, resorting to defiance. 'That's what they *want* her to think. They aren't going to let her in on their top-secret operation, are they?'

'Millie,' Nick tried gently, 'that's not how it works. If there really was an undercover operation, they'd warn her off. They wouldn't have to tell her any details. Just order her to drop the case. As it is, she's more fired up than ever. She thinks they're straight-out criminals, and she's going all out to catch them.'

'She still may not be allowed to,' Leon said. 'I'd guess this is one for the Serious Organized Crime Agency. They'll take her off the case.'

Nick felt an unexpected sympathy for the determined little inspector. She had taken professional risks for him and his family. Raiding Ed Harries' house. Letting the girls tell their story off-record.

Had she managed to make her enquiries about the SBS involvement without giving the source of her information away? She'd evidently talked only to people more senior than herself. Did that mean the girls' identity was safe?

More and more, the chilling fear was mounting. Everyone had become a suspect, a possible source of danger. Even in Police HQ.

Suddenly it seemed too exposed to be standing out here in the dark street, not knowing who might be only a few paces away.

A burst of light illuminated the fog as the pub door opened. Two figures came out, blurred shadows. They started along the pavement towards the Fewings.

'Come on,' Nick said urgently. 'We shouldn't be talking out here. Let's get indoors.'

He wanted to throw his arms round the girls, like a hen gathering her chicks under her wing. Would his physical presence really be enough to keep them safe? And he couldn't be with them always.

Perhaps they should leave St Furseys. Tomorrow morning. Two hundred and fifty miles away in the West Country they should be out of reach of whoever had wanted to silence Millie and Anna . . . Shouldn't they?

When they turned into Beach Street, the surrounding silence deepened. Not even the curlews were calling now. Their footsteps came back to them muffled. The fog pressed like a damp cloth smothering Nick's face.

They were almost at the cottage at the bottom of the street when his straining eyes began telling him that there was a darker bulk looming out of the mist ahead. His heart raced. He grabbed Millie and Anna by the shoulders and brought them to a halt.

'Dad! What are you . . .?' Millie started to protest.

'Shh.'

Suzie, Leon and Tom had stopped behind them.

'There's a car parked outside your house,' he told Leon in a low voice.

'I think you're right.'

There was hardly light enough to examine each other's expression.

'I'll go,' offered Tom. 'See what's up.'

Suzie gave a little cry of protest, but before anyone could stop him, Tom was striding the last few metres to Rogues Roost. He even whistled a little, to convey a nonchalant innocence.

A few moments later he was back.

'There's someone in it.' His voice was guarded. 'Must be waiting for you, Leon.'

'Or us,' said Nick.

There was a hesitation. Then Leon said, 'Well, we can't stay out on the pavement all night. I can't think who'd be visiting me this time of the evening. I don't know that many people here well. Unless it's old Malcolm, with his ears flapping for some juicy gossip.'

'Didn't look like the flash kind of car I'd expect him to drive,' Tom said.

Leon went forward with Tom. Nick held the girls back. He
heard the car door open, dimly saw a figure get out.
Leon's cry of alarm rang suddenly loud. 'Jacqui!'
'Oh, help!' gasped Anna. 'It's my mother.'

From ages ago – was it only this morning? – Nick remembered Leon making that difficult phone call to his estranged
wife. Telling her that Anna was back, but not yet saying where
she'd been. Anna herself, returning sullenly from talking to
her mother. Jacqui had threatened to drive to St Furseys and
take Anna home. They'd none of them remembered that, as
the more terrifying truth unfolded.
He wasn't aware of taking the last few steps to join his
brother by the garden gate. But they were all listening to the
full blast of Jacqui's anger.
'What do you think you're playing at? It's taken me five
hours to drive here through the fog. And I find the house
in darkness. You've been at the *pub*? Didn't it occur to you
for one minute to tell me where you were? Where Anna
was?'
'I'm sorry,' Leon stumbled over the words. 'It's been such
a day, it went out of my head. I didn't know you were coming.'
'Did you honestly think I'd leave Anna with you, after what
happened?'
'It wasn't his fault,' Anna broke in. 'Millie and I just set
out for a walk and got lost. Millie dropped her phone. And
my battery was dead. And we were out there in the middle
of all these reed beds when it started to get dark, and we
didn't know which way to go. So we just waited till daybreak
and then came home.'
Nick gazed down at his niece in astonishment. The light
from the open car door showed that obstinate tilt of her chin,
the toss of her dark curls. Whatever Anna had reluctantly told
Leon, it wasn't the story she was giving her mother.
What would Jacqui do if she heard about the tunnel packed
with drugs, the ropes and blindfold, the threats?
No prizes for guessing the answer to that.
He gave her shoulder an avuncular squeeze. Anna clearly
wanted to stay here with Millie.
His hand dropped away. Should Leon let her? Should he
and Suzie let Millie stay? Shouldn't they be getting away

from St Furseys as fast as they could? Away from a man with an ice-cold voice, who wanted them silenced. Who might have driven Kevin Cook to crash upside down in a water-filled drain?

'Well, are you going to keep me waiting all night on the pavement? Or do I get something to eat?'

In the warmer light of Leon's living room, Nick was caught by surprise. Jacqui's usually meticulous make-up had been sketchily applied. Her stylishly cut hair was awry. Unlike Suzie, whose femininity was softly natural, Nick's former sister-in-law had always donned clothes, cosmetics and coiffure as a sort of armour, so that the rest of the world saw only what she chose it to. He had never really warmed to Jacqui, but now he felt a rush of fellow feeling. The mask had slipped. For the moment, she was letting them see the distraught parent behind the facade.

'Sit down,' said Leon, hurrying to light the driftwood fire.

The cottage room had felt crowded enough with six of them. Now they seemed to fill every available space. An awkwardness hung in the atmosphere. Nick sensed Leon's feeling of guilt. So much had happened that neither of them had taken seriously the possibility that Jacqui might make good her threat, and come to take Anna home. They should have done. Leon and Jacqui had always lived with the expectation that whatever Jacqui said would happen.

The brothers hadn't discussed, with the girls or with each other, how much they would tell her. Now Anna had pre-empted that decision. Only the six of them, and Inspector Davis, knew what had really happened last night, and about that man – Kevin Cook? – who had made the astonishing choice to let them go. Anna had clearly decided she would not break her oath of secrecy to anyone else. His doggedly truthful niece was lying now.

One of the logs settled in a shower of sparks, as the kindling burned through. Something shifted in Nick's mind. A flash of altered awareness.

Anna and Millie had made that promise to someone they believed to be an SBS agent. If the inspector's sources had told her the truth, the man's story was a lie. There was no covert SBS operation. The man was simply what he had first appeared to the girls to be: one of a despicable gang importing cocaine. Ruining lives across the country.

So why? Why would he take such a huge personal risk to free the girls, if the fate of so many teenage girls like them mattered so little to him?

Nick rubbed his tired eyes. It didn't make sense.

Leon was reciting for Jacqui the contents of his depleted freezer.

'You know I've never liked pasta.'

'I could pop out for some fish and chips,' Tom offered.

Jacqui shuddered. 'Very well, then. If that's the best you can do, I'll put up with a meal-for-one lasagne. Is that really what you live off these days, Leon?'

'I get good fresh fish on the quay.'

'Thank goodness you don't expect me to gut it.'

Her hair might have lost its manicured look, but the edge of criticism in her voice was as sharp as ever.

'Please, Mum,' Anna was saying. 'I don't know why you had to come all this way. Particularly in the fog. I'm perfectly all right. I know what happened last night sounds a bit silly. But we were actually trying to be *sensible*. We didn't want to end up drowned in one those drains in the marsh.'

Cold crept up on Nick, despite the leaping flames. That man who had dumped them in the marsh, blindfolded and bound. Is that what he had wanted to happen? Was he not really setting them free at all?

But, then, why take such a risk? Why not carry out the orders of that more terrifying figure, and drop them out at sea?

Jacqui, predictably, was not inclined to be mollified. Would he, if he were honest, have let Millie stay here, if the situation had been reversed?

'But you *said* I could come for a week,' Anna protested. 'Millie and I have never spent this long together. And Uncle Nick and Auntie Suzie are doing all this really interesting detective work on family history. They let me help. I'm finding out all sorts of things about how you use Record Offices and libraries. It's really useful stuff.'

Jacqui had insisted that Anna go to a private girls' school, though Leon would have preferred the perfectly good local comprehensive. She placed a high value on education, of the

particular sort she herself had received. It was clever of Anna
to try and make their fun holiday activity sound like an educa-
tional project.

'The Fewings? I thought they were northern mill workers.'
The scorn was evident.

'It's the Margersons, actually,' Leon said levelly. 'Our
mother's family.'

'And they were from round here? Then I suppose they'll
have been mixed up in smuggling or wrecking, and that sort
of disreputable activity.'

There was a surprised silence. She had come so close.

'It's not quite like that,' said Leon, through tight lips. 'Great-
grandfather Margerson was a lifeboatman and a local hero.'

'They have photos of him in the museum,' Anna put in.

'Hmm. I notice you've never asked me about *my* family. I
suppose successful, respectable, chapel-going bankers aren't
colourful enough for you.'

The microwave pinged. Nick sensed Jacqui's shiver of
distaste. But when Leon set the meal in front of her, she set
to readily, despite her avowed dislike of pasta. Leon poured
her a glass of wine and made coffee for the others.

The conversation lapsed. There was so much they needed
to talk about. But it was impossible in front of Jacqui. Leon
could have overruled Anna, and told her mother the whole
story. But he knew, as his daughter did, how dangerous that
might be. Jacqui could certainly not be relied upon to keep
quiet about the information.

Did that matter now?

Nick felt a sudden overwhelming certainty that it did. Until
the smuggling chain was caught and broken, the girls'
continued safety might depend on their silence.

Then doubt crept in.

Or was that silence itself their greatest danger? If whoever
was in charge believed they *hadn't* talked, he could still take
steps to make sure they never did.

He fought his growing panic. It was too late now to think
that fleeing St Furseys would work. This end of the operation must be run by someone living near here. He, or she,
would know by now all about the Fewings. There would
certainly be enough money at stake to ensure that someone
in his employ tracked the girls down to their homes.

Should he ask Inspector Davis for police protection?

He hadn't noticed Leon leave the room. But now his brother came back carrying a sleeping bag and a pillow.

'You're sleeping in my studio,' he told his ex-wife. 'Up in the loft. I'll use the sofa.'

And still nothing had been resolved about what would happen in the morning.

The girls had gone to their own room. Anna was still sulky at the thought of having to leave Millie next day. Tom sat in his favourite window seat. He had his earphones on, lost in his personal world.

Nick found it hard to contribute to the stilted conversation of the four adults. The only thing he really wanted to talk about couldn't be mentioned. He felt the burden of responsibility heavy on him. Somehow, he had to keep Millie safe until the police had cleaned up the smuggling racket. There was nothing else he could do. He didn't know the people in St Furseys. He couldn't identify that chilling presence who had ordered Millie and Anna's deaths. He had no clue where they had been imprisoned. A windowless room, piled with empty cardboard boxes. A rancid smell . . .

His head shot up. Leon must have caught the sudden movement. His eyes met Nick's, questioning.

Nick tried to keep his voice offhand. 'If no one minds, I think I'll take a turn outside before I go to bed. Shake off the cobwebs.' He looked hard at Leon.

'I'll come with you,' his brother said, putting on a smile. 'Make sure you don't get lost in the fog.'

'I think it's lifting.' Tom had taken off one earphone. 'I can see more lights from the village. Is it OK if I come too?'

Nick was caught wrong-footed. He had wanted to try out his theory privately on Leon. But he could hardly say no to Tom.

'Don't mind us,' Suzie smiled. 'We'll enjoy a chance for some girl talk.'

Can she mean that? Nick wondered. She really doesn't mind being left alone with Jacqui? To be fair, she had never been as critical of Leon's wife as Nick had. But Suzie was still looking at him with more than usual meaning. As if she positively wanted the men to stay away. He nodded, only half understanding.

Outside, they found that Tom was right. A light breeze was teasing the edges of the mist, tearing it into rags, fluttering it away. He could see the lights on the beach wall reflected in the flooding tide.

By unspoken agreement, they turned towards the sea. The path that led to the village centre and the creek also followed the sea shore north. Nick steered them in that direction. Occasional lamps threaded the darkness for a short distance, before petering out at the edge of the village.

There was only room for two to walk abreast. Tom strode ahead, hands in pockets.

'What's up?' Leon said in a low voice. 'You didn't bring me out here just to get my body mass index down.'

'No. I had an idea. I was racking my brains to think of some clue in what the girls told us that would put the finger on someone. Someone here in St Furseys. Someone you wouldn't suspect of being behind all this.'

'What, you mean a pillar of the community? Like Malcolm Partridge?'

'No. Someone even more unlikely. Ed Harries.'

Leon stopped short on the path. 'Oh, come on now, Nick. The man's a nut case. Probably a paranoid schizophrenic.'

'Yeah! What did Millie say? That's why he'd make the perfect cover.' Tom had turned to face them. 'Well done, Dad.'

'You weren't supposed to hear that,' Nick said.

'Too bad. All is revealed.'

'But why, Nick?' Leon protested. 'Why, out of all the perfectly sane people in the village, would you want to finger *him*?'

'Ever since the girls told us where they'd been locked up all night, it's been bugging me. That smell that was still on their clothes. Somewhere where hygiene was definitely not the top priority. A little room full of empty boxes. And suddenly I remembered. Last night, when the police raided the old Noah's Ark, because we thought the girls might be there, I went with the inspector and her DS sidekick round the house, while you and Tom did the barns. And there *was* a storeroom like that. I know, because I turned over the boxes, looking for clues.'

'But you didn't find any.'

'No. Because we searched it *before* the girls were

taken there. They were still in the tunnel at nightfall.'

'But Ed was behaving like a raving lunatic. You said he had to be handcuffed to a door.'

'As Tom says, the perfect cover. Who's going to suspect a paranoid nutter of masterminding a drugs ring? And we've already found reason to believe that, when Alfred Margerson ran the Noah's Ark, he also worked the land with the entrance to the tunnel. The house isn't a pub now, but couldn't Ed Harries still be the owner of both?'

The others digested this in silence.

'Are you going to ring the inspector?' Leon asked.

Nick consulted his watch. 'It's getting a bit late. I've got her mobile number. But the poor woman was at Brandon Head with the search party early this morning. She's been over twice to question the girls, here and at Parwold. She's been making the telephone lines red hot to get to the bottom of that SBS story. I think she deserves a night's rest. I'll ring her first thing in the morning. She might be readier to listen to me then.'

'I'd certainly sleep easier in my bed, once that lot are behind bars.'

'Me too.'

There was no need to say what they both feared for their daughters.

'Well, shall we join the ladies?'

They turned back towards the village.

Excitement coursed through Nick's veins. He had felt so help-less to protect Millie and Anna. Now at last he had made the breakthrough. He almost regretted not telling the inspector straight away. But it was going to be difficult to convince her. He needed her to be fresh, on the ball, ready to consider a new theory.

It was one thing for the police to raid Ed Harries' house because they thought he was a mad old man who might have imprisoned two girls he found trespassing. It was quite another to finger him as the secret spider at the centre of the web, whose menace Nick had felt thrumming in the White Swan. How those in the know must have laughed as the police pursued their enquiries, not dreaming this village idiot might be the mastermind they were looking for.

He pushed away the thought that this theory might look a lot less credible, even to him, in the cold light of morning. That was precisely the beauty of it. The sheer ludicrousness of it to the outward eye. Clever. Very clever.

Clever enough to present a real threat to Millie and Anna as long as the man was free. Perhaps even after that.

More soberly, he turned with the others into Beach Street.

Indoors, Suzie met them with a smile that had more than a hint of self-satisfaction about it.

'Had a good walk? How's the fog?'

'Nearly gone,' Leon said. 'A nice little breeze has got up. Should be fine by morning.'

'Thank goodness for that,' Jacqui said. 'I certainly don't want a repeat of today's journey. Trust you to go and live somewhere at the back of beyond.'

'Jacqui and I have been having a chat.' Suzie's smile persisted. 'She needs to leave early in the morning. Without the fog, she should get back in time for work.'

The men stared at her.

'Anna?' said Leon.

'I said we'd drop her off on our way home on Saturday. If that's all right?' she appealed to Nick.

'Er, yes. Fine. It's not much out of our way.'

'Good. That's settled.' She beamed at him.

'Under the circumstances, I think I'll go to bed,' Jacqui said, to no one in particular. 'It was a hell of a drive in the fog.'

'Yes, of course,' Leon said. 'I'm really sorry about all this. We were scared ourselves. Had half the village out searching for them. Police, coastguard. They don't think of the trouble they're causing, do they?'

'Yes, Leon. I think we get the point, that you're blaming it all on the girls.'

She swept off, up to the studio.

Leon let out a long breath. He turned to Suzie. 'How did you do it?'

'I told her how lovely it was to be able to get to know Anna better. What a good influence she was on Millie. How she'd been the more sensible of the two last night. I let her give me a lecture on the importance of paying for the right school. She's really proud of Anna, you know, Leon. She was frightened out of her wits when she heard the girls were missing. Anna's all she's got now.'

'Not counting her fancy bloke.'

'I'm not sure she *is* counting too much on him.' A frown replaced Suzie's smile. 'So what were you being so secretive about? All this stuff about blowing away the cobwebs. You don't usually go for a brisk walk before bedtime.'

'I could hardly discuss it in front of Jacqui, could I? But I think, I just think, I've cracked it. The St Furseys man who's at the centre of all this. The one with the cold, quiet voice, who wanted them dead . . .'

Suzie listened incredulously. 'Ed Harries? The "an Englishman's home is his castle" guy? "Get back over the drawbridge or I'll shoot you"?'

'You've not met him, have you? But that's a fair description of the persona he's built up for himself. Nobody would believe, (a) that he had the intelligence to plan a drug import ring, and (b) that he could organize a team of people to help him.'

'And terrify them into obeying him,' Leon added. 'If Kevin Cook's accident is part of this.'

'And could he, really? You talked about Ed Harries screaming his head off at you. Not quiet and icy, like Millie described.'

Nick shrugged. 'He must be a very good actor. I can't think of any other explanation. I'm positive that's where the girls were for most of last night.'

TWENTY-FIVE

Nick woke early to sounds from the bathroom next door. He stifled a groan. Jacqui must be preparing to drive back to the Midlands for a nine o'clock start at her office. He shook Suzie gently.

'Mmm?'

'Jacqui's in the shower. Do you think we should get up and see her off?'

There was a sleepy silence. Then Suzie struggled upright. She yawned widely.

'I suppose you're right. Goodness knows when we'll see her again, now that she and Leon have split up.'

'Saturday, I thought you said. We're dropping Anna off.'

Suzie yawned again. 'You're right. Still, you can't help feeling sorry for her. At least when Millie went missing I had you.'

Nick pulled on his dressing gown, but Suzie dressed in trousers and sweater. She even, Nick noticed with a fond smile, took a few moments to apply foundation and powder to her shiny morning face. That was the effect Jacqui had on other women.

'You look lovely just as you are.' He put an arm round her and kissed her nose.

Leon was up too, making breakfast for Jacqui and silently putting up with criticism about the inadequately browned toast.

'I suppose it's too much to expect that my daughter should bother to see me off. Even though I came all this way because of her.'

Leon went upstairs.

A few moments later, Anna appeared, tousled and sleepy-eyed. 'Hi, Mum. You off?'

'What does it look like?'

Jacqui's overnight bag was already by the door, her handbag on the table.

Anna hesitated, then went across and put her arms round her mother's shoulders. 'Thanks for coming. I'm really sorry for scaring you. Millie and I just never thought we could get lost so easily. We'll be more careful from now on.'

'Well, be sure you keep an eye on Millie in future. Remember, she hasn't had your advantages.'

Nick winced. Suzie frowned at him to hold his tongue. She turned to Jacqui.

'Don't worry about Anna. We'll take good care of her. And we'll see you on Saturday.'

'Yes, well. Enjoy the rest of your family history trail. At least this is one holiday I haven't got Anna at home saying how bored she is. Perhaps I should get her to research my own family.'

'Great idea. You can let me know if she needs any help.'

Jacqui drove to the end of the street to do a three-point turn, then shot off in the direction of the main road.

The four of them visibly relaxed.

Anna slipped her hand through her father's arm. 'Poor Mum. She never seems to be able to enjoy herself, does she?'

He turned his troubled face to her. 'I wouldn't think "enjoy" was the best word to use about this week.'

Her face fell.

Can she really have forgotten already? Nick thought incredulously. *She's home, safe, the centre of attention. Can that terrifying experience really have left no scars?*

They turned to go indoors. Suzie's words echoed in Nick's head. *Don't worry about Anna. We'll take care of her.*

Could they promise that?

A cold terror gripped him. Too late, he wanted to call back Jacqui's BMW. To hustle Anna inside. To get her away from St Furseys until every last one of that drugs ring was behind bars.

His own car was in front of Leon's garage. They could leave this morning, straight after breakfast.

And what? Sit and wait at home for the man at the centre of this to move against Millie, from a quarter Nick could not predict? In a part of the country where the police force knew nothing of what had happened here, and would probably not take the risk seriously?

His fists tightened as he thought of Ed Harries, pretending to be a paranoid householder, with a reputation for seeing off anyone who set foot on his property. Living in squalor, while running a drugs racket that must be earning him millions. He must have been laughing his socks off, saving the money up until . . . Until what?

But now Millie and Anna had put all that in danger.

It was still early, but he couldn't risk waiting any longer. He rang Inspector Davis.

Nick put down his mobile and sat on the edge of the bed, contemplating the clothes he had laid out ready, but not moving to put them on. He lifted his eyes to Suzie.

'She wasn't impressed. She admits the girls might have been held there. It would have been a clever move to shift them somewhere that had already been searched. The lab tests on the girls' clothes might prove it. But she says after meeting Ed Harries she doesn't believe it can be him at the bottom of it. It's possible someone else might have roped him in as a bit player, if there was money for him in it. Someone who knew the tunnel entrance was on Ed's land. And that he had a house where visitors weren't welcome.'

'And what about you? Do you still think Ed Harries is that man Millie keeps talking about? The one with the low, creepy voice?'

'He'd have to be a pretty good actor,' Nick admitted. 'I've only ever heard him yelling his head off or snarling. But with that much money at stake, he could be.'

Suzie sat down in front of the mirror. Her reflected eyes met his. 'If we knew more about this village . . . Whether Ed Harries has always lived here. There must be people who knew him when he was younger. Was he always like this? Ranting at people and waving weapons? Was it something that changed suddenly?'

Nick rubbed his head. He stood up and started to dress. 'I'm not sure I'd want to go around asking that sort of question. Last night in the pub, after Kevin Cook's accident, there was a feeling in the bar, and it wasn't good. As though this was all our fault. And only hours before, they'd been out searching for the girls.'

'Did the inspector have any news of Kevin Cook? Did she say?'

'He's in a coma. They can't say when she'll be able to question him. If ever.'

'Is she still on the case? They haven't handed it over to this . . .?'

'SOCA. Serious Organized Crime Agency. She's meeting them this morning.'

'She'll have to tell them what really happened to Millie and Anna, won't she?'

'I'm afraid so. Now we know there was never any SBS involvement.'

'And will the story be all over the police force?'

'I think she'll have her own reasons for keeping it secret, if she can.'

'You're still worried about a local informer on the inside? So what do we do now?'

'Wait. She wants Millie and Anna to be on standby, because it's likely the big boys will want to question them further. In the meantime, she suggests we either stay indoors, or take them off for the day. Somewhere not too obvious.'

Suzie spun round on her stool. 'So she does think they're still in danger.'

'We've no idea whether Kevin Cook's car crash has anything to do with this. It could be just a coincidence. But she's sending DS Vine over to us as a precaution.'

'I'm not sure I fancy sitting around indoors, just wondering who's outside. So where shall we go?'

He attempted a smile. 'I'm sure there must be somewhere in those family history files you haven't introduced me to yet.'

Leon was talking on the house telephone at the foot of the stairs. Suzie and Nick edged their way round him. The fire was unlit, the sky beyond the window mostly blue, promising sunshine. A brisk breeze was chasing the few clouds and setting the daffodils in the garden opposite nodding.

Nick drew a deep breath. 'Spring! What a difference from yesterday.'

Leon was saying, 'That's very kind of you. Yes, I'm sure they'd love to . . . All of us? Are you sure? Right, then, we'll see you down at the harbour, nine thirty . . . What? Oh, I see. No problem. I'm sure we'll find it . . . See you then, if we can prise the younger generation out of bed.'

He put down the phone and turned to them. The tension

of Jacqui's visit had faded. A smile lit up his features.

'That was Malcolm. Good news. He says it's a perfect day for sailing. He's not just inviting Tom for a spin in his yacht, but all of us. For the last few weeks, I've been sitting on the waterfront painting, and wishing I had the sort of money to join the yachting fraternity. I've been rather hoping that Malcolm might invite me out with him, once the season got under way.'

Nick looked at Suzie. He saw the relief in her face.

'Great idea,' he told Leon. 'Tom will be thrilled. Especially if he gets to handle a rope or two, or even get his hands on the wheel. Malcolm was pretty decent about that with his inflatable.'

'And there's another reason,' Suzie said more seriously. 'Inspector Davis has told Nick it might be a good idea for us to take ourselves away from St Furseys, while they sort this drugs thing out. I was wondering what that would be like. Having to keep looking over our shoulders. Wondering if anyone was following us. Thinking about that Land Rover upside down in the ditch. But on a yacht out at sea, nobody could touch us.'

'That's settled then. All we have to do now is get three teenagers awake, dressed and breakfasted. Not necessarily in that order.'

'What do we wear?' Millie asked sleepily, over her cereal. 'In case you've forgotten, the police haven't brought our jackets back yet. Not to mention my favourite trainers.'

Somewhere lab technicians would be at work, examining traces from the girls' clothing, to see where they had been. Just in case they had still not told the whole truth?

'The only thing Malcolm was particular about was footwear. No hard shoes. Trainers or Wellingtons would do. Yachtsmen are a bit finicky about their decks, apparently. That pair you've got on will be fine. Oh, and he advised dressing up warmly. It's always colder out at sea than it is on land. We can rustle up some spare coats for you, like yesterday.'

'Thanks. We could set a fashion in scarecrow chic.'

The doorbell rang. Nick went to answer it.

His heart lurched with shock as he recognized the policeman on the doorstep, even though he wore plain clothes. Detective

Sergeant Vine. In a dark, polo-necked sweater and a hiking jacket. Then, with a guilty intake of breath, Nick remembered. Inspector Davis had said she would send him to watch over the girls' safety.

'Come in,' he invited.

'Looks like you're going somewhere.'

Leon came forward. 'Dr Partridge has invited us out on his yacht. Do you remember him? He helped with the search of Ed Harries' house.'

The sergeant pulled a wry face. 'He'd be a difficult guy to forget. Not exactly a shrinking violet, is he?'

'Malcolm's all right. You'd have had a lot more trouble getting inside that house if he hadn't talked to Ed Harries like a Dutch uncle.'

'The crazy guy still went berserk once the good doctor took himself off to the barns.'

Nick listened. Had Inspector Davis told Vine about his certainty that the girls had been held prisoner at the old Noah's Ark, later? Of his horrible suspicion that Harries might not be the unstable idiot he pretended to be? That the run-down place might be the hub of a criminal web in which the girls had been caught?

No ground was secure now. No one could be trusted. Not even the police.

He said nothing.

DS Vine looked round the room full of Fewings, like a sheepdog assessing its flock. 'I'll see you down to the harbour, and safely aboard. You should be OK, out of reach of the shore. But I'll keep an eye on you. If there's any sign that another vessel might be trying to intercept you, I'll call the coastguard out. In fact, I'll give Dennis Gaiman a ring right now. Just so he's on the alert.'

A sudden picture came into Nick's mind. The burly coastguard organizing the search of the rocks at Brandon Head. The sound of a deep voice talking to Malcolm Partridge. Hadn't Millie said the second man, with his back to the tunnel entrance, had been wearing a dark peaked cap?

A shiver seemed to start in his guts and work its way up to his throat. Should he tell DS Vine? Surely he was becoming paranoid himself to fear that Davis's closest colleague was not to be trusted?

If the real threat was from the coastguard Vine was trusting to get them out of danger, he had to know.

He put out a discreet hand to Vine. 'Wait a minute,' he murmured. 'I need to talk to you.'

The party set out. At the end of the street, above the shingle beach, Leon turned left, instead of right to the creek.

'Hey, where are we going?' Tom objected. 'His boat's that way.'

Leon turned his head. 'Not this morning, apparently. She's anchored off his house now. He's got a place right on the shore, just out of the village. Even got his own boathouse. Lucky chap.'

They set off along the coastal path that Leon, Nick and Tom had followed the night before. Nick let the others get ahead of them and fell back beside Sergeant Vine.

'How much has Inspector Davis said to you about what this is all about?'

Vine eyed him guardedly. 'She isn't giving much away. I gather she's got a high-up meeting about some case this morning. Would I be right in guessing it has something to do with your two girls?'

They were skating around each other, each afraid of revealing too much.

'Did she tell you I thought Ed Harries might be behind it?'

He saw the flicker of surprise in Vine's eyes. So the inspector was being discreet.

'Let's suppose she didn't.'

'Well, I know it sounds unlikely, but I did think that. In fact, its unlikelihood seemed like a pretty strong argument. But I have to admit that in the cold light of morning it makes a bit less sense. The girls described a big man, and they were particularly scared by his voice. Low and icy cold, they said. A man who could order them to be put to death by dropping them out at sea, without a hint of emotion. Ed Harries would have to be a superb actor to carry off his impersonation of a mad old householder, even if he made sure not many people came near him. And he's not that big, though I grant you, he could have looked bigger than he was, to a couple of terrified teenagers. And then again, why earn millions from drugs trafficking, and live in a pigsty?'

'Yes, and your point is . . .'

'When you mentioned the coastguard, I had this sudden memory of him. Dennis Gaiman fits the bill. A big guy, wearing a dark peaked cap. And his voice, if I remember rightly, was pretty deep. He could easily have made it sound really cold and nasty, when he knew the girls had found out too much. Is it really safe for us to put out to sea? It seemed like a good idea when Leon suggested it.'

'Thanks. I'll pass that on. And I'll put the Revenue and Customs people on standby, not Dennis Gaiman. They've got pretty fast boats. I'll let the inspector know what you're thinking. We'll get a tail on him.'

Nick breathed more easily.

They had passed the last lamp post on the sea wall. Houses were giving way to fields. Ahead of them was a stand of trees. From it, a wooden jetty ran out into the shallow water. On the landward side was the dark outline of a boathouse. A little distance from the far end of the jetty, the yacht rode at anchor in deeper water. At the top of sloping lawns, a wide, double-fronted house, with a classical portico, overlooked the scene.

'Hey, Dad! Can I switch to medicine?' Tom turned round to joke with his father. 'How about this for a retirement pad? Yacht and all. I fancy it.'

A familiar splash of yellow showed where Malcolm was waiting for them by the boathouse. At the edge of his land, the path veered inland to skirt the house.

'Enjoy yourselves. And don't worry too much. I'll watch your back.'

Sergeant Vine lifted his hand to Nick and carried on along the path, as though he was just another holidaymaker out for a walk. At some point, Nick supposed, he would wait in the cover of a clump of bushes to watch them set sail.

Nick looked out to sea. The bare-masted yacht rode only a short distance from the end of the jetty. He wanted to cross that space quickly now. He longed to get the family aboard, to see the sails climb the mast, to be out on the freedom and the safety of the open sea. They should still be in reach by mobile phone. If the inspector wanted the girls back, she could contact them. It was comforting to know that Sergeant Vine would be watching them from the shore, that someone else would be keeping an eye on the coastguard.

Malcolm Partridge was, as ever, dressed for the part, in the yellow oilskins and yachting cap he had worn yesterday. He beamed with pleasure as they came up to him. He really was, Nick thought, like Mr Toad. He took a childish pleasure in showing off his latest toys. For his own part, Nick felt like a landlubber, wrapped up in hiking clothes and the Wellington boots he used for gardening.

'Glad you could all make it. This time of year, I can't wait to get out on the water. First hint of sunshine, a good breeze, and I'm off. Perfect weather today.' He turned to Tom. 'Last time, when we went out in the RIB, you wanted me to take a detour and look for your smugglers' cave. You still up for that?'

Tom looked startled. He swiftly recovered himself. 'Sure. Fine. Could we do that?'

Nick was relieved that Tom hadn't given away how much they now knew about that cave and tunnel. Malcolm might be a good ally, and a magistrate, but this morning Nick didn't feel inclined to trust even him with the girls' story.

'Certainly we could. We can sail by Brandon Head. See what it looks like from the sea. Never taken that smuggling story seriously, myself. Still, you never know. Maybe you'll prove me wrong. How about you girls? Fancy learning how to manage the sails?'

'Yes, please!' Anna, at least, sounded eager.

Millie, Nick thought, looked nervous. He threw her a comforting smile.

Malcolm led the way into the cavernous shadows of the boathouse. Nick experienced a shock that was both surprise and recognition. One half of the space was taken up by Malcolm's large inflatable. The still black water gave back a faint reflected gleam of the nearest outboard motor. He should not have been surprised to find it there, but he had temporarily forgotten that the doctor owned more than the yacht.

In the other half of the boathouse was tied a fibreglass dinghy.

'Well, now, I think we'll take you out in style. Normally I'd use the dinghy for shore to ship, when it's just me. But it would take all morning to get six of you aboard, and we don't want to waste this wind.'

Narrow decking ran around the sides of the boathouse. They

picked their way carefully along it. Malcolm handed them
into the RIB. The craft rocked beneath Nick. As he settled
himself in the stern and looked ahead at the sunlit water, he
felt his spirits soaring. This was how seaside holidays should
be spent. Messing about in boats, out on the open waves.
Recreating, in a small way, all the generations of lives he was
discovering.

Leon and the girls took up position in the bows. Tom joined
Nick at the stern.

'This way, dear lady. These are the best seats.'

Suzie, once more, was cajoled to the little wheelhouse
amidships, to sit beside the doctor. She caught Nick's eye,
with a little grimace, before turning to smile up at Partridge.
Good old Suzie. She was doing what was expected of her as
a guest. Laughing at the doctor's jokes, blushing prettily at
his flattery.

'Ready to cast off, Tom?' Malcolm shouted back.

'Aye, aye, Cap'n.'

'Let go.'

Tom slipped the painter. The engines sprang into life, then
settled to a steady thrum. The powerful craft edged its way
with surprising delicacy out of the boathouse into the sunshine
alongside the jetty.

Nick sat back with the beginnings of relief. Only a few
minutes now. That little stretch of water ahead. All they had
to do was clear the jetty, nose alongside the yacht and climb
aboard. For a few hours, the girls would be untouchable.

He turned back to see if DS Vine was watching them. There
was no sign of a dark figure on the coastal path. But there
were clumps of willow and alder that could easily hide him.

Suddenly, Tom gripped his arm. His voice was low and
urgent. 'Dad! Have you seen?'

Whatever he had been going to say was lost in a surge of
power. The engines roared. Nick was flung back against the
stern as the RIB leaped forward in a burst of spray and shot
beyond the jetty. It raced past the moored yacht, out to sea.

TWENTY-SIX

'**W**hat the hell . . .?'

Nick struggled to sit upright. He was reeling with the physical shock of his fall. His mind was whirling. What was going on?

The three in the bows had been flung backwards. Leon had grabbed hold of Anna. But Millie skidded back almost as far as the wheelhouse. She lay face downward in a slopping pool of water.

Nick tried to haul himself to his feet to go and help her.

What was Partridge playing at? This was beyond a prank.

The doctor had his large yellow-clad back to Nick. He was driving the RIB forward at a seemingly irresponsible speed. To his bewilderment, Nick saw the moored yacht receding behind them, her tall masts rocking in their wake. Partridge had made no attempt to stop.

Tom was grabbing his arm. 'Look! What did I tell you?'

He forced Nick round to look down at the stern. The sight punched Nick between the eyes.

Where, before, two 250-horsepower engines had been bolted to the stern, today there were – he made a rapid, incredulous count – eight.

Malcolm had said the two outboards would give him a top speed of fifty knots. Nick tried to imagine what eight would do.

Tom spoke his thoughts. 'This has to be faster than just about anything else on the water. I bet it could leave any Customs boat standing. You know what this means, Dad?'

Nick threw a desperate glance back. Over the churning wake, the shore was already too far away to distinguish a lone figure watching them.

How far was the nearest Revenue and Customs boat? And what use was that, against this speed? Was there anything else that could intercept them?

Already the yacht was dwindling far behind. Unless this was some mad joke, it had never been Partridge's intention to go aboard her. However sleek her lines, she was evidently far too slow for whatever he was planning. They were heading out across the North Sea.

As they slammed into another wave, Nick was jolted back to the present. He had to go to Millie's help. He started forward, fighting unsteadily against the bucking motion of the inflatable.

'Get back and stay there,' the doctor roared.

'Not till I've got Millie.'

The voice dropped lower. 'I rather think you will do exactly what I say.'

Nick was close enough to the wheelhouse to hear the words distinctly, though they came now, not as a roar, but a low, slow, ice-cold command.

His stomach lurched, sickeningly. The big man with the dark, peaked cap. The second man the girls had seen in the tunnel. The man who gave the orders that meant life or death.

Nick stopped dead, struggling for his balance. Millie was lifting her face to him, pleading. He took another unsteady step forward.

'I do hope you won't force me to do anything unpleasant to dear Suzie.'

And only then Nick saw. Partridge had one hand firmly on the wheel. The other was holding a small handgun to Suzie's temple. She was pinned into her chair, with her back to Nick, unable to move.

Slowly, Nick retreated. He collapsed on the stern seat beside Tom.

'Now you.' Partridge nodded his head towards Leon, Anna and Millie, motioning them to move astern too.

Clumsily, Leon and Anna made their way back past the wheelhouse, grabbing for handholds. Anna was shooting scared looks at the doctor as she passed. Leon's face was grim.

Partridge had slowed the engines a little, after that first mad roar, but the craft was still plunging on at speed.

Millie struggled on to her hands and knees. The front of her clothing was soaked. She bit her lip as she stumbled past the doctor to join them. Nick grabbed her and pulled her close.

'It's him, isn't it?' she whispered. 'What's he going to do to us?'

'I don't know what he's planning. But there are six of us, and only one of him.'

'He's got a gun. And he's got Mum.'

'I know.'

Nick longed to see Suzie's face. If only he could catch her eye and do something to give her courage.

Could he? What unspoken promises could he make? What could he possibly do to help her?

'He's going to drown us, isn't he?'Millie said in a small voice. 'Like he meant that other man to do.'

'We'll see about that.'

Brave words. Could he stop it? The alternative appalled him. His whole family – wife, daughter, son, brother, niece – wiped out in a single morning.

The irony hit him. They had come to St Furseys to discover his family history. Now the Fewings line might end here, because of that.

A cold far more deadly than the wind and sea of an April morning held him rigid in his seat.

'It's been a pleasure knowing you.' Malcolm Partridge allowed himself a cold smile. He had to raise his voice above the engines, but it was still without emotion, belying his words. 'I'm sorry you won't be painting any more pictures, Leon. Just when you'd found your true vocation. And, Nick, all those homes you'll never now design. And Suzie, the great family history detective. There will be no more mysteries solved after today. Because you failed to crack this one. A pity. You three passed on just too many of your inquisitive genes to your daughters.'

'You won't get away with this.' Nick's voice surprised him with its hoarseness. 'Detective Sergeant Vine's been watching this. The alarm bells will already be ringing.'

'And just what will he be able to do? Scramble the coast-guard? Good old Dennis Gaiman? Bring up the Customs cutter from twenty miles down the coast? Call out the Special Boat Service? I think we'll be lost to sight long before any of those can catch up with us, don't you?'

To prove his point, he gunned the engines again. With most of the weight in the stern, the bows shot high in the air. The RIB slammed across the waves, which were rising ever higher as they streaked out into the North Sea.

*   *   *

A horrifying thought was growing in Nick's mind. He tried to fight it away. But the logic persisted as the shore receded. Dr Partridge could be taking them out here for one reason only: to get rid of them. They had, as he had tried to reassure Millie, the advantage of numbers, but Partridge had the gun, and he was holding it to Suzie's head.

That was becoming more difficult. The doctor was struggling to control the RIB one-handed, as she smashed her way across the rising waves. If Nick and Leon, and maybe Tom, rushed him, there was a good chance they could overpower him. But Suzie would almost certainly die, and perhaps others among them as well.

Could he bring himself to do that? Lose Suzie? In the hope of saving the children?

He sat numbed with the reality, not daring to decide.

'What's the point?' Leon shouted at Partridge. 'The girls have told their story to the police. Smuggling drugs is one thing. But not murder.'

'You think I'm a common drug runner? Give me credit for a little more class. Besides, I don't think your friends on shore are going to catch me, do you? And I have a reputation to keep up. Oh, no. Not the one you think. Not the jackass doctor, showing off his—'

The boat lurched. A bigger wave reared under the port bow, threatening to roll her sideways. For a brief moment, Partridge snatched his other hand away from Suzie, wrestling the wheel back on course.

Leon and Nick leaped to their feet. But they lost their balance as the RIB bucked. Nick hit the floor hard. When he clawed his way ignominiously back to his feet, the inflatable was again meeting the swell head on. Dr Partridge stood perfectly balanced at the wheel, one hand locked against Suzie's skull.

'Luckily for your wife I'm not trigger-happy. I do only what needs to be done. But I do it without pity. So you needn't waste your breath pleading for your daughters. It's that reputation that makes me so successful, and so feared. Your little ladies swore to keep quiet, and they didn't. There are people around the world who need to learn what happens when my orders are not carried out. First Kevin Cook, and now you.'

Nick felt in his stomach what Millie had meant about that

voice. This was not the genial, boastful Dr Partridge they had known. The voice was colder than the sea around them. Raised only just enough for them to hear him clearly. The voice of a man whose emotions were under icy control.

The engines were slowing. No longer did Nick feel pinned back against the stern by the speed of their passage. The inflatable was dipping and rolling more naturally to the swing of the waves. Whatever was going to happen would happen soon.

'I think here will do nicely.'

With a startled flash of belated observation, Nick knew what was missing. Yesterday, for the short voyage out to the archaeological survey ship, the doctor had handed out slim life jackets for them to wear around their necks. Today, they had none. It had not seemed necessary, just to transfer from the boathouse to the yacht. Here, even with them, with the sea at its coldest at the end of winter, they could not survive long.

All the same, he began to ease off his Wellington boots. If they filled with water, they would drag him down.

'Shh.' He nudged Millie and made a small gesture for her to do the same.

Partridge's voice halted him.

'I think we'll take Millie first, so that you can all watch.' He fixed his gaze on the girl's pale face. 'Jump.'

Her eyes went from the doctor to Nick, questioning in terror.

This was the moment that Nick had dreaded. The moment when he would be forced to make a choice.

But it was no choice, was it? Millie might be first, but Suzie would follow. He couldn't save all of them, but he might save some. His muscles clenched.

'Too late!' Tom had spun round in his seat and was pointing behind them, over the creaming fan of their wake. 'The helicopter's coming.'

Partridge's head jerked up, staring past Millie to the sky beyond her.

Nick willed himself not to look, though everyone else was craning round. Even Suzie had turned her white face at last.

Nick flung himself forward. But even as he did so, he heard the sickening crack of a gun firing.

TWENTY-SEVEN

'**N**o!'

Nick hurled himself across the intervening space, even though there was nothing he could do except to catch Suzie's falling body in his arms.

He hit the wheelhouse chairs.

He was struggling to make sense of the scene in front of him. Confusingly, Suzie was still upright. She was grappling with Partridge, forcing his right arm above his head. But it could not last. He was far stronger than she was.

Nick threw her aside and lunged at Partridge.

But he was hampered by the helmsman's chair. He had to reach across it to grab the doctor. He couldn't launch his full weight behind his grip. The yellow oilskins were slippery. Gradually, Partridge was bringing down the hand that held the gun.

Next moment, the world tilted crazily. The port bow was rearing above them both. Nick was slithering backwards.

He saw a large flash of yellow catapulting through the air. Then the inflatable cast a monstrous panoply over him, shutting out the light. Slowly, inexorably, the wave rolled the RIB over.

Nick hit the water with a shock of cold that made him gasp.

He came up floundering for air. He was terrified that his head would break the surface and he would find himself trapped underneath the boat.

He opened his eyes on sunshine and tossing green waves. 'Thank God!'

He retched up seawater and breathed deeply.

Something grabbed his arm. He turned his head to find Tom, attempting a grin. With his other hand, Tom was clutching a grab rope on the side of the upturned boat. He dragged Nick towards him, so that it was within his reach too. Nick gripped the rope harder than was necessary, though his hands were already beginning to grow numb with cold.

He looked around frantically for the others.

To his enormous relief he made out three heads bobbing by the stern. One fair, one grey, one dark. Leon had his arms round both of the girls, anchoring them to the hull.

A flash of terror shot through Nick. Those eight engines at the stern. Surely their screws could rip the girls apart? Or send the RIB shooting across the waves out of sight, leaving them alone and helpless?

It was eerily quiet. Only the slop of waves, beating against the boat now with their own natural rhythm.

He turned to Tom in confusion. 'We're not moving! At least . . .' A bigger wave lifted them up and dropped them sickeningly into its trough.

Tom's grin was wide with pride, even though his teeth were chattering. 'I was on my way to help you. But then the boat started to flip over, so I hit the Stop switch. I didn't fancy being in the drink, while our only buoyancy aid took off over the horizon.'

'Where's Partridge?'

Tom nodded behind them. As another wave rolled past, Nick saw on its lifting side a patch of yellow. It seemed to be within the wave, rather than riding on it.

The doctor had hit the water seconds before Tom cut the engines. He was not far behind them, but too great a distance to reach. Nick thought of those sea boots filling with water, pulling him down. He felt his own stockinged feet.

And only then, far, far too late, the most important truth hit him.

'*Suzie!*'

He twisted round. There was no sign of the white jacket Suzie had been wearing. No long brown hair spread out on the water.

In desperate haste, he worked his way to the stern.

'Suzie?' he gasped at Leon. 'Is she round the other side?'

Leon craned to look. He shook his head dumbly.

There was only one place she could be. With horrifying clarity, Nick knew she must be under the capsized boat. He drew a deep breath and dived.

It was frighteningly dark. When his head surfaced under the hull, there was room to breathe, but he could see nothing. He scrabbled wildly, panting with terror. He ought to search the enclosed space systematically, but he couldn't order his thoughts.

He bumped into something soft. Hands clutched him.

'Nick?'

He held her close. He was not sure which of them was sobbing.

Common sense returned.

'We just need to dive and we'll be out. Not too far down. Just take a deep breath and hold on to me.'

He filled his lungs and plunged. For horrible moments he found he had made a mistake. He was weighed down by his clothes, and by Suzie as well. He fought to get past the hull and then to force his way up to daylight.

The dragging weight lifted from him. Suzie had let go. She rose to the surface beside him. They turned and smiled at each other wordlessly.

Suzie gripped the ropes that held the fenders. She looked instantly, as Nick had done, for the children. From this side, they could see only Anna's head and Leon's shoulder.

'Millie? Tom?'

'Millie's at the stern with Leon. Tom's round the other side.'

'And . . .?'

'Partridge went overboard first. He's somewhere behind us. He was still afloat when I saw him. Sort of. I'm not sure his head's above water.'

Suzie said nothing.

Tom appeared, working his way around the bows. His anxious face broke into a laugh of relief.

'You made it! I was just wondering if I should dive down after you. Mum, you're a heroine.'

Nick tried to sound light-hearted too. 'All we need now is that helicopter you invented. It was good ploy of yours to get him off guard.'

'I didn't invent the helicopter, Dad. Can't you hear it?'

The silence of the sea was giving way to a drone that grew ever nearer.

Nick felt the tension go out of his limbs. He sagged against the upturned boat. It might not be too late, after all.

The shadow of the helicopter loomed over them. The downdraught of its rotors flattened the waves into pimpled planes.

'No markings. It's not the coastguard, or Air-Sea Rescue. Bet it's the SBS,' Tom chortled. 'Millie *will* be pleased.'

A man was descending on a winch rope. Nick watched him slip a harness over Anna and the two of them were drawn back into the open belly of the small helicopter. Millie followed. Her dripping figure looked heartbreakingly fragile, even in her winter clothes. Nick shut his eyes in thankfulness as she disappeared inside.

Suzie was next. The winchman, in his orange survival suit, dropped into the water beside them.

'You're OK, love. Hot cup of tea coming up any moment now.'

'You ought to take the men first,' Suzie argued. 'Women can stand the cold better. We've got more fat.'

'Don't let Millie hear you say that,' Tom joked through shivering lips.

'We're old-fashioned types. Women and children first.'

As he clipped her sling into place, he said over his shoulder to Nick, 'Where's the doctor?'

Nick nodded astern.

'Out of harm's way, then. Well, hang on in there. 'Fraid this isn't a Sea King. There's a limit of three for this trip. But more help's on its way.' A look of concern crossed his face. 'No life jackets?'

Nick shook his head.

'We can fix that, at least.'

He and Suzie rose, swaying, in the air. Three orange life jackets descended. Nick grabbed one gratefully and passed another to Tom.

The door closed behind the winchman. The helicopter's engines faded away towards the shore.

It was a relief to let the life jacket take the weight of his numbed body. But still he had to cling on to the boat with chilled hands.

He turned his head. Tom looked ill. His face was bluish-white, his lips tinged with purple. He had stopped talking. Suzie was right. The boy was still a gangly teenager, with no fat on his long limbs. Nick knew he should try to keep up a conversation, to force his son to hold on to the present.

But a lethargy was creeping over Nick too. It was not entirely unpleasant. It would be seductively easy to close his eyes, let his grip on the rope slacken, allow himself to succumb to the cold and the wet and drift away.

Was this how it had been in those last moments, for Solomon Margerson and the boy Peter Sullivan, when they had been swept from the lifeboat and drowned? Just drifting into death? No. Honesty struck back at him. It had been nothing like this. They had died on a night of terrible storm, in pitch blackness, engulfed by enormous waves. A night of terror. Nick forced himself to open his eyes and look around him. The water was cold, but above him was a sky of April sunshine. These waves might look huge to him, but they were probably no more than a moderate swell to an experienced seaman. Unlike Sollie Margerson, he had a chance to survive. If help was not too long coming. If the cold didn't get to him first.

He looked the other way, at Leon. His brother was quiet too, holding on to the stern with grim determination.

Nick started to move towards him, hand over hand along the side of the hull. It was alarmingly more difficult than it had been before. There seemed no strength in his arms. Every time a big wave lifted them, he felt his grip would be torn from the RIB.

'Do you think we could pull ourselves on to the boat?' he called, when he was near enough. 'Get out of this freezing water?'

'Not sure . . . I can.'

Leon's voice was weak. He seemed to have trouble moving his stiff lips. Hadn't there been some scare last year about a heart murmur? How long could his brother's body stand the cold?

Nick studied the hull above them. It might just be possible to use the outboards as ledges to climb up. But the upturned inflatable would be slippery, with no handholds. They could easily be washed or tipped off.

More help is on its way. He had to hold on to that.

He was losing the sense of where the shore lay. He could see nothing but heaving waves. He peered upward. There was no sign of another helicopter.

A darkness rose in front of Nick. A gigantic grey wave that must overwhelm him this time.

The grey wall stilled. It hung motionless over them. There was a sound that was not wind and waves, but an engine running.

Voices were calling, but he could no longer make sense of them.

Suddenly his attention focused. He saw Tom's grip break away from the fender rope. With his last strength, Nick threw out his arm to grab his son. But the boy's dark head above the orange life jacket was moving away through the water, faster now. Did Nick have the courage to let go and swim after him? What chance of survival would either of them have?

More voices. Clearer now.

'Come on!'

'You're nearly there.'

'That's it.'

'Got you!'

Nick's straining neck turned again to face that towering grey wall.

A ship rode the rolling swell. He gazed at it with more incredulity than belief.

Its deck was not so very far above them as he had thought. There was a ladder over the side. Hands were hoisting Tom up. Nick saw him reach the rail, hauled up on to the deck. The boy stumbled forward. More hands caught him. Someone threw a blanket round him and helped him away.

Nick watched the scene with a feeling of unreality.

More shouts. Gradually Nick realized that they were calling to him; that now it was his turn. But his mind seemed frozen into immobility. His numb hands would not let go of the rope. The short gap between the two boats seemed impossible to cross.

Now there were people on either side of him. Divers in black suits supporting him. They prised his fingers away and carried him through the water between them. He couldn't climb the ladder. It looked impossibly high, and he felt as weak as a kitten. There was a rope around him. He was being pulled up.

Like Tom, he almost fell on to the deck. Arms supported him. A blanket over his soaked clothes shut out the wind. There was spring sunshine on his face. He was alive.

'Well, we didn't expect to see *you* aboard again.'

The ginger-bearded archaeology professor met his eyes with an anxious laugh.

*   *   *

The survey ship didn't run to complete changes of clothing. But the students and crew managed to rustle up an assortment of sweaters and waterproofs for the three of them. Hot chocolate coursed like fire through chilled bodies.

Nick stood beside the skipper at the wheel.

'It was somewhere around here. The engines were still running when we started to capsize, and he was the first to go overboard. I got a glimpse of him astern of us.'

The engines of the survey ship slowed.

'There he is!' a girl's voice called.

They crept alongside. The yellow figure was wallowing face downwards. The yachting cap had gone. Only the crown of the balding head broke the surface.

There was silence on the boat. Someone held the body stationary with a boathook.

The two divers climbed down again and fastened a rope around it. Nick stood back as they brought the heavy figure with difficulty on board.

The body of Malcolm Partridge, if that was his real name, fell on to the deck. Nick stared down at it, unable to feel the triumph he might have done. This was the man who had ordered the killing of Millie and Anna. Who had then decided to murder the whole Fewings family, as a warning to his associates. The man who must have controlled an empire doing untold harm to thousands of others.

Yet Nick could feel only an inexplicable sorrow for the lifeless body at his feet. He had not willed this death. It was not his doing. He would rather have seen the doctor face justice than take his life away like this.

'Well, let's get you ashore,' said the professor briskly. 'Apparently there's an ambulance waiting at St Furseys. Then *perhaps* we can get back to marine archaeology before my grant runs out.'

He strode away.

Dr Kapoor turned her small face up to Nick with a friendlier smile in her dark eyes.

'He's actually thrilled to bits. Did he tell you? We've found the wreck of the *Caractacus*. The ship whose passengers and crew your great-grandfather was trying to rescue when he drowned.'

TWENTY-EIGHT

L eon, Millie and Anna were waiting in the Murchington Hospital foyer when Nick and Suzie brought Tom down. To his embarrassment, Tom had been the only one kept in overnight with hypothermia.

'And don't you dare say anything to Millie about women being fatter,' Suzie whispered at the foot of the stairs.

'Well, another fine day,' Leon greeted them. 'What trouble are you lot planning to get us into today?'

'I thought we . . .' Suzie began.

The lift doors opened. Inspector Davis stepped out, accompanied by a grey-haired, square-set man. Startled by the encounter, Nick searched his memory for the name.

Superintendent John Radford, from SOCA, the Serious Organized Crime Agency. He had debriefed them yesterday, after their medical checks.

Inspector Davis stopped in surprise, too. 'Is Tom all right? Oh, yes. I can see he is. You're a tough lot, you Fewings. Hard to keep down.'

Millie pressed forward. 'Have you been to see Kevin Cook? Is he going to be all right? *Was* he the man in the tunnel?'

The inspector held up her hand. 'Steady on!' She looked questioningly at Radford. He shrugged his shoulders. 'Yes, I'm glad to say he's recovered consciousness, though they're still sedating him. We were only able to question him for a short time. And yes, Millie.' She lowered her voice. 'Keep this to yourselves, please, but he admits he *was* the man.'

'The man who set us free in the marshes, instead of drowning us?' Anna whispered. 'Why?'

'Because not everyone in the criminal underworld is quite as cold-hearted as the late doctor. He found he couldn't go through with it. Apparently, his plan was to wait until it was just starting to get light, then drop you into the sea, not too far from the shore. He hoped you'd make it. The doctor might be furious with him, but Cook would blame a freak current.

People *have* survived in these seas, and come ashore alive, against expectations.'

'But he didn't,' said Millie, struggling to keep her voice from rising. 'He never even put us in a boat.'

The superintendent was beginning to look uneasy. But the inspector carried on, her voice no more than a murmur.

'No. He hadn't bargained on the fact that we'd be out searching Brandon Head for you at the crack of dawn. When he saw the size of the search party, he panicked. He says the only thing he could think of was to drive off in the opposite direction and dump you in the marshes instead. Unfortunately, when you turned up safe and well, he didn't have a convincing enough story to save him from Partridge's fury. If he thought telling you to switch suspicion to the archaeologist would keep his boss happy, he made a very serious mistake.'

'And anyway, we didn't,' said Anna. 'Because it wasn't the professor.'

'Quite.'

Nick glanced around. People were looking at them curiously, skirting around the eight of them. Were any of them from St Furseys? Would they catch anything of what they were saying?

'So what will happen to Kevin now?' he asked in a low voice. 'He saved the girls, but drug running's a pretty nasty crime.'

'If it *was* drug running,' muttered Superintendent Radford.

'What do you mean?' Leon asked. 'The boat, the cave, the cargo they were shifting at night? What else would it be?'

Like Nick, Superintendent Radford looked around the busy foyer, criss-crossed by outpatients and visitors. 'Shall we?'

He guided them out of doors. To the right of the entrance a garden had been set with wooden benches. The sun shone down on its gravel and dwarf conifers. At this time of the morning it was deserted. They settled themselves to listen.

'I'm not suggesting there isn't drug running on the North Sea shore. But we don't have the same problem we do on the Channel coast.'

'Makes sense,' Tom was trying to follow him. 'I was beginning to wonder about that. If we're talking about shipments from North Africa, and stuff.'

'Exactly. I wouldn't put anything above him, if there was

money in it. But we found something rather interesting on Malcolm Partridge.'

Their eyes were riveted on him.

'I'm speaking in confidence, mind. I hope you all understand that. If you want us to catch the ring behind this, none of you will breathe a word.'

The Fewings nodded.

'We found his passport. In the last three years alone, he's made no fewer than ten visits to Russia. For business purposes, according to his visas.'

'*Russia?*' said Suzie. 'But we thought the funny lettering the girls saw must have been Arabic, so it had to be cocaine, from South America via North Africa. I even suspected poor Isabella da Souza at the museum, because she could be Brazilian rather than Portuguese. I thought there might be a connection.'

'Partridge wouldn't have been unhappy for you to think that. A useful red herring. Since it wasn't true, nobody could prove that connection against him.'

'Then what? Heroin from Afghanistan, via Russia?'

'It's not impossible. But from some things Kevin Cook told us, I think it may be something else altogether. After the war, a lot of art works looted from Germany by the Russians went missing. Nobody knows to this day where most of them are. And a century ago, Russian Orthodox churches were loaded with priceless works of art: icons, crucifixes, communion vessels. Under Communism, thousands of churches and monasteries were closed, or even pulled down. Some of their treasures ended up in museums. Who knows where the rest went?'

'And you think Partridge was shipping these art works out?' Nick asked. 'To sell to collectors?'

'On the black market, yes.'

'Icons!' cried Millie, turning in excitement to Anna. 'That flat-pack furniture!'

'And he was prepared to kill for that?' Suzie spoke slowly. 'For sacred icons of Mary and the Christ child? For a chalice that held communion wine? For a cross with the figure of Jesus crucified?'

'To him, they would just be money. In some cases, very big money. It's only a theory yet, but we're working on it.'

For a while, no one found anything to say. Sparrows flew down and hopped around the gravel at their feet, as if they expected crumbs.

Nick frowned. 'But he couldn't have got away with it. Taking us out to sea and drowning us. Suspicion would be bound to fall on him when he came back alone.'

'I don't think he was planning to come back. The RIB would have been found floating upside down. No sign of any survivors. Some of you might or might not have been washed ashore eventually. In spite of the gun, he'd have tried to avoid any bullet wounds. The doctor would have been presumed dead, like the rest of you. He probably had a rendezvous with a boat in the North Sea. He'll have had plenty of money to start again with a new identity, somewhere else, and take up his – shall we say – import business where he left off.'

'And he'd just walk away and leave that house, the yacht, everything?' Tom sounded incredulous.

'I'm sure he'd have taken care of that. There'll have been a will. The supposed heir would turn up, claim his inheritance, then sell it and hand the loot over to his master.'

'Or make off with it himself.' There was a nervous edge to Millie's laughter.

The superintendent turned a sympathetic look at her. 'I don't think so. Malcolm Partridge appears to have been very keen to preserve his reputation as a man nobody crosses.'

Again that silence.

Millie broke it. 'You never did say what's going to happen to Kevin Cook. He saved our lives.'

'He was only a small cog in the machine. But I think he's going to give us some valuable leads. The only person he could have testified against directly was Malcolm Partridge. But *he's* not going to come to court now. So I think we can come to some arrangement with Kevin about the rest of his evidence.'

The superintendent rose. 'Well, if you'll excuse us, I think it's time we left you to get on with the rest of your holiday.'

Nick looked at the others. 'I think this calls for a celebratory lunch.'

'Can we go back to that Italian restaurant?' Millie cried. 'The one near the Record Office.'

They parked the cars and walked through the streets of the market town. Millie paused in front of a tall brick building with gilt lettering above the ground floor windows.

'*Murchington Herald*. That's the newspaper you got us finding all those stories from, about our family. Solomon Margerson and all the rest of the lifeboatmen. Only it's not going to happen with us, is it? They're never going to put our story in the paper. About Anna and me being tied up in that tunnel, and Dr Partridge ordering Kevin to kill us. And being locked up in Ed Harries' house. And then everything that happened on the boat. Mum grabbing his arm to stop him firing. The RIB capsizing. Being rescued by a helicopter, and everything. I can't *believe* it. Nothing. There isn't going to be a single line. And we're not allowed to say a word about it to our friends when we get home. It's such a *waste*.'

'Think of the Special Boat Service,' Tom grinned. 'A secret mission. Millie Fewings, Special Agent.'

She punched him.

As the others walked on, Nick stood looking up at the old-fashioned newspaper office windows. Suzie turned her head, then came back to join him.

He smiled at her ruefully. 'There's so much we don't know. Stuff we'll never know. When Aunt Eleanor left me that photograph of Great-grandfather Sollie, it set us looking for stories here. And we've found far more evidence than I dreamed we would. But there must have been so much more that never got into the newspapers. Lives saved, crimes no one discovered, how people died. Centuries of them.' He shook his head.

Suzie linked her arm through his. 'Our own lives are like that. A secret history. Much of it nobody's going to write down, unless we do it. Perhaps that's what we should be doing. Leaving evidence of ourselves for the next generation.'

He squeezed her arm and looked along the street, at the backs of their family heading for the restaurant. Tom's laughter. An exasperated punch from Millie.

Nick laughed. 'And we do *have* a next generation. Family history or not, that's what matters.'

AUTHOR'S NOTE

The people, places and institutions in this book are fictitious. But I am indebted to many real-life people and organizations who have done so much to help my own family history research in ways which have inspired this book, or contributed further information. They include the following:

Alan March, great-grandson of Charlie Cox
Ancestry.co.uk
'A Smuggler's Song', Rudyard Kipling
Great Expectations, Charles Dickens
Cromer Museum
RNLI Cromer Lifeboat Station
RNLI Henry Blogg Museum, Cromer
The Deal Maritime and Local History Museum
Devon Record Office
West Country Studies Library
Jamaica Inn, Daphne du Maurier
IGI: www.familysearch.org
The Wreckers, Bella Bathurst
History of Deal, John Laker
The Longshoreman, Herbert Russell
www.hoax-slayer.com/drug-runner-boat.shtml

While I have given free rein to my imagination here, many details owe their original inspiration to discoveries in my own family history research:

The framed photograph of the lifeboatman – Charlie Cox of Cromer, in the possession of Alan March.

The lifeboatman's funeral – Charlie Cox, Cromer, 1834.

Census results, Solomon Margerson's family – Charlie Cox's family, www.ancestry.co.uk

Online photographs of Solomon Margerson – Charlie Cox. www.museums.norfolk.gov.uk. Search under Cromer Museum and surname.

Suzie's great-uncle drowned in the Scillies – gravestone of Richard Lee and family, St Budeaux churchyard, Plymouth.

The creek at St Furseys – the river Blyth between Southwold and Walberswick.

The family portrait in St Furseys Museum – Thomas Cory and family in Deal Maritime and Local History Museum.

Television documentary on wreckers – *Timewatch*, BBC2, Feb 2007. Bella Bathurst on 'The Wreckers'.

Noah's Ark Inn – the Noah's Ark Inn in Deal was used by smugglers. 'It was situated amid fields and gardens in the rear of the town.'

Alfred Margerson – Richard Cory moved from Milton Keynes to Deal before 1807, to become both the licensee of the Noah's Ark and a gardener. His sons became boatmen.

The Customs officer killed boarding a smugglers' vessel – Customs Officer Alistair Soutar of Dundee was killed in 1996 while boarding the *Jubilee* off the Scottish coast. Nine men were arrested and several tons of cannabis seized.

The smugglers' vessel hauled up to a cave – the Kent coast near Ramsgate, reported in *The Longshoreman*, Herbert Russell.

The soldier killed by smugglers – in 1794 Pte. John Elbeck of the Westmoreland Militia received fatal wounds while guarding a captured cargo at Deal.

Burning the boats – in 1784, a troop of the 13th Light Dragoons smashed and burned all the boats on Deal beach.

The Rigid Inflatable Boat with eight 250-horsepower outboard motors – boats like these have been made in the UK and taken to the Mediterranean, for use in transporting drugs and contraband. They are capable of speeds up to sixty knots.

St Furseys church – St Peter and St Paul, Cromer.

Graveyard plans – Moretonhampstead, Mariansleigh.

Reed beds – Suffolk coast between Walberswick and Dunwich.